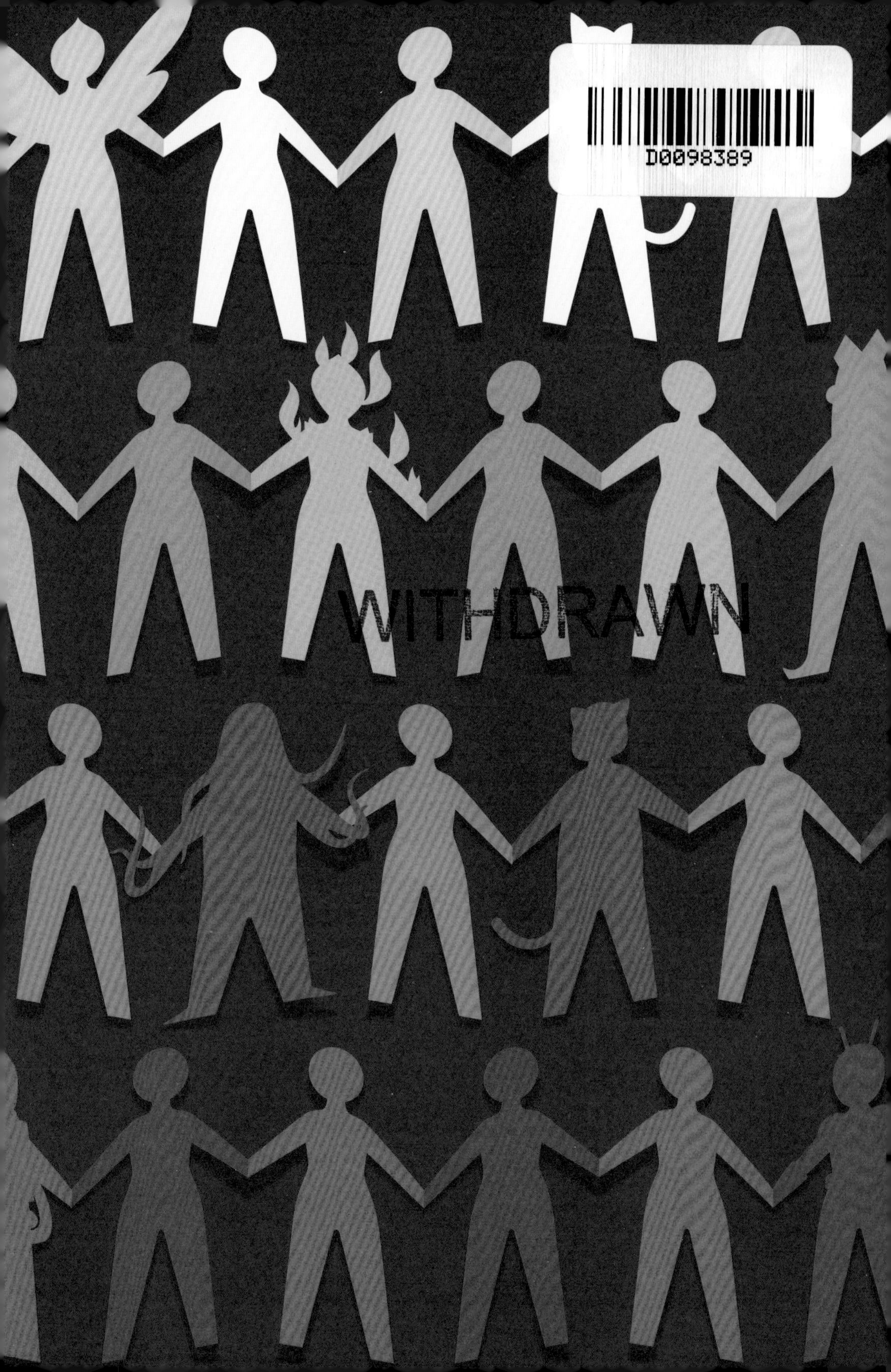

SCHOOL FOR EXTRATERRESTRIAL GIRLS

PAPERCUTZ

THE SMURFS #21

BRINA THE CAT #1

CAT & CAT #1

THE SISTERS #1

ATTACK OF THE STUFF

GERONIMO STILTON #17

THEA STILTON #6

GERONIMO STILTON RREPORTER #1

THE MYTHICS #1

GUMBY #1

ANNE OF GREEN BAGELS #1

BLUEBEARD

THE RED SHOES

THE LITTLE MERMAID

FUZZY BASEBALL

HOTEL TRANSYLVANIA #1

THE LOUD HOUSE #1

MANOSAURS #1

THE ONLY LIVING BOY #5

ONLY LIVING GIRL #1

MORE GREAT GRAPHIC NOVEL SERIES AVAILABLE FROM

PAPERCUTZ™

papercutz.com

All available where ebooks are sold.

SCHOOL FOR EXTRATERRESTRIAL GIRLS

GIRL ON FIRE

JEREMY WHITLEY   JAMIE NOGUCHI

PAPERCUTZ
NEW YORK

School for Extraterrestrial Girls
#1 "Girl on Fire"

By Jeremy Whitley and Jamie Noguchi
©2020 Jeremy Whitley and Jamie Noguchi
All other editorial material © Papercutz.
Written by Jeremy Whitley
Art and color by Jamie Noguchi
Coloring assists by Shannon Lilly
Lettering by Wilson Ramos Jr.

Special thanks to Moe Ferrara

Managing Editor — Jeff Whitman
Editorial Interns — Eric Storms, Izzy Boyce-Blanchard
Jim Salicrup
Editor-in-Chief

Papercutz books may be purchased for business or promotional use. For information on bulk purchases please contact Macmillan Corporate and Premium Sales Department at (800) 221-795 x5442.

Hardcover ISBN: 978-1-5458-0492-6
Paperback ISBN: 978-1-5458-0493-3

Printed in Turkey
August 2020

Distributed by Macmillan
First Printing

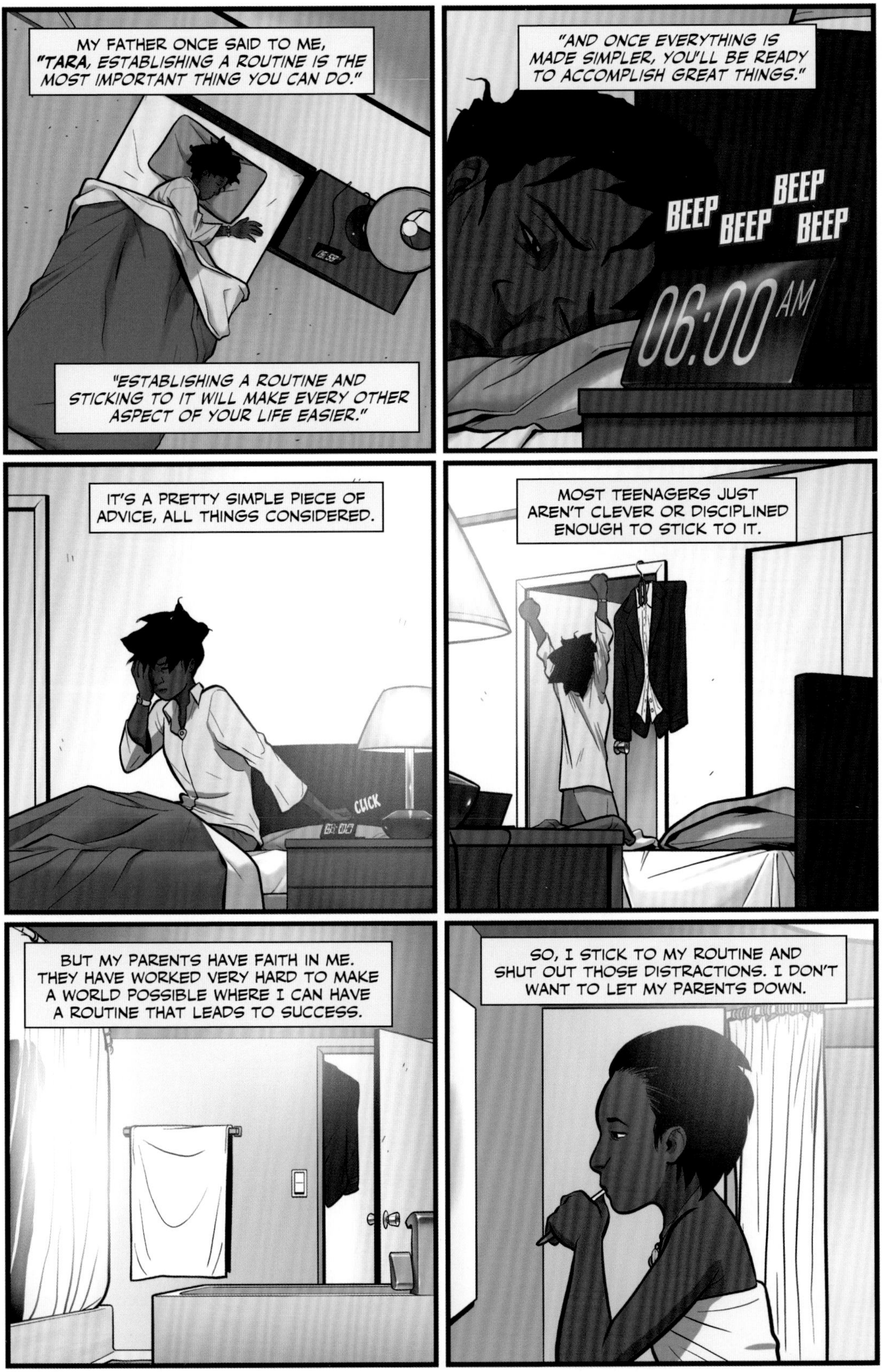
MY FATHER ONCE SAID TO ME, "TARA, ESTABLISHING A ROUTINE IS THE MOST IMPORTANT THING YOU CAN DO."
"ESTABLISHING A ROUTINE AND STICKING TO IT WILL MAKE EVERY OTHER ASPECT OF YOUR LIFE EASIER."
"AND ONCE EVERYTHING IS MADE SIMPLER, YOU'LL BE READY TO ACCOMPLISH GREAT THINGS."
BEEP BEEP BEEP BEEP
06:00 AM
IT'S A PRETTY SIMPLE PIECE OF ADVICE, ALL THINGS CONSIDERED.
CLICK
MOST TEENAGERS JUST AREN'T CLEVER OR DISCIPLINED ENOUGH TO STICK TO IT.
BUT MY PARENTS HAVE FAITH IN ME. THEY HAVE WORKED VERY HARD TO MAKE A WORLD POSSIBLE WHERE I CAN HAVE A ROUTINE THAT LEADS TO SUCCESS.
SO, I STICK TO MY ROUTINE AND SHUT OUT THOSE DISTRACTIONS. I DON'T WANT TO LET MY PARENTS DOWN.

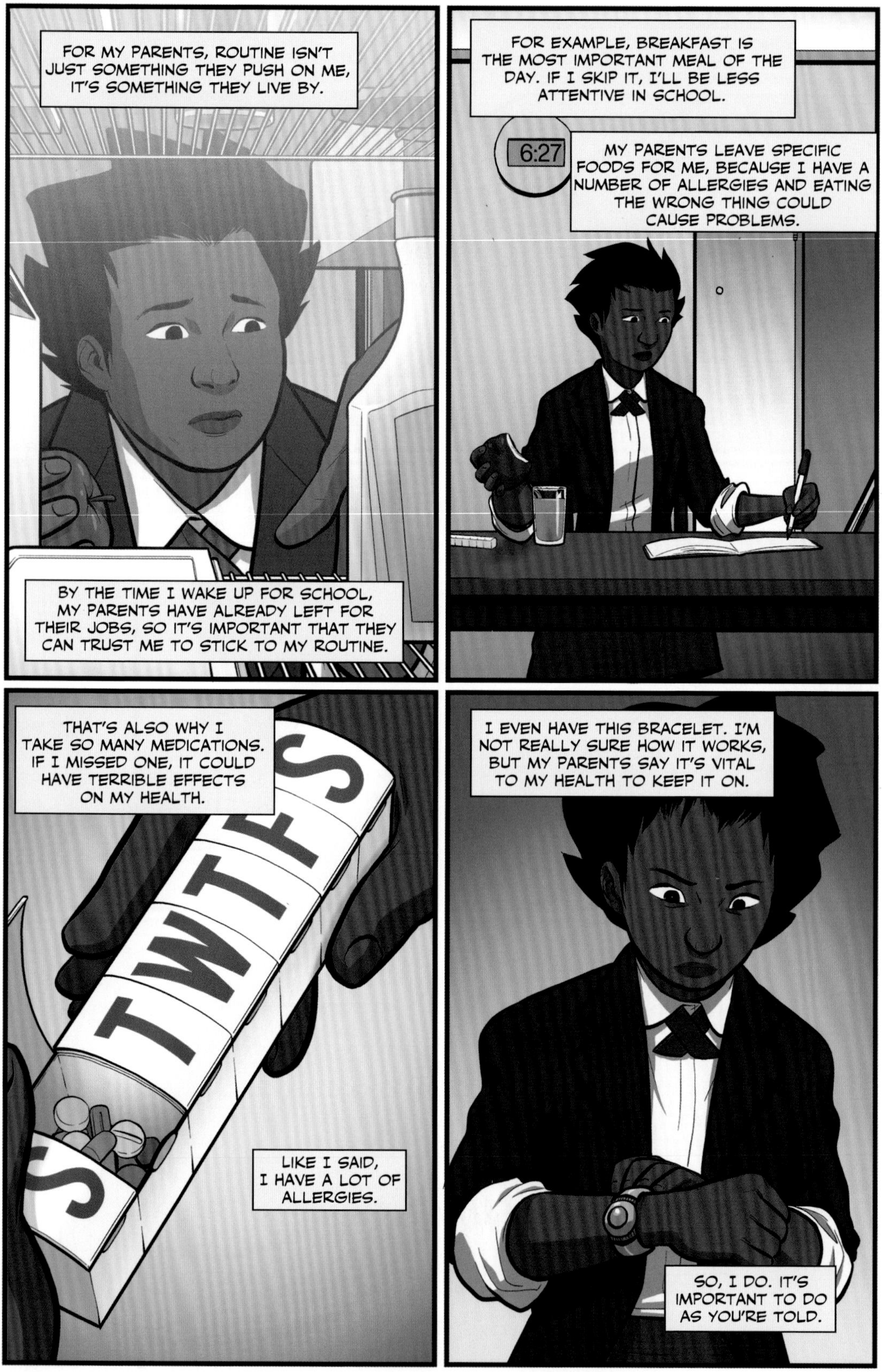
FOR MY PARENTS, ROUTINE ISN'T JUST SOMETHING THEY PUSH ON ME, IT'S SOMETHING THEY LIVE BY.
BY THE TIME I WAKE UP FOR SCHOOL, MY PARENTS HAVE ALREADY LEFT FOR THEIR JOBS, SO IT'S IMPORTANT THAT THEY CAN TRUST ME TO STICK TO MY ROUTINE.
FOR EXAMPLE, BREAKFAST IS THE MOST IMPORTANT MEAL OF THE DAY. IF I SKIP IT, I'LL BE LESS ATTENTIVE IN SCHOOL.
6:27
MY PARENTS LEAVE SPECIFIC FOODS FOR ME, BECAUSE I HAVE A NUMBER OF ALLERGIES AND EATING THE WRONG THING COULD CAUSE PROBLEMS.
THAT'S ALSO WHY I TAKE SO MANY MEDICATIONS. IF I MISSED ONE, IT COULD HAVE TERRIBLE EFFECTS ON MY HEALTH.
S T W T F S
LIKE I SAID, I HAVE A LOT OF ALLERGIES.
I EVEN HAVE THIS BRACELET. I'M NOT REALLY SURE HOW IT WORKS, BUT MY PARENTS SAY IT'S VITAL TO MY HEALTH TO KEEP IT ON.
SO, I DO. IT'S IMPORTANT TO DO AS YOU'RE TOLD.

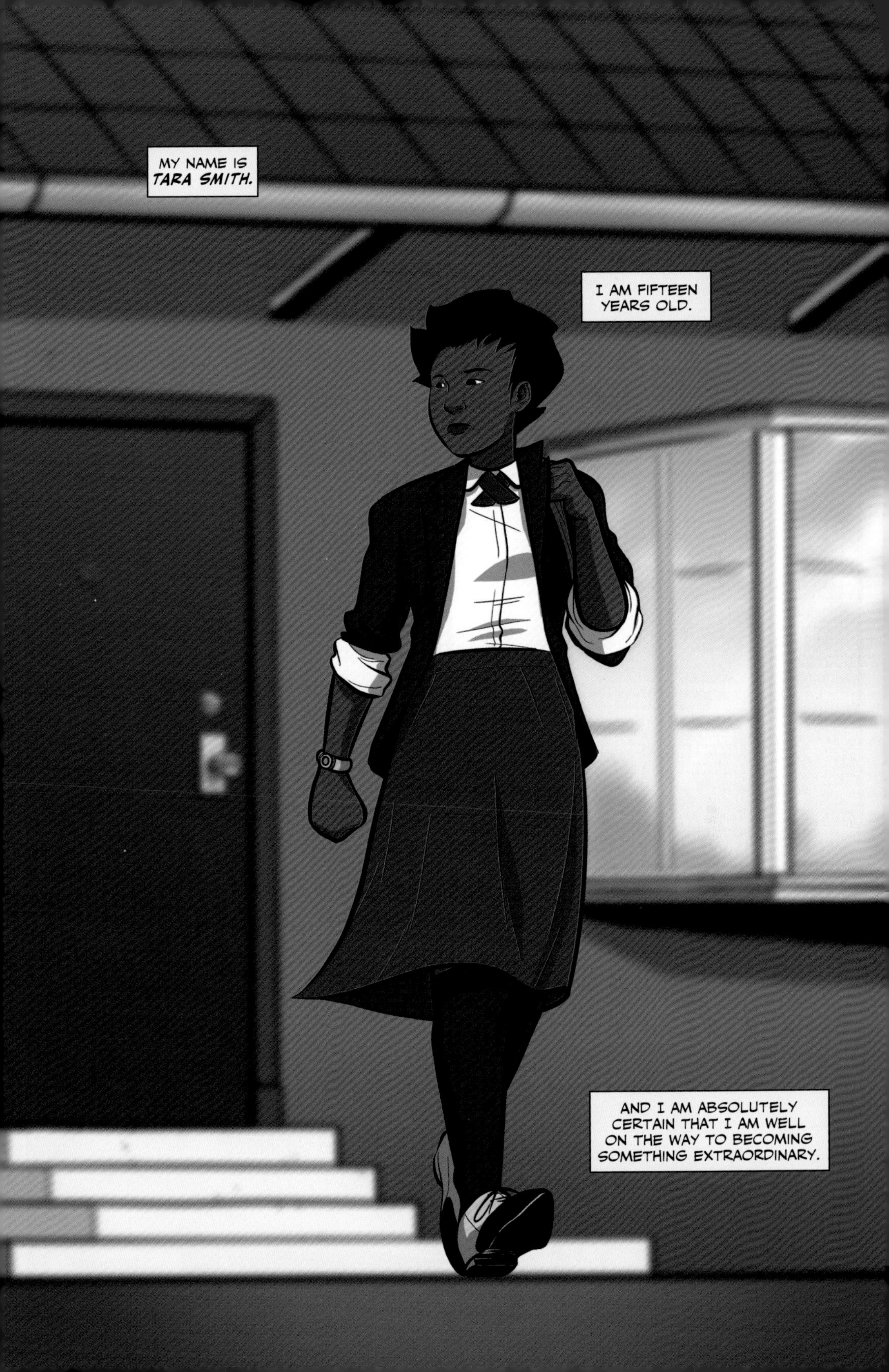
MY NAME IS TARA SMITH.
I AM FIFTEEN YEARS OLD.
AND I AM ABSOLUTELY CERTAIN THAT I AM WELL ON THE WAY TO BECOMING SOMETHING EXTRAORDINARY.

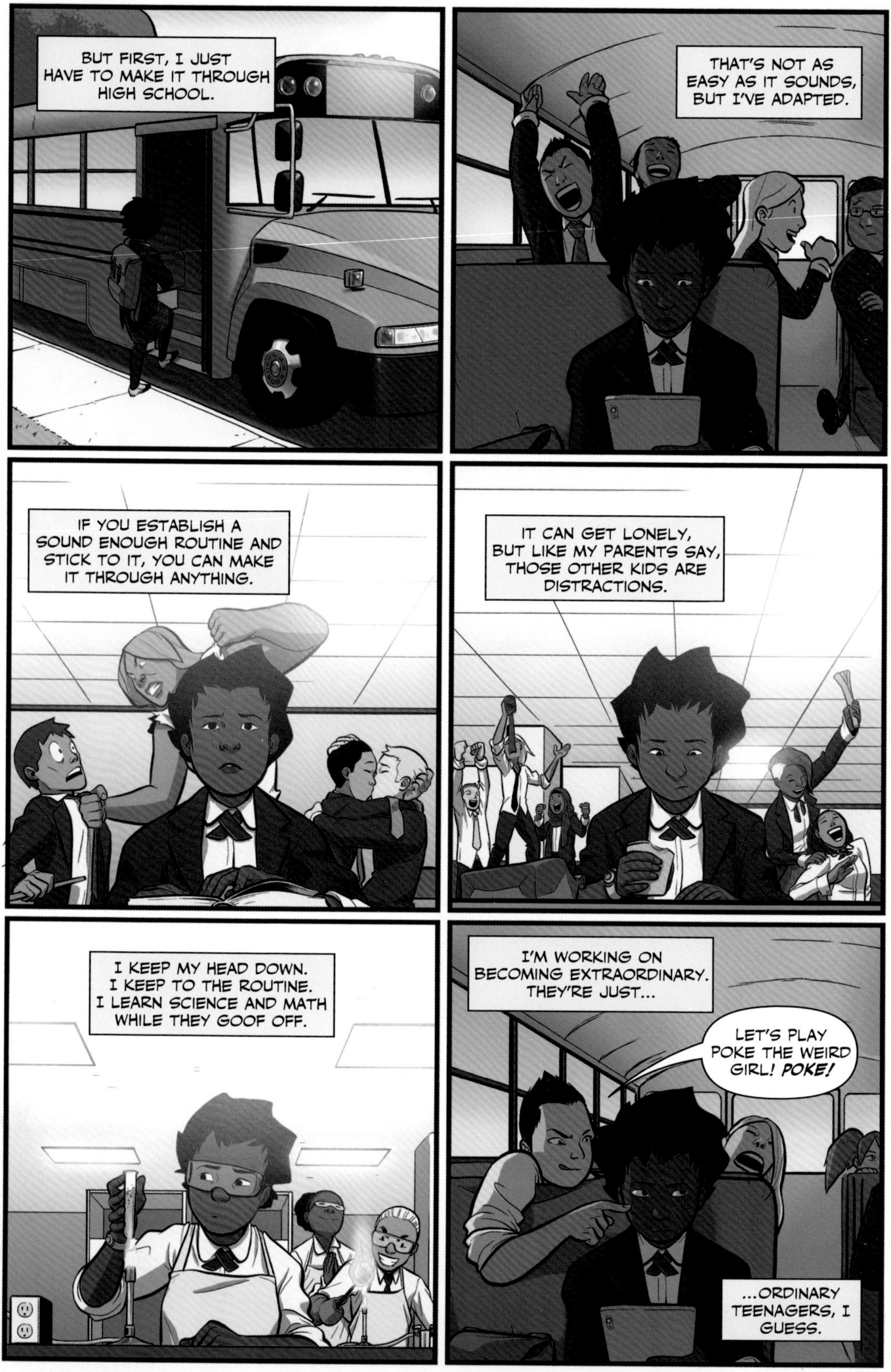
BUT FIRST, I JUST HAVE TO MAKE IT THROUGH HIGH SCHOOL.
THAT'S NOT AS EASY AS IT SOUNDS, BUT I'VE ADAPTED.
IF YOU ESTABLISH A SOUND ENOUGH ROUTINE AND STICK TO IT, YOU CAN MAKE IT THROUGH ANYTHING.
IT CAN GET LONELY, BUT LIKE MY PARENTS SAY, THOSE OTHER KIDS ARE DISTRACTIONS.
I KEEP MY HEAD DOWN. I KEEP TO THE ROUTINE. I LEARN SCIENCE AND MATH WHILE THEY GOOF OFF.
I'M WORKING ON BECOMING EXTRAORDINARY. THEY'RE JUST...
LET'S PLAY POKE THE WEIRD GIRL! *POKE!*
...ORDINARY TEENAGERS, I GUESS.

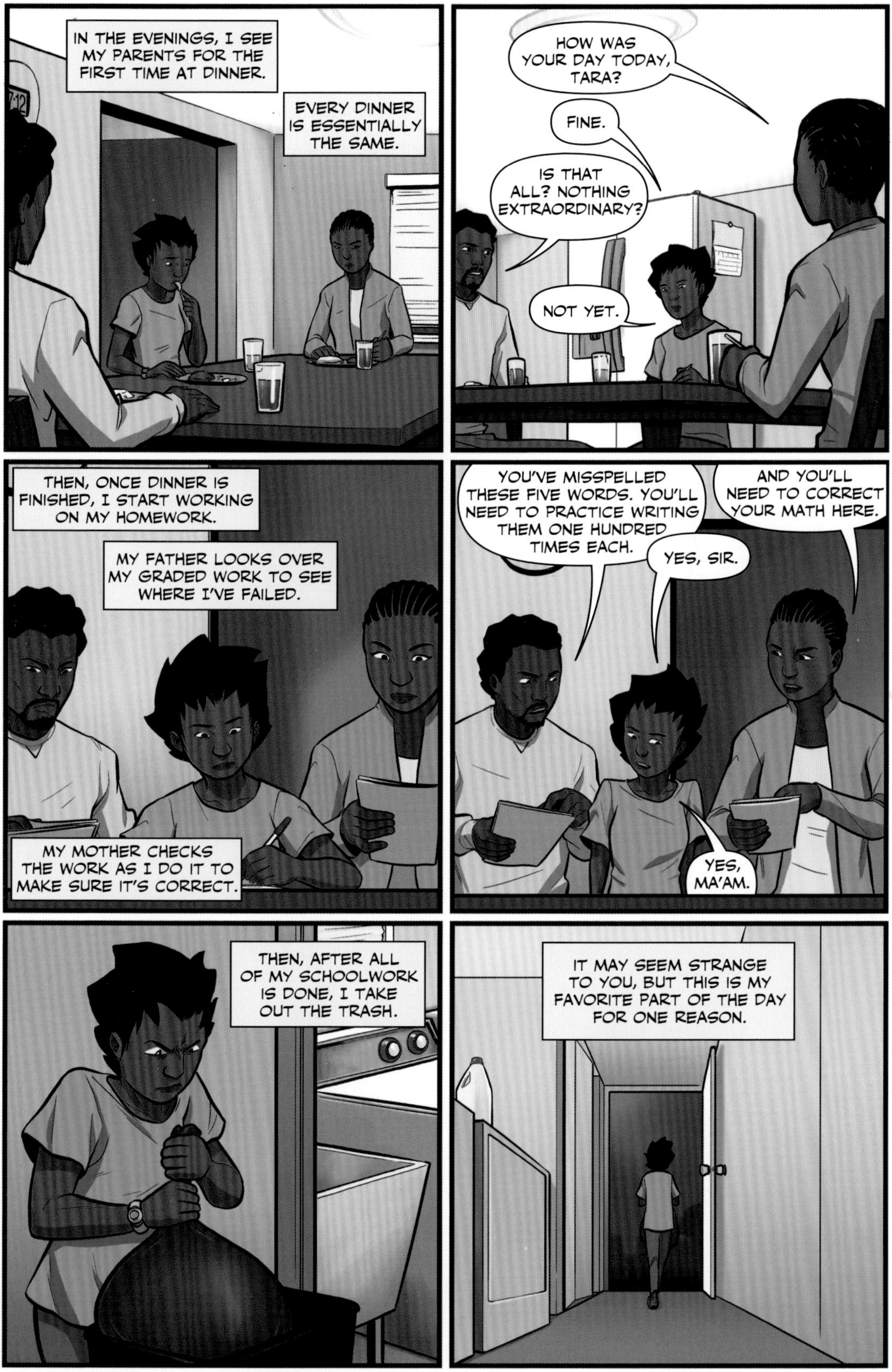
IN THE EVENINGS, I SEE MY PARENTS FOR THE FIRST TIME AT DINNER.
EVERY DINNER IS ESSENTIALLY THE SAME.
7:12
HOW WAS YOUR DAY TODAY, TARA?
FINE.
IS THAT ALL? NOTHING EXTRAORDINARY?
NOT YET.
THEN, ONCE DINNER IS FINISHED, I START WORKING ON MY HOMEWORK.
MY FATHER LOOKS OVER MY GRADED WORK TO SEE WHERE I'VE FAILED.
MY MOTHER CHECKS THE WORK AS I DO IT TO MAKE SURE IT'S CORRECT.
YOU'VE MISSPELLED THESE FIVE WORDS. YOU'LL NEED TO PRACTICE WRITING THEM ONE HUNDRED TIMES EACH.
YES, SIR.
AND YOU'LL NEED TO CORRECT YOUR MATH HERE.
YES, MA'AM.
THEN, AFTER ALL OF MY SCHOOLWORK IS DONE, I TAKE OUT THE TRASH.
IT MAY SEEM STRANGE TO YOU, BUT THIS IS MY FAVORITE PART OF THE DAY FOR ONE REASON.

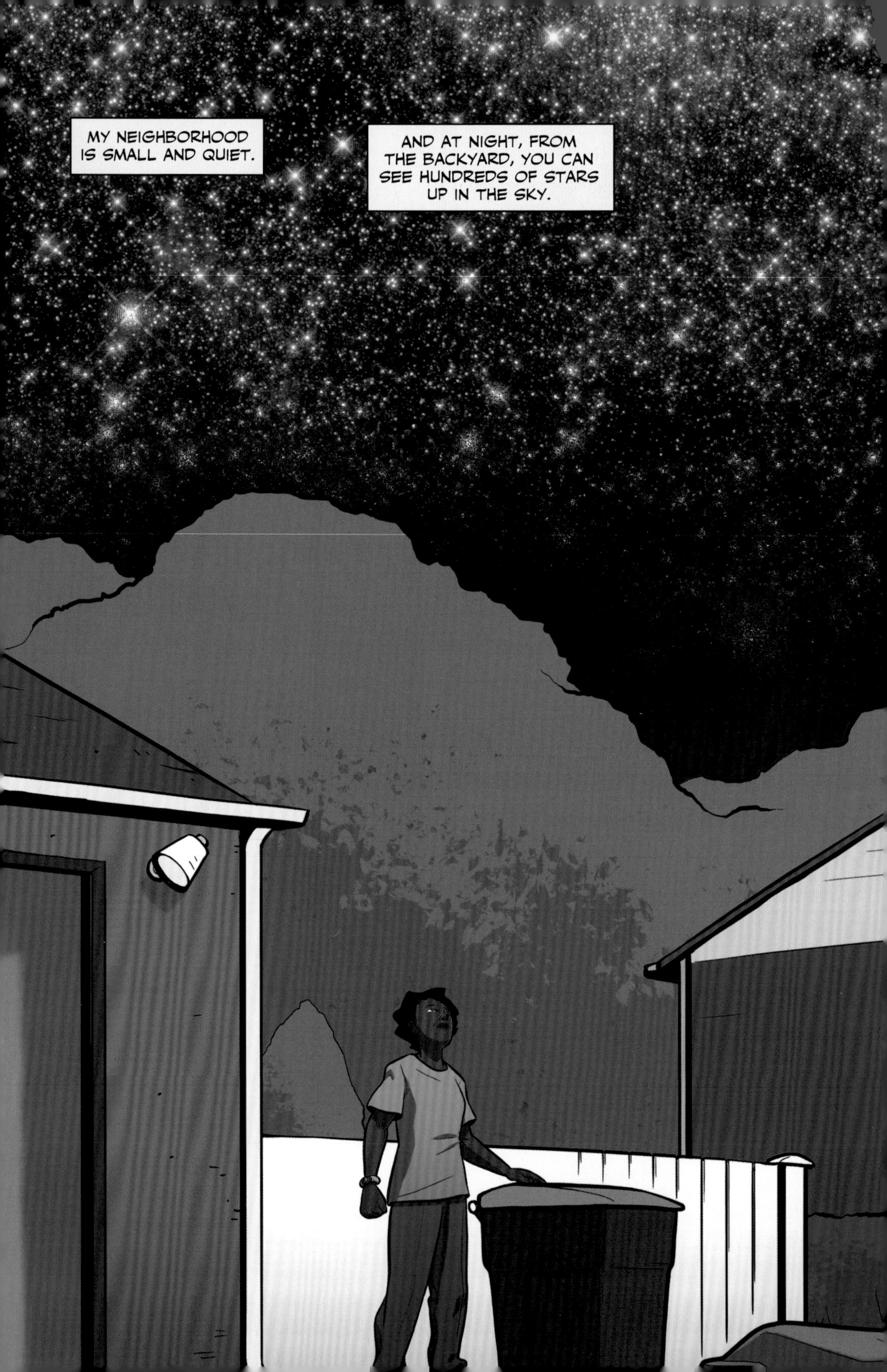
MY NEIGHBORHOOD IS SMALL AND QUIET.
AND AT NIGHT, FROM THE BACKYARD, YOU CAN SEE HUNDREDS OF STARS UP IN THE SKY.

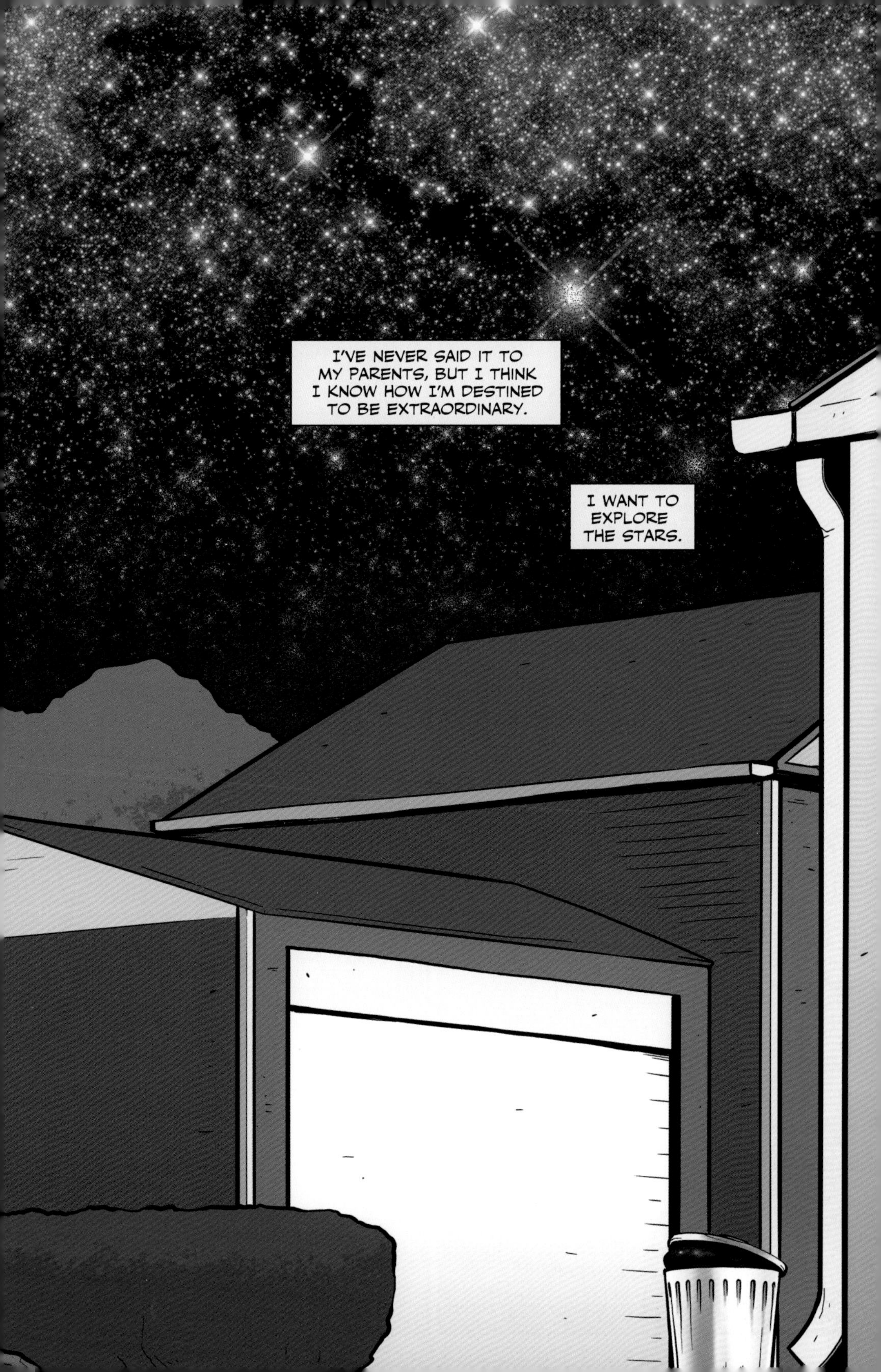
I'VE NEVER SAID IT TO MY PARENTS, BUT I THINK I KNOW HOW I'M DESTINED TO BE EXTRAORDINARY.
I WANT TO EXPLORE THE STARS.

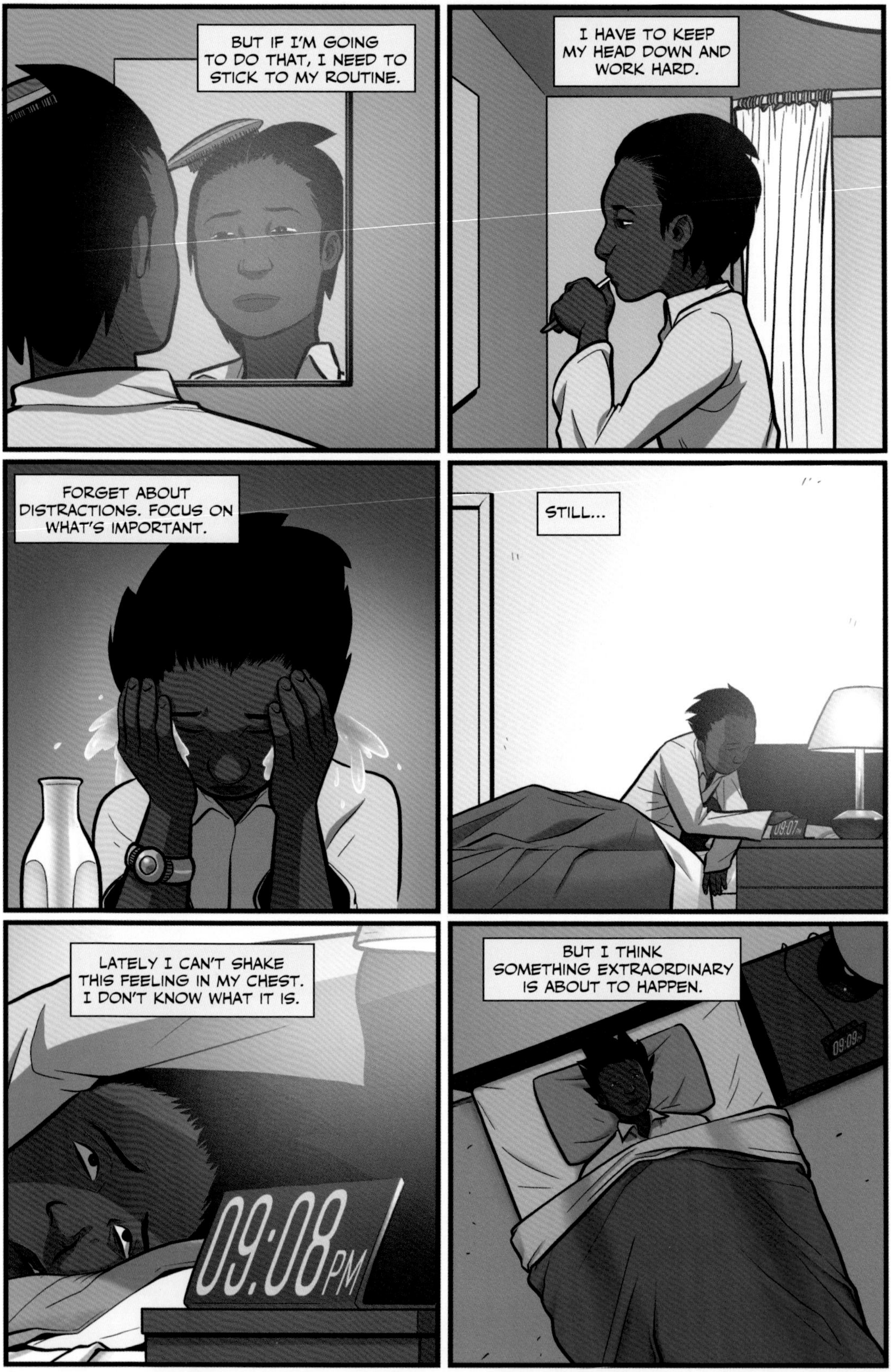
BUT IF I'M GOING TO DO THAT, I NEED TO STICK TO MY ROUTINE.
I HAVE TO KEEP MY HEAD DOWN AND WORK HARD.
FORGET ABOUT DISTRACTIONS. FOCUS ON WHAT'S IMPORTANT.
STILL...
09:07PM
LATELY I CAN'T SHAKE THIS FEELING IN MY CHEST. I DON'T KNOW WHAT IT IS.
09:08PM
BUT I THINK SOMETHING EXTRAORDINARY IS ABOUT TO HAPPEN.
09:09PM

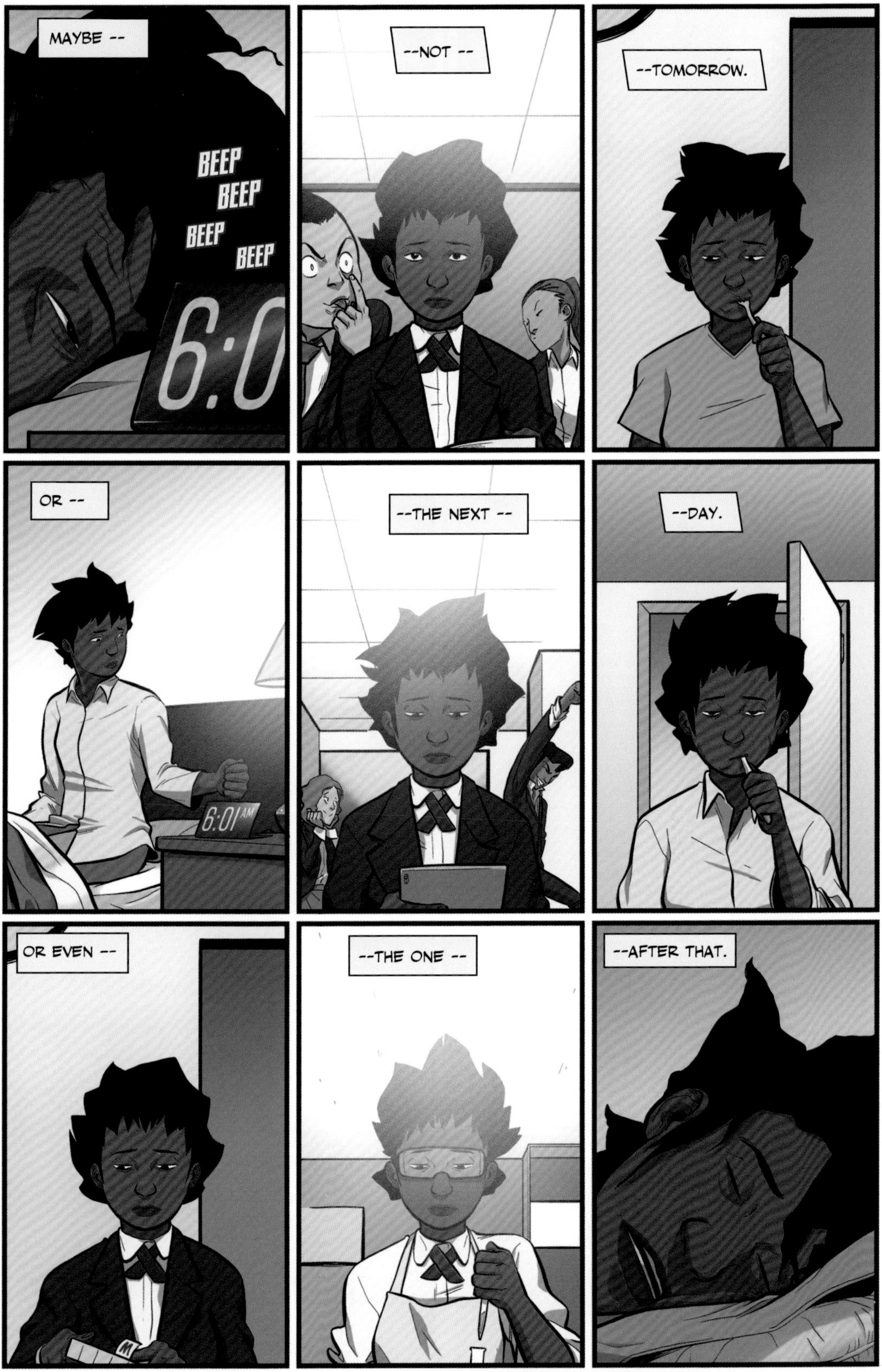
MAYBE --
BEEP
BEEP
BEEP
BEEP
6:0
--NOT --
--TOMORROW.
OR --
6:01AM
--THE NEXT --
--DAY.
OR EVEN --
--THE ONE --
--AFTER THAT.

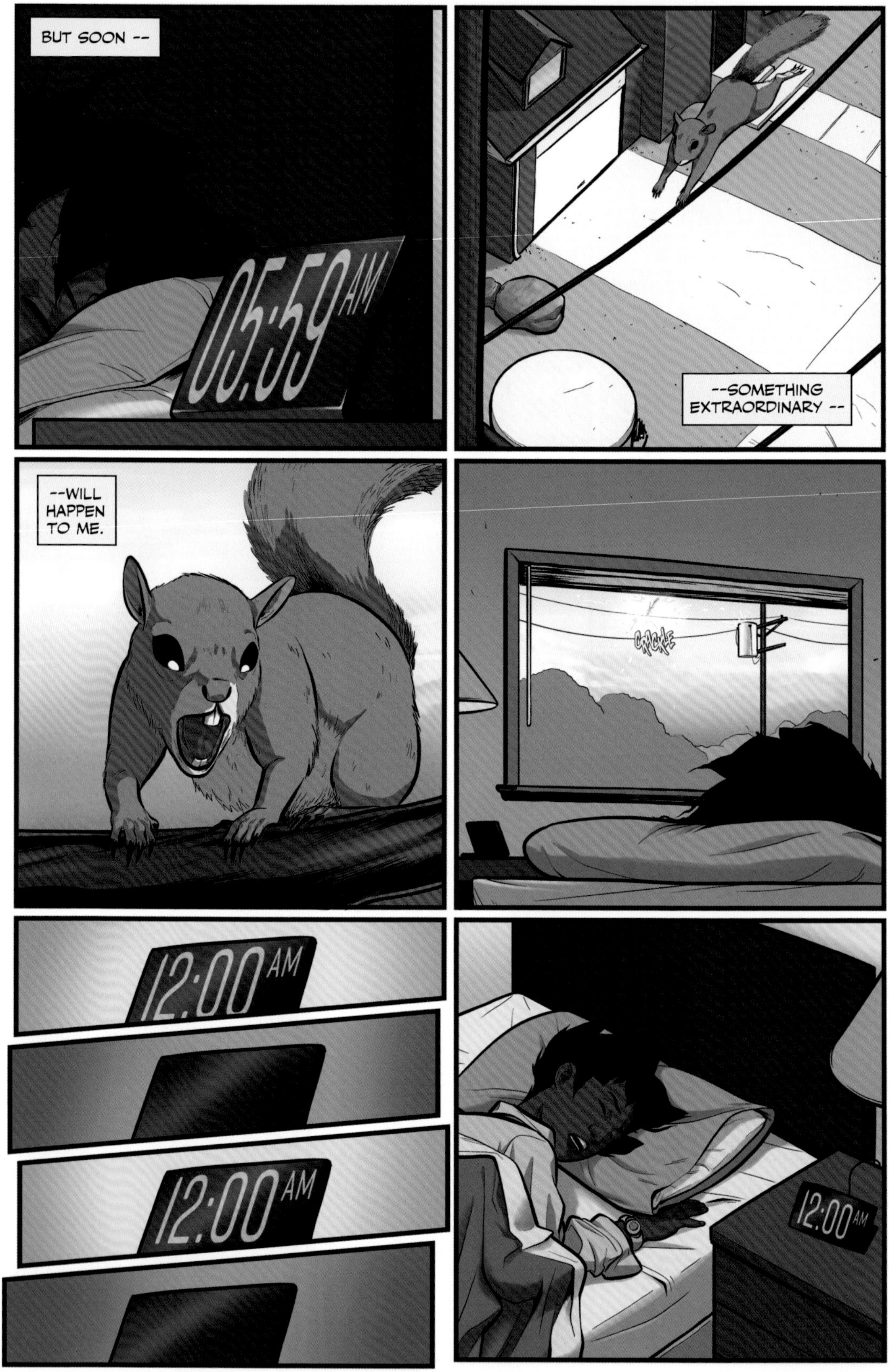
BUT SOON --
05:59 AM
--SOMETHING EXTRAORDINARY --
--WILL HAPPEN TO ME.
CRACKLE
12:00 AM
12:00 AM
12:00 AM

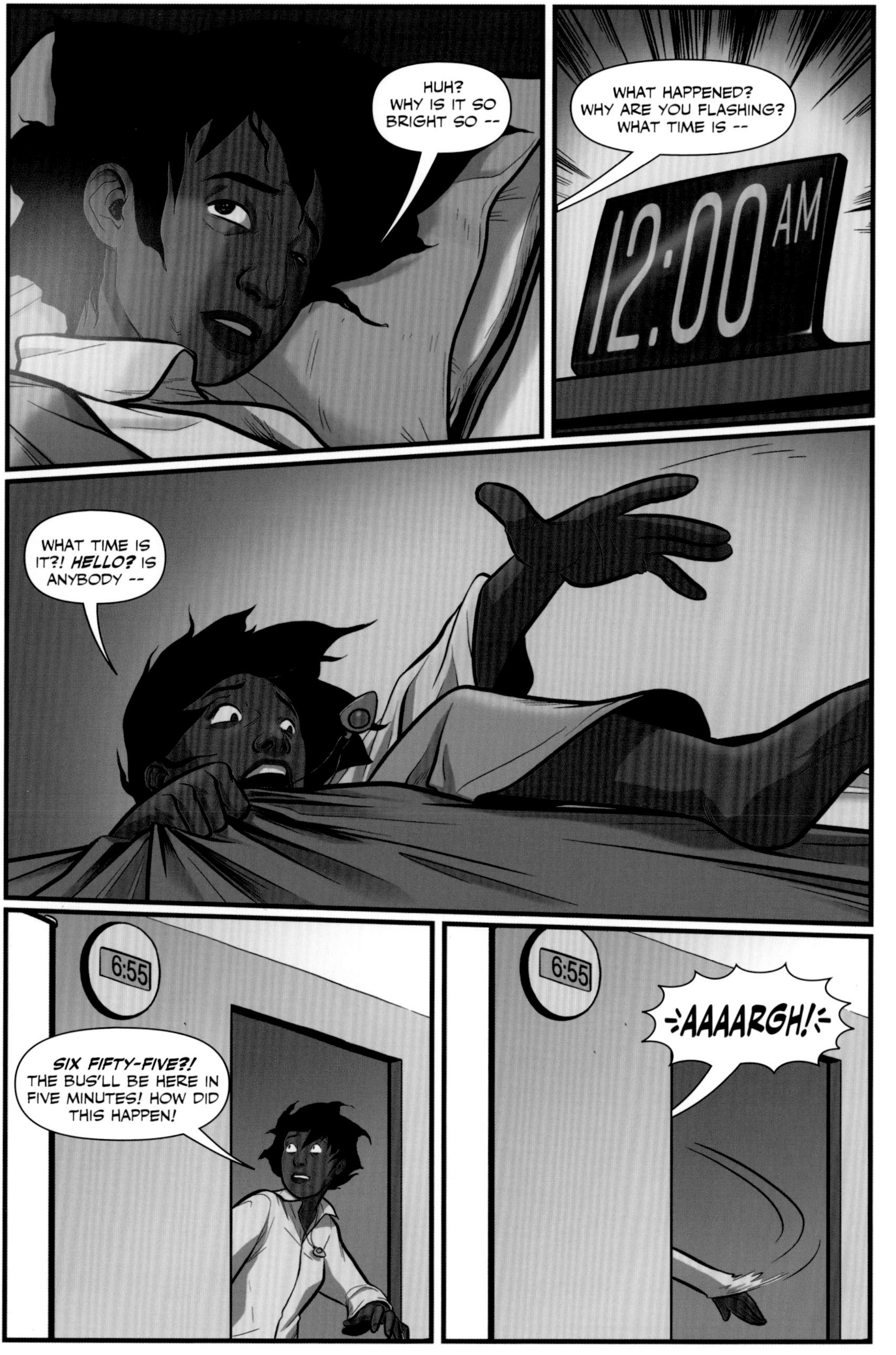
HUH?
WHY IS IT SO
BRIGHT SO --
WHAT HAPPENED?
WHY ARE YOU FLASHING?
WHAT TIME IS --
12:00 AM
WHAT TIME IS
IT?! *HELLO?* IS
ANYBODY --
6:55
SIX FIFTY-FIVE?!
THE BUS'LL BE HERE IN
FIVE MINUTES! HOW DID
THIS HAPPEN!
6:55
AAAARGH!

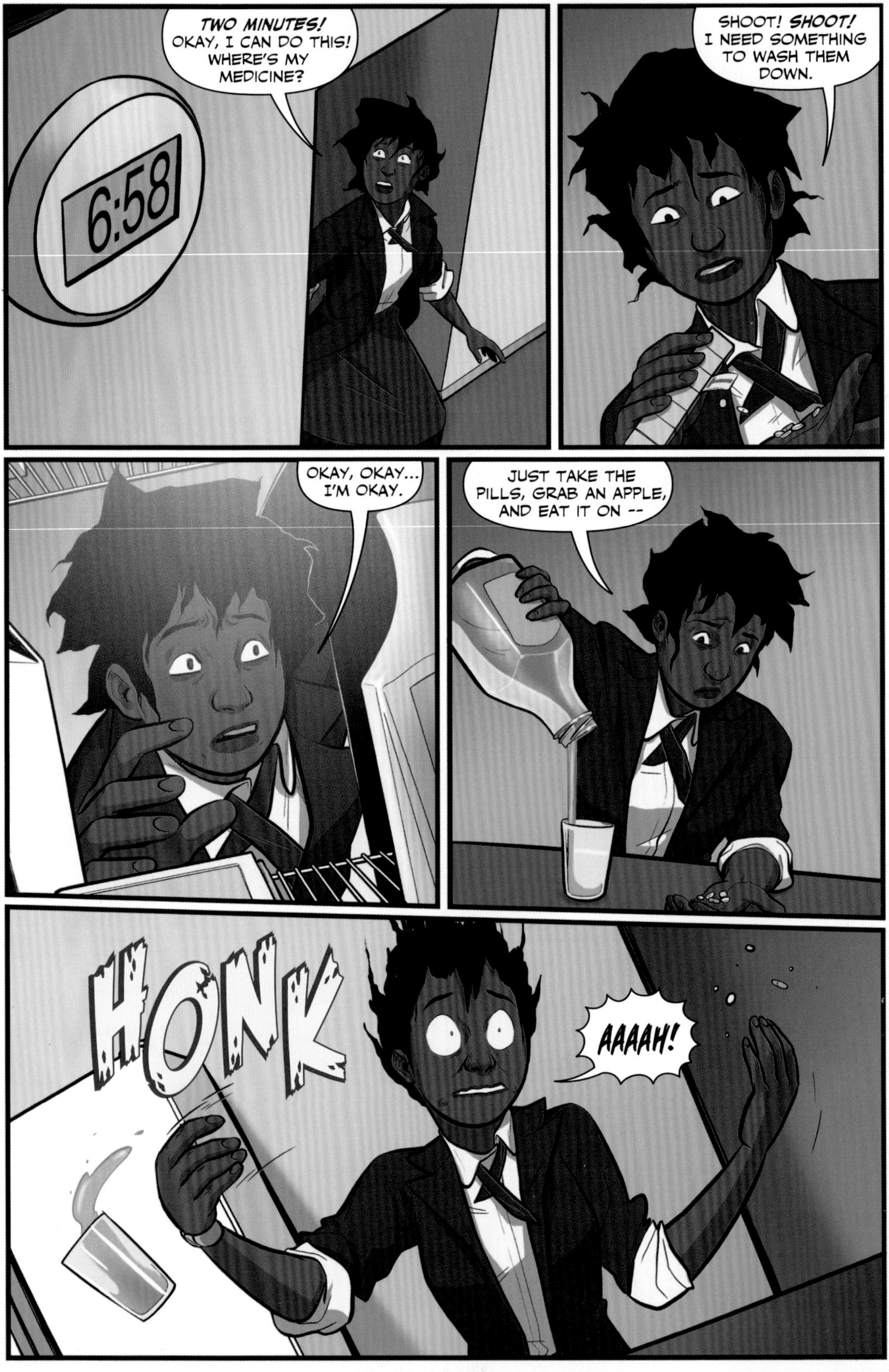
TWO MINUTES! OKAY, I CAN DO THIS! WHERE'S MY MEDICINE?
6:58
SHOOT! SHOOT! I NEED SOMETHING TO WASH THEM DOWN.
OKAY, OKAY... I'M OKAY.
JUST TAKE THE PILLS, GRAB AN APPLE, AND EAT IT ON --
HONK
AAAAH!

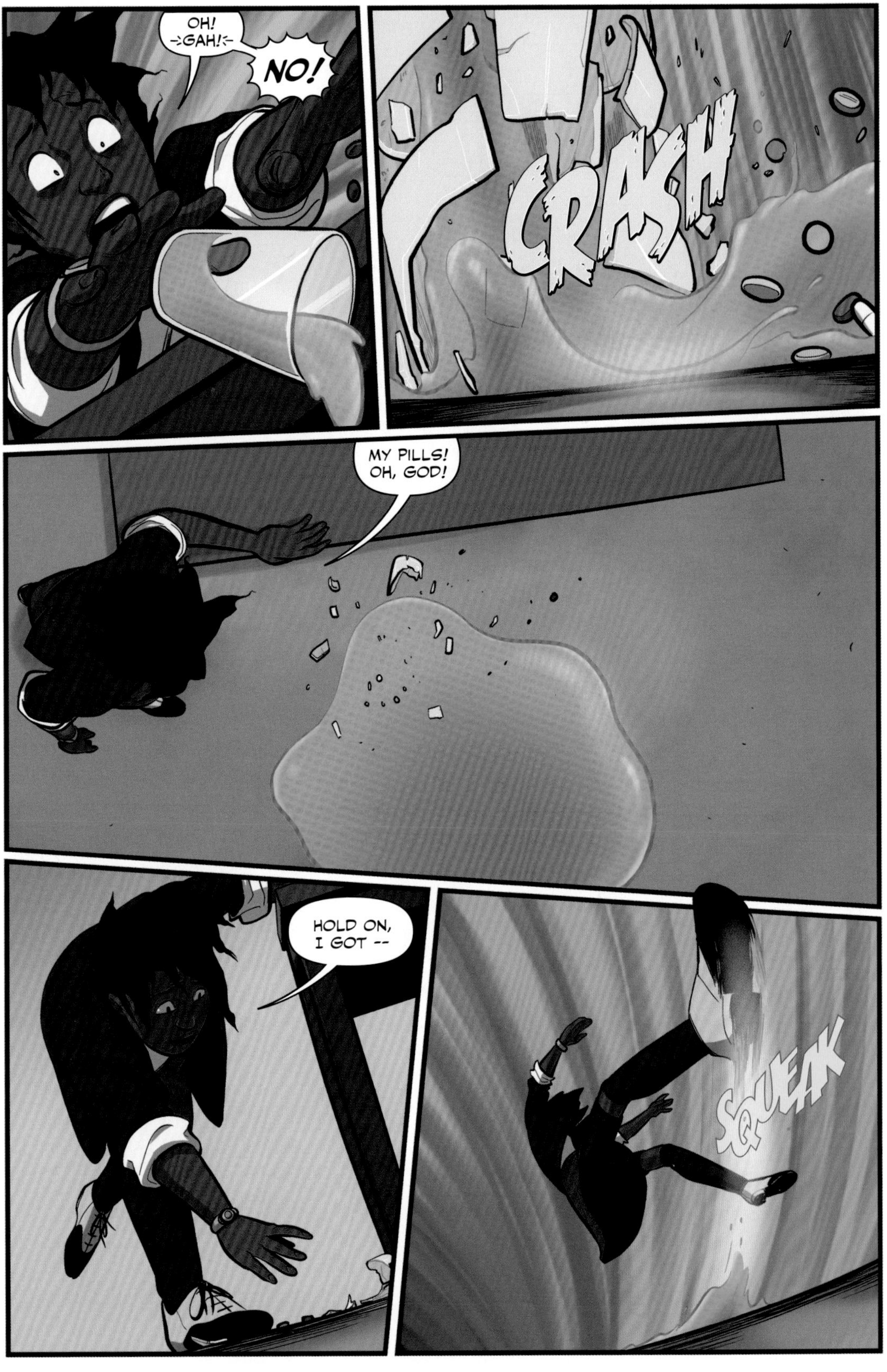
OH! -GAH!-
NO!
CRASH
MY PILLS! OH, GOD!
HOLD ON, I GOT --
SQUEAK

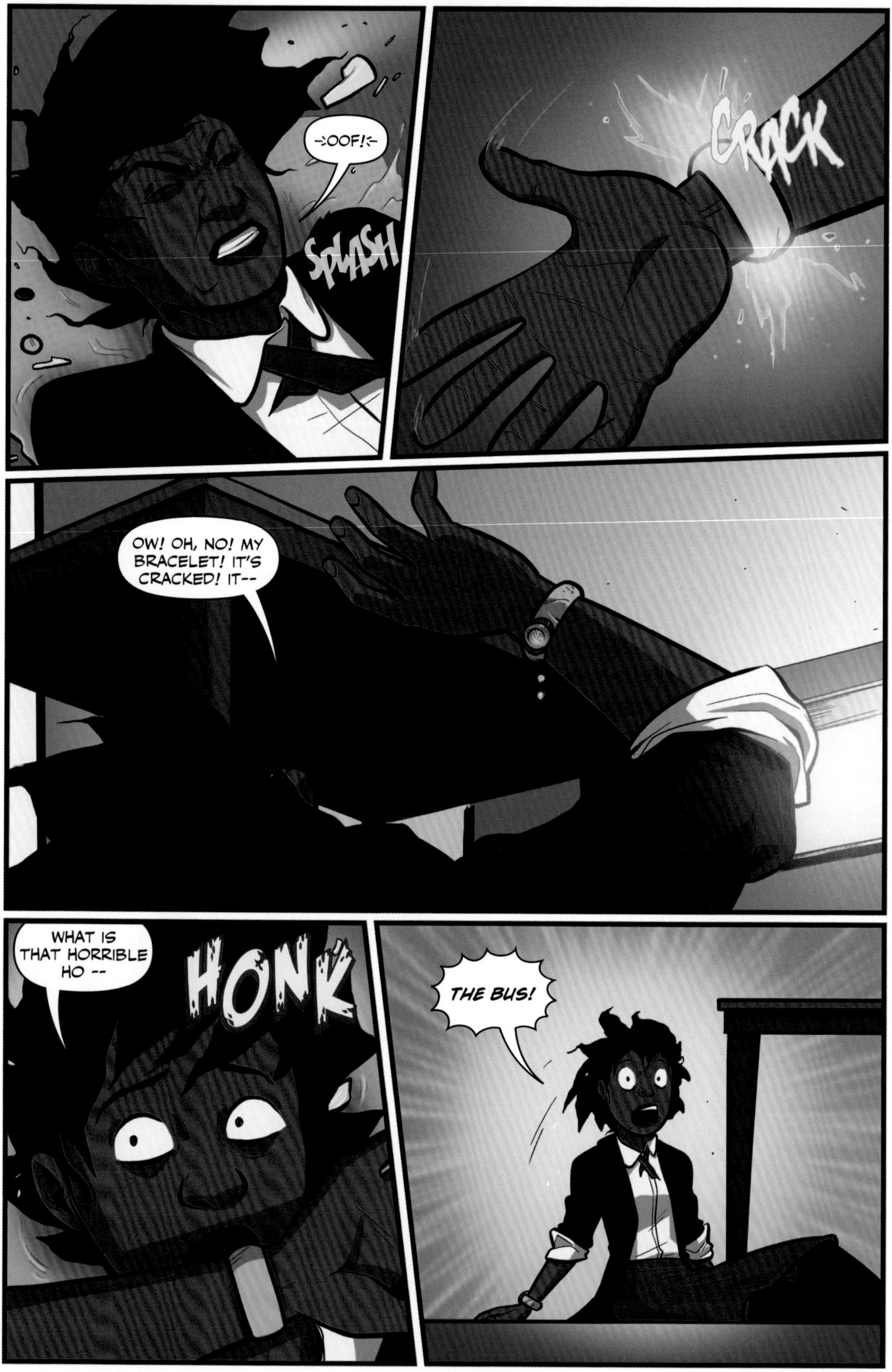
-OOF!-
SPLASH
CRACK
OW! OH, NO! MY BRACELET! IT'S CRACKED! IT--
WHAT IS THAT HORRIBLE HO --
HONK
THE BUS!

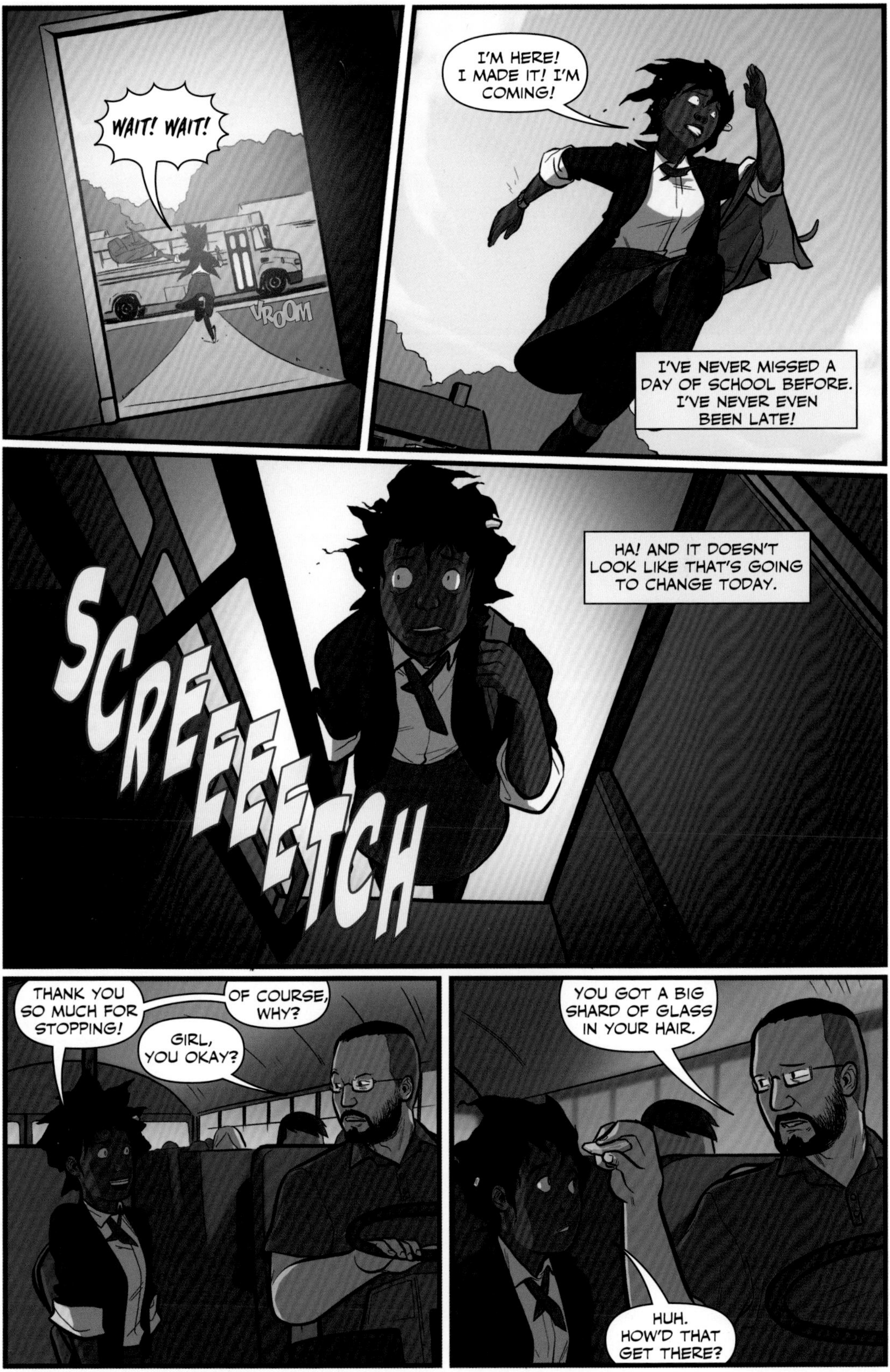

WAIT! WAIT!
VROOM
I'M HERE! I MADE IT! I'M COMING!
I'VE NEVER MISSED A DAY OF SCHOOL BEFORE. I'VE NEVER EVEN BEEN LATE!
HA! AND IT DOESN'T LOOK LIKE THAT'S GOING TO CHANGE TODAY.
SCREEEETCH
THANK YOU SO MUCH FOR STOPPING!
OF COURSE, WHY?
GIRL, YOU OKAY?
YOU GOT A BIG SHARD OF GLASS IN YOUR HAIR.
HUH. HOW'D THAT GET THERE?

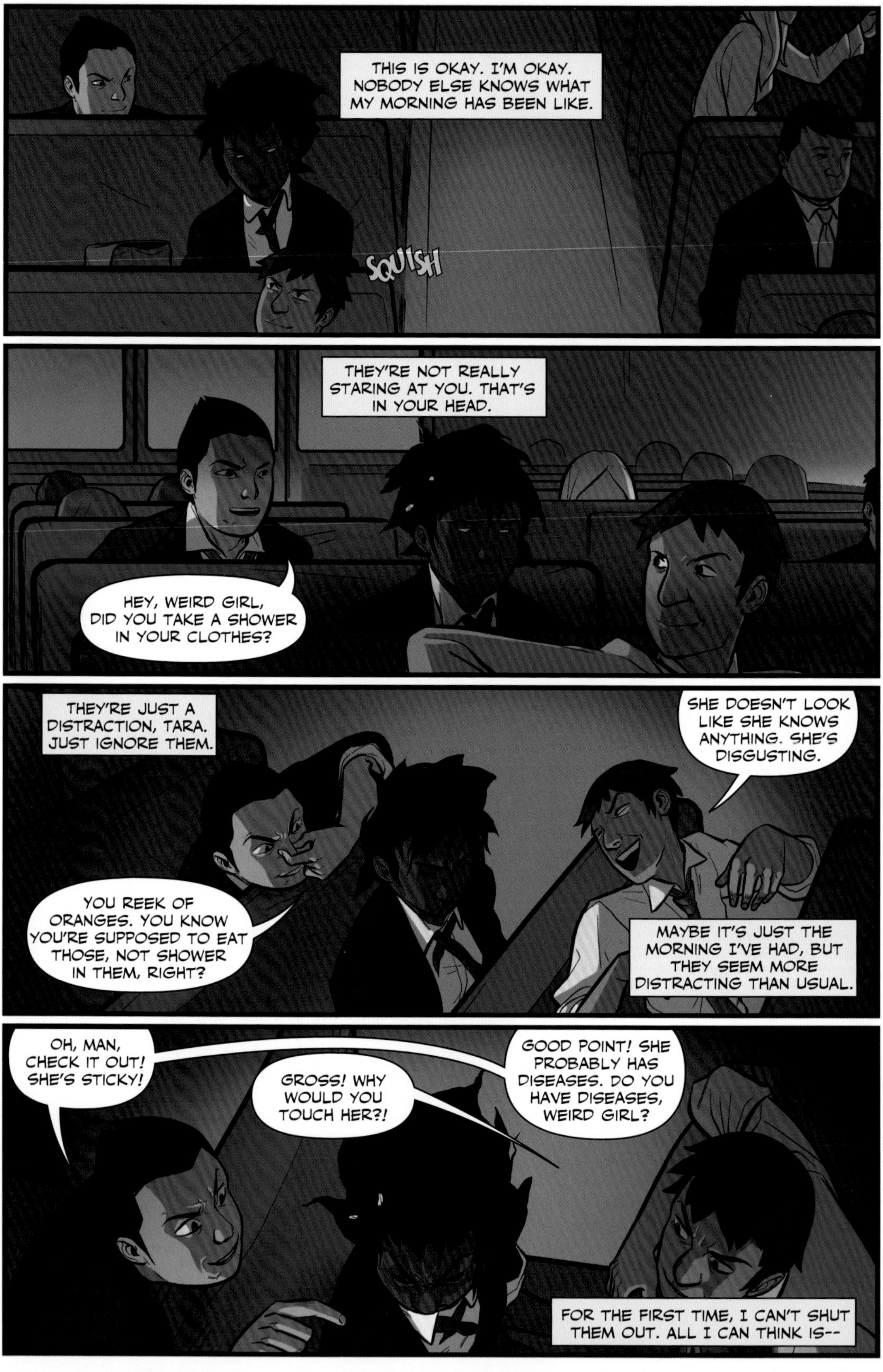
THIS IS OKAY. I'M OKAY. NOBODY ELSE KNOWS WHAT MY MORNING HAS BEEN LIKE.
SQUISH
THEY'RE NOT REALLY STARING AT YOU. THAT'S IN YOUR HEAD.
HEY, WEIRD GIRL, DID YOU TAKE A SHOWER IN YOUR CLOTHES?
THEY'RE JUST A DISTRACTION, TARA. JUST IGNORE THEM.
SHE DOESN'T LOOK LIKE SHE KNOWS ANYTHING. SHE'S DISGUSTING.
YOU REEK OF ORANGES. YOU KNOW YOU'RE SUPPOSED TO EAT THOSE, NOT SHOWER IN THEM, RIGHT?
MAYBE IT'S JUST THE MORNING I'VE HAD, BUT THEY SEEM MORE DISTRACTING THAN USUAL.
OH, MAN, CHECK IT OUT! SHE'S STICKY!
GROSS! WHY WOULD YOU TOUCH HER?!
GOOD POINT! SHE PROBABLY HAS DISEASES. DO YOU HAVE DISEASES, WEIRD GIRL?
FOR THE FIRST TIME, I CAN'T SHUT THEM OUT. ALL I CAN THINK IS--

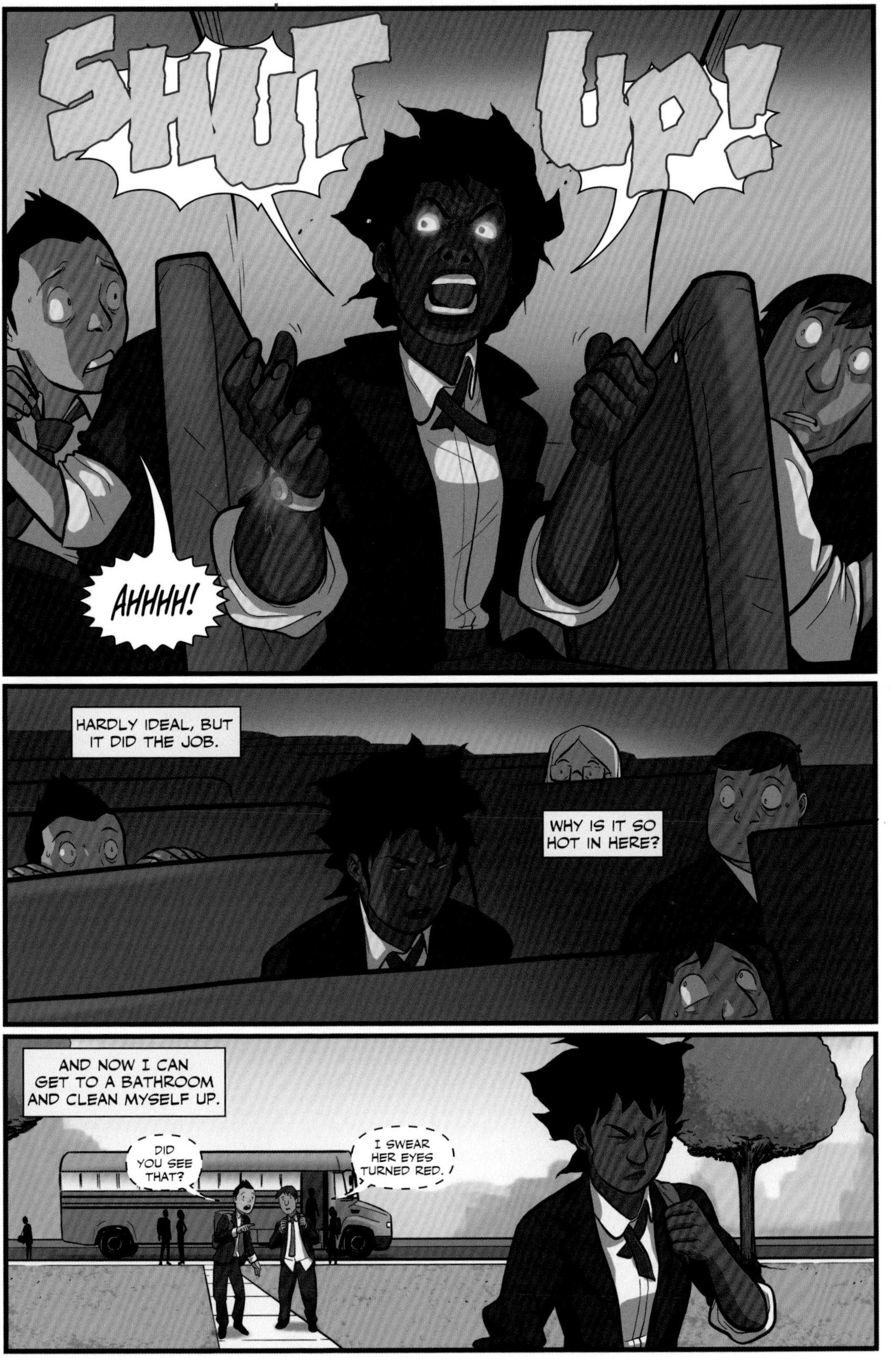
SHUT UP!
AHHHH!
HARDLY IDEAL, BUT IT DID THE JOB.
WHY IS IT SO HOT IN HERE?
AND NOW I CAN GET TO A BATHROOM AND CLEAN MYSELF UP.
DID YOU SEE THAT?
I SWEAR HER EYES TURNED RED.

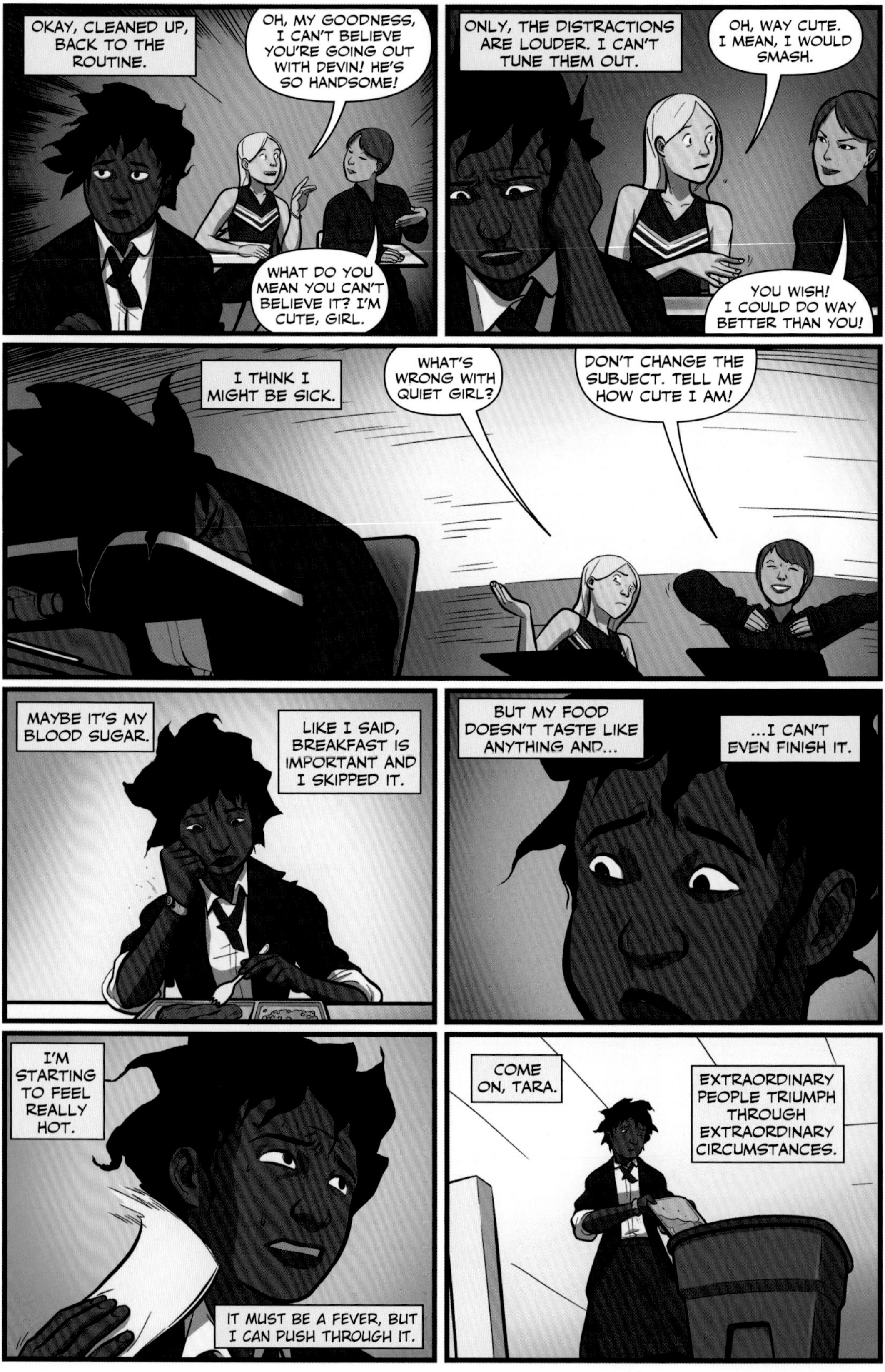
OKAY, CLEANED UP, BACK TO THE ROUTINE.
OH, MY GOODNESS, I CAN'T BELIEVE YOU'RE GOING OUT WITH DEVIN! HE'S SO HANDSOME!
WHAT DO YOU MEAN YOU CAN'T BELIEVE IT? I'M CUTE, GIRL.
ONLY, THE DISTRACTIONS ARE LOUDER. I CAN'T TUNE THEM OUT.
OH, WAY CUTE. I MEAN, I WOULD SMASH.
YOU WISH! I COULD DO WAY BETTER THAN YOU!
I THINK I MIGHT BE SICK.
WHAT'S WRONG WITH QUIET GIRL?
DON'T CHANGE THE SUBJECT. TELL ME HOW CUTE I AM!
MAYBE IT'S MY BLOOD SUGAR.
LIKE I SAID, BREAKFAST IS IMPORTANT AND I SKIPPED IT.
BUT MY FOOD DOESN'T TASTE LIKE ANYTHING AND...
...I CAN'T EVEN FINISH IT.
I'M STARTING TO FEEL REALLY HOT.
IT MUST BE A FEVER, BUT I CAN PUSH THROUGH IT.
COME ON, TARA.
EXTRAORDINARY PEOPLE TRIUMPH THROUGH EXTRAORDINARY CIRCUMSTANCES.

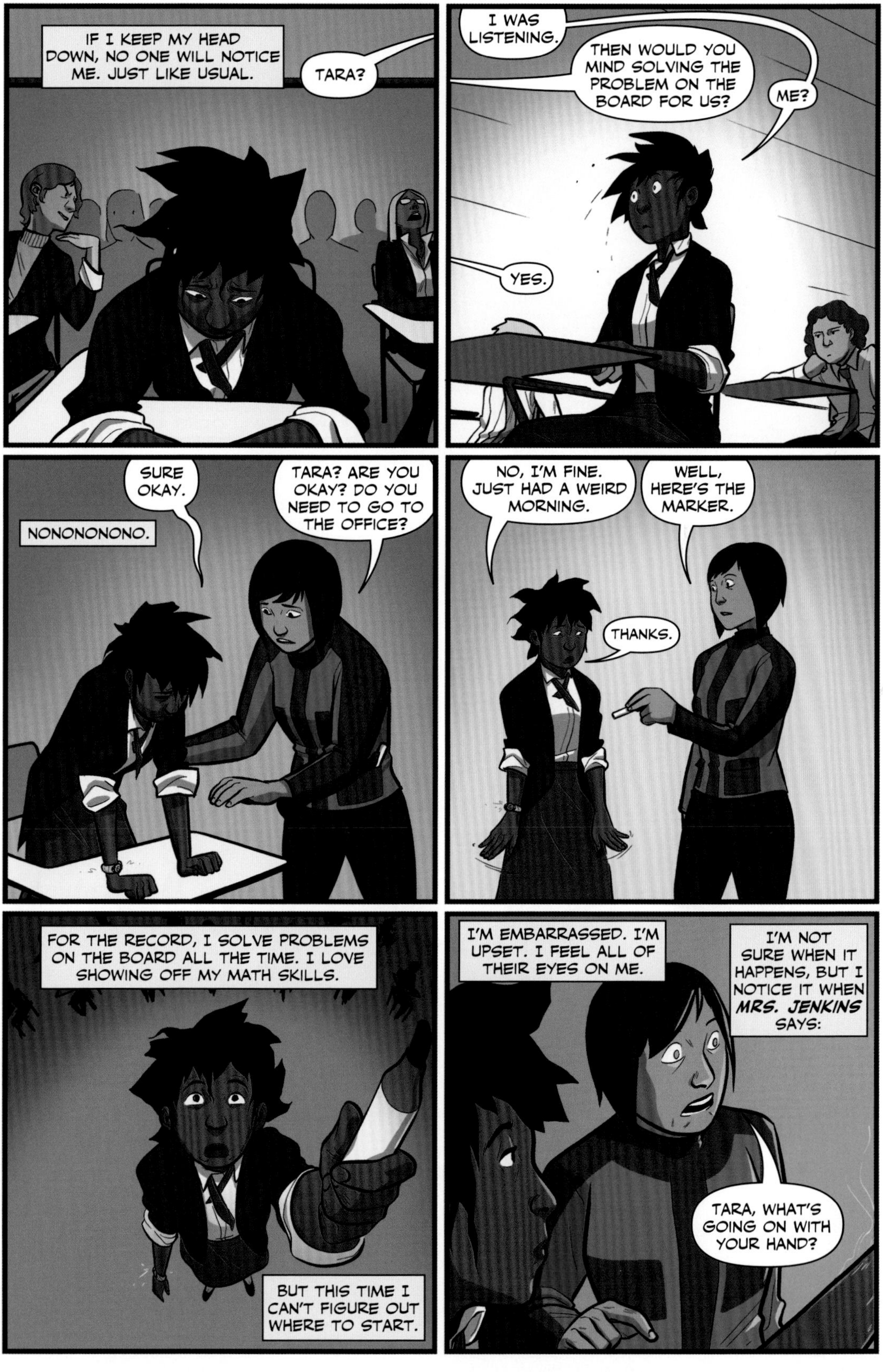
IF I KEEP MY HEAD DOWN, NO ONE WILL NOTICE ME. JUST LIKE USUAL.
TARA?
I WAS LISTENING.
THEN WOULD YOU MIND SOLVING THE PROBLEM ON THE BOARD FOR US?
ME?
YES.
NONONONONO.
SURE OKAY.
TARA? ARE YOU OKAY? DO YOU NEED TO GO TO THE OFFICE?
NO, I'M FINE. JUST HAD A WEIRD MORNING.
WELL, HERE'S THE MARKER.
THANKS.
FOR THE RECORD, I SOLVE PROBLEMS ON THE BOARD ALL THE TIME. I LOVE SHOWING OFF MY MATH SKILLS.
BUT THIS TIME I CAN'T FIGURE OUT WHERE TO START.
I'M EMBARRASSED. I'M UPSET. I FEEL ALL OF THEIR EYES ON ME.
I'M NOT SURE WHEN IT HAPPENS, BUT I NOTICE IT WHEN *MRS. JENKINS* SAYS:
TARA, WHAT'S GOING ON WITH YOUR HAND?

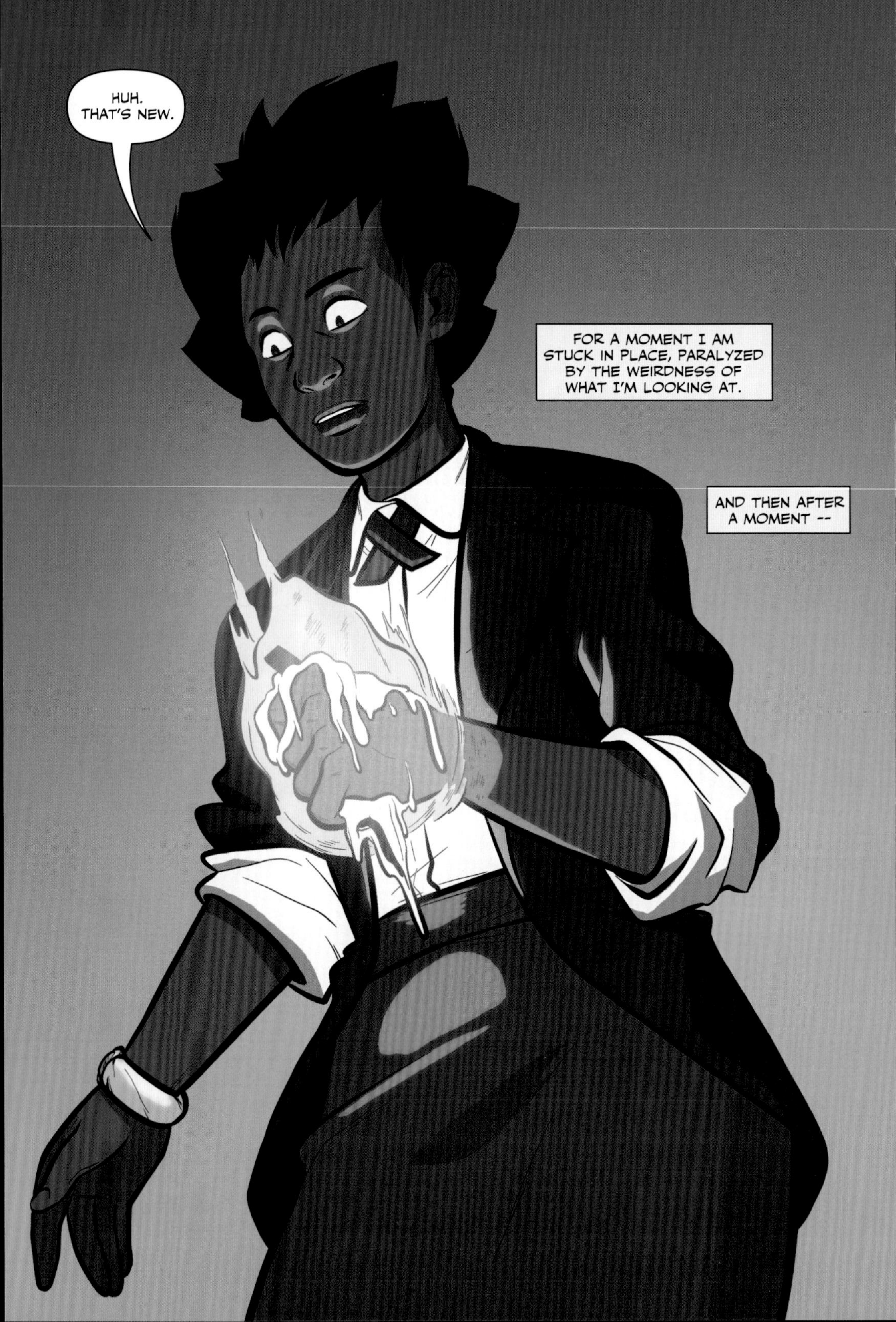
HUH. THAT'S NEW.
FOR A MOMENT I AM STUCK IN PLACE, PARALYZED BY THE WEIRDNESS OF WHAT I'M LOOKING AT.
AND THEN AFTER A MOMENT --

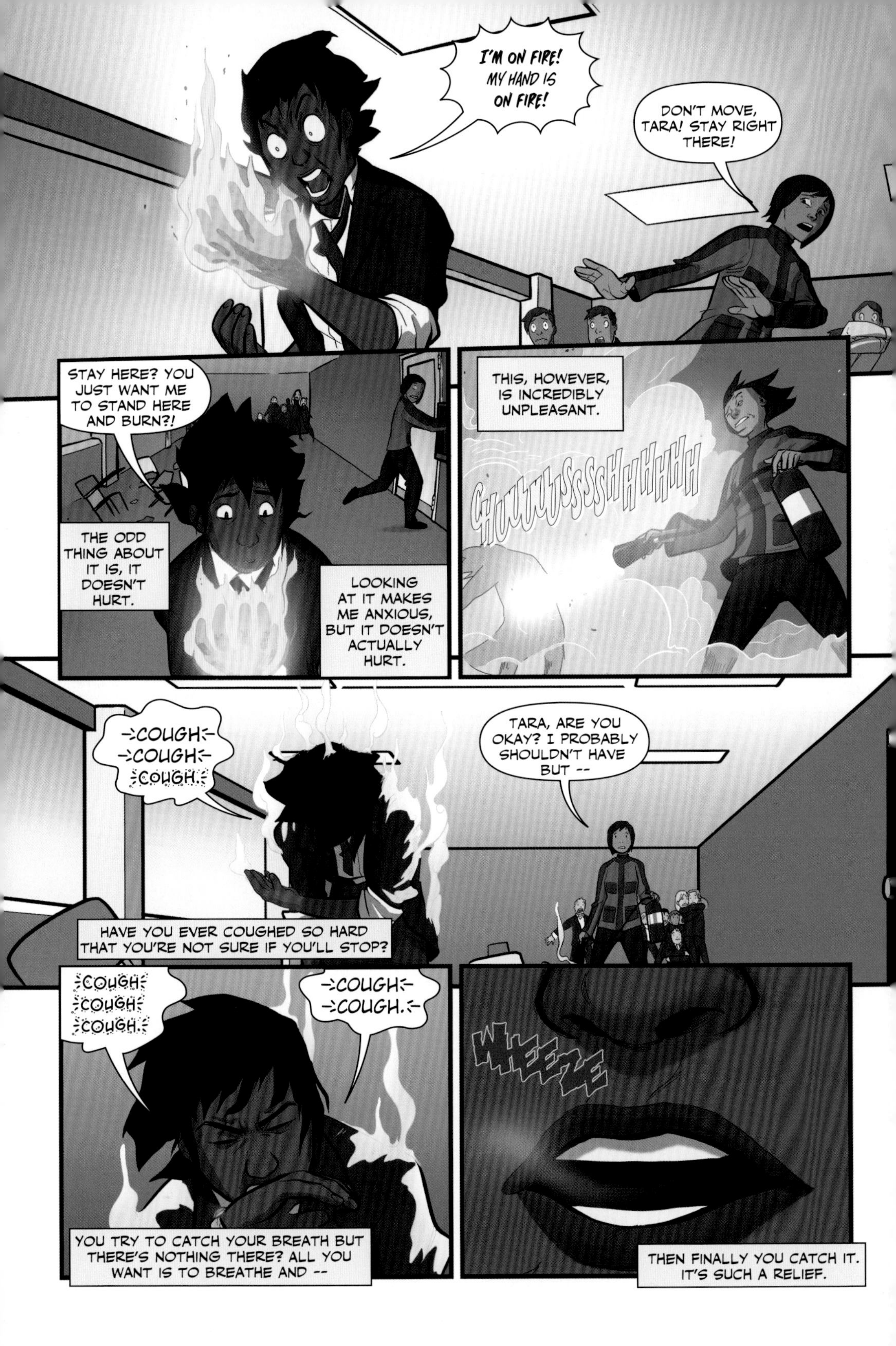
I'M ON FIRE! MY HAND IS ON FIRE!
DON'T MOVE, TARA! STAY RIGHT THERE!
STAY HERE? YOU JUST WANT ME TO STAND HERE AND BURN?!
THE ODD THING ABOUT IT IS, IT DOESN'T HURT.
LOOKING AT IT MAKES ME ANXIOUS, BUT IT DOESN'T ACTUALLY HURT.
THIS, HOWEVER, IS INCREDIBLY UNPLEASANT.
CHUUUUSSSSHHHHHH
COUGH COUGH COUGH.
TARA, ARE YOU OKAY? I PROBABLY SHOULDN'T HAVE BUT --
HAVE YOU EVER COUGHED SO HARD THAT YOU'RE NOT SURE IF YOU'LL STOP?
COUGH COUGH COUGH.
COUGH COUGH.
YOU TRY TO CATCH YOUR BREATH BUT THERE'S NOTHING THERE? ALL YOU WANT IS TO BREATHE AND --
WHEEZE
THEN FINALLY YOU CATCH IT. IT'S SUCH A RELIEF.

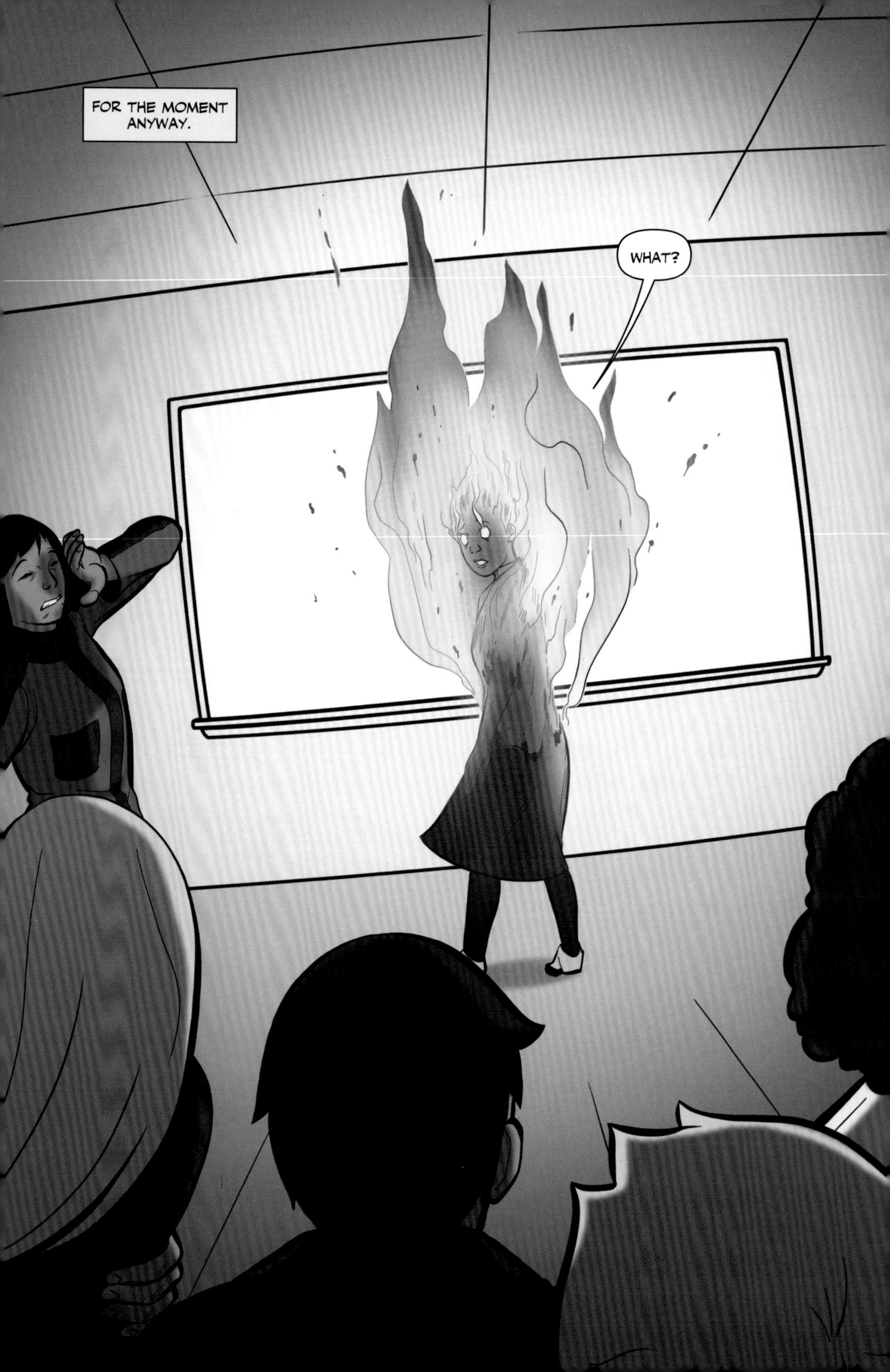
FOR THE MOMENT ANYWAY.
WHAT?

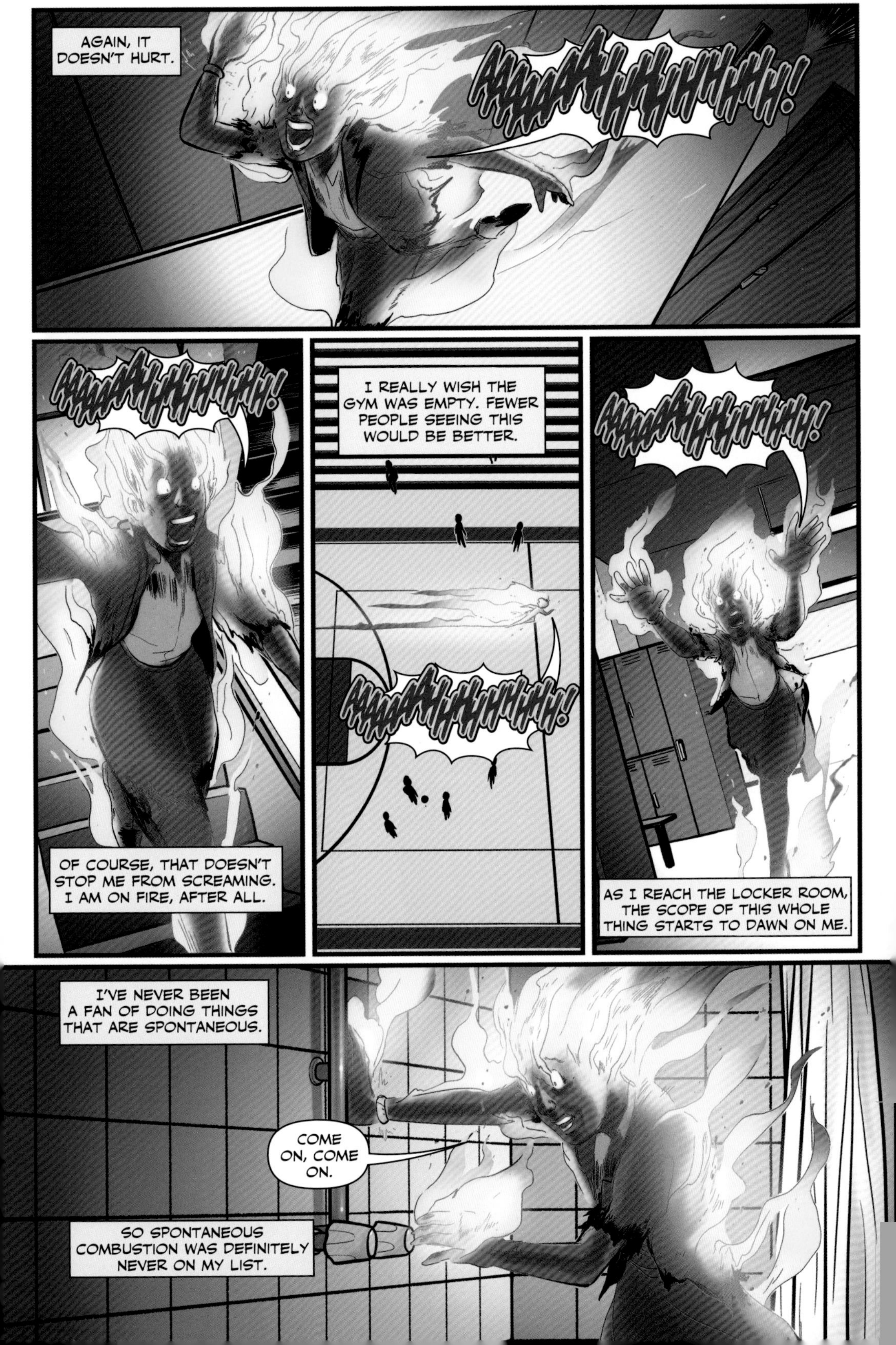
AGAIN, IT DOESN'T HURT.
AAAAAAAHHHHHHHHHHH!
AAAAAAAHHHHHHHHHHH!
OF COURSE, THAT DOESN'T STOP ME FROM SCREAMING. I AM ON FIRE, AFTER ALL.
I REALLY WISH THE GYM WAS EMPTY. FEWER PEOPLE SEEING THIS WOULD BE BETTER.
AAAAAAAHHHHHHHHHHH!
AAAAAAAHHHHHHHHHHH!
AS I REACH THE LOCKER ROOM, THE SCOPE OF THIS WHOLE THING STARTS TO DAWN ON ME.
I'VE NEVER BEEN A FAN OF DOING THINGS THAT ARE SPONTANEOUS.
COME ON, COME ON.
SO SPONTANEOUS COMBUSTION WAS DEFINITELY NEVER ON MY LIST.

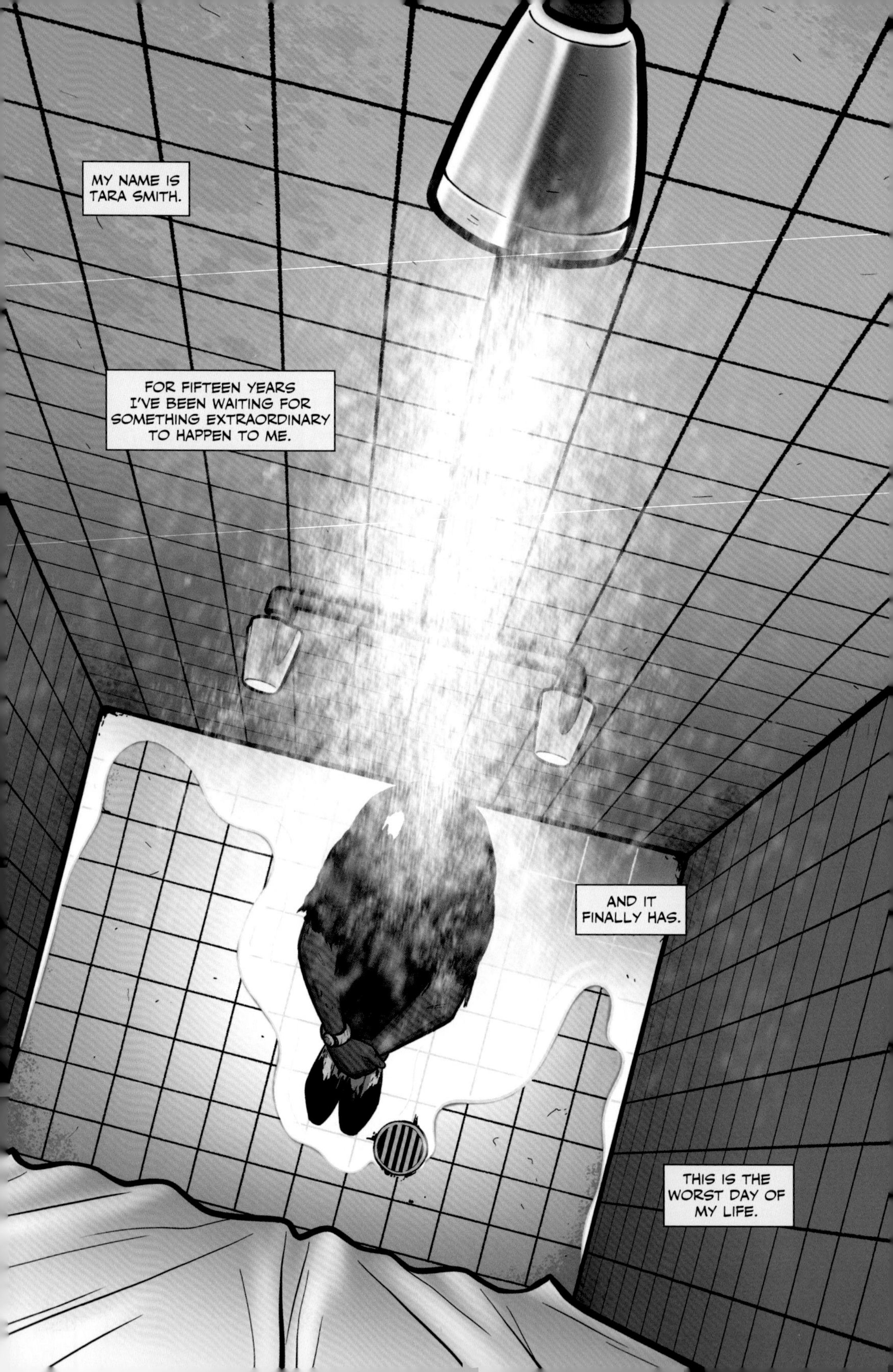

MY NAME IS TARA SMITH.
FOR FIFTEEN YEARS I'VE BEEN WAITING FOR SOMETHING EXTRAORDINARY TO HAPPEN TO ME.
AND IT FINALLY HAS.
THIS IS THE WORST DAY OF MY LIFE.

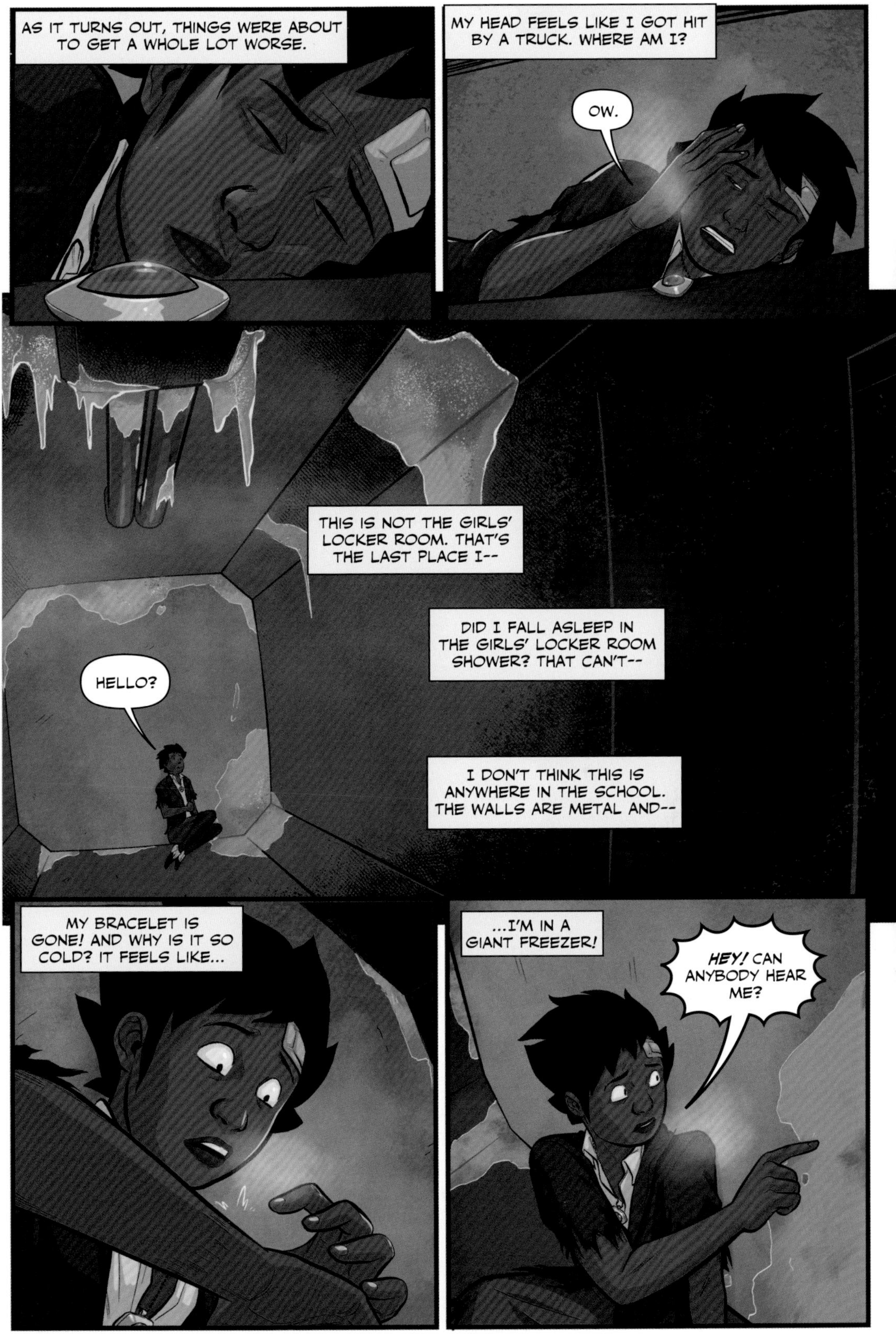
AS IT TURNS OUT, THINGS WERE ABOUT TO GET A WHOLE LOT WORSE.
MY HEAD FEELS LIKE I GOT HIT BY A TRUCK. WHERE AM I?
OW.
THIS IS NOT THE GIRLS' LOCKER ROOM. THAT'S THE LAST PLACE I--
DID I FALL ASLEEP IN THE GIRLS' LOCKER ROOM SHOWER? THAT CAN'T--
HELLO?
I DON'T THINK THIS IS ANYWHERE IN THE SCHOOL. THE WALLS ARE METAL AND--
MY BRACELET IS GONE! AND WHY IS IT SO COLD? IT FEELS LIKE...
...I'M IN A GIANT FREEZER!
HEY! CAN ANYBODY HEAR ME?

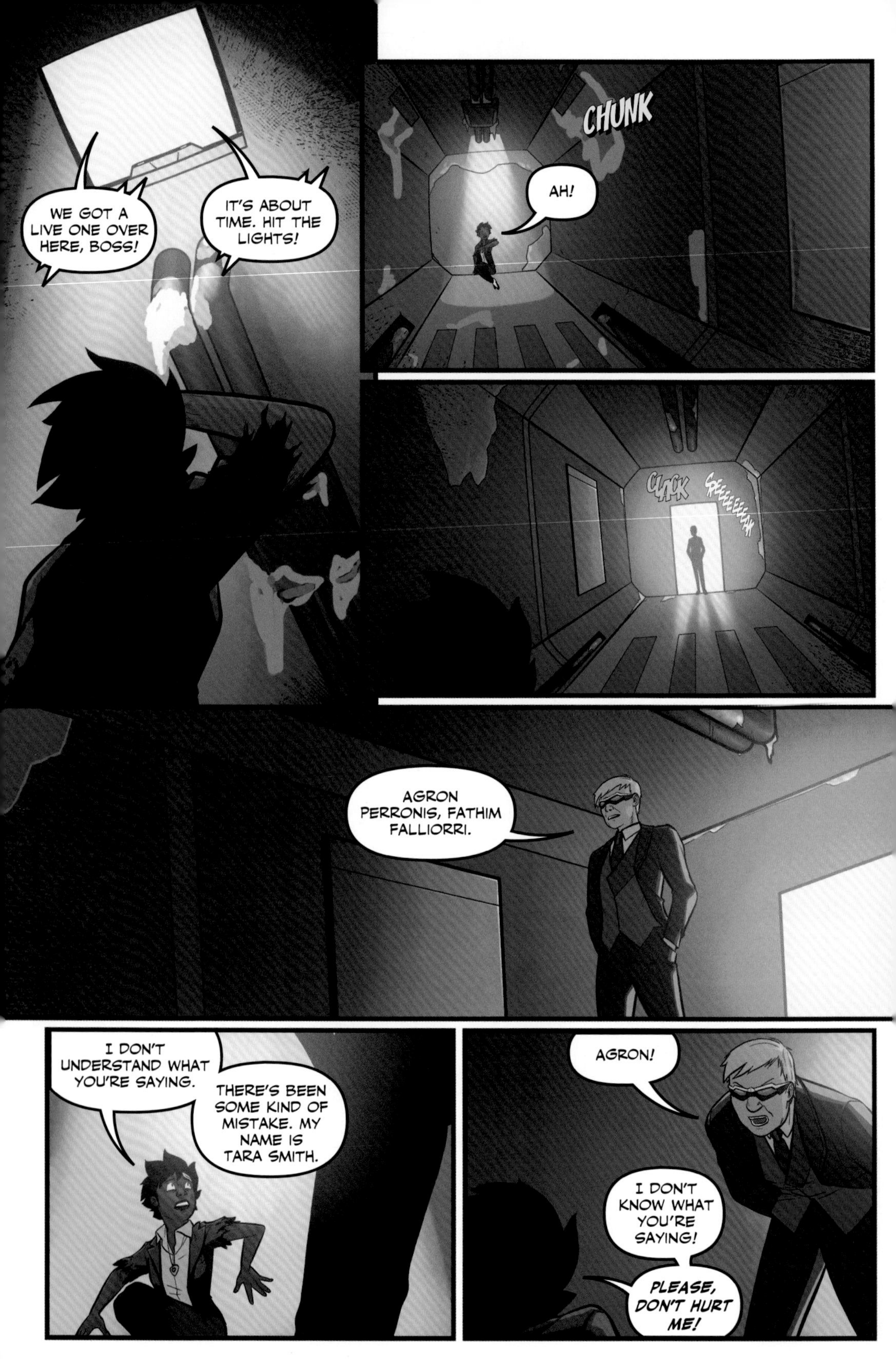
WE GOT A LIVE ONE OVER HERE, BOSS!
IT'S ABOUT TIME. HIT THE LIGHTS!
CHUNK
AH!
CLACK
SPEEEEEECH
AGRON PERRONIS, FATHIM FALLIORRI.
I DON'T UNDERSTAND WHAT YOU'RE SAYING.
THERE'S BEEN SOME KIND OF MISTAKE. MY NAME IS TARA SMITH.
AGRON!
I DON'T KNOW WHAT YOU'RE SAYING!
PLEASE, DON'T HURT ME!

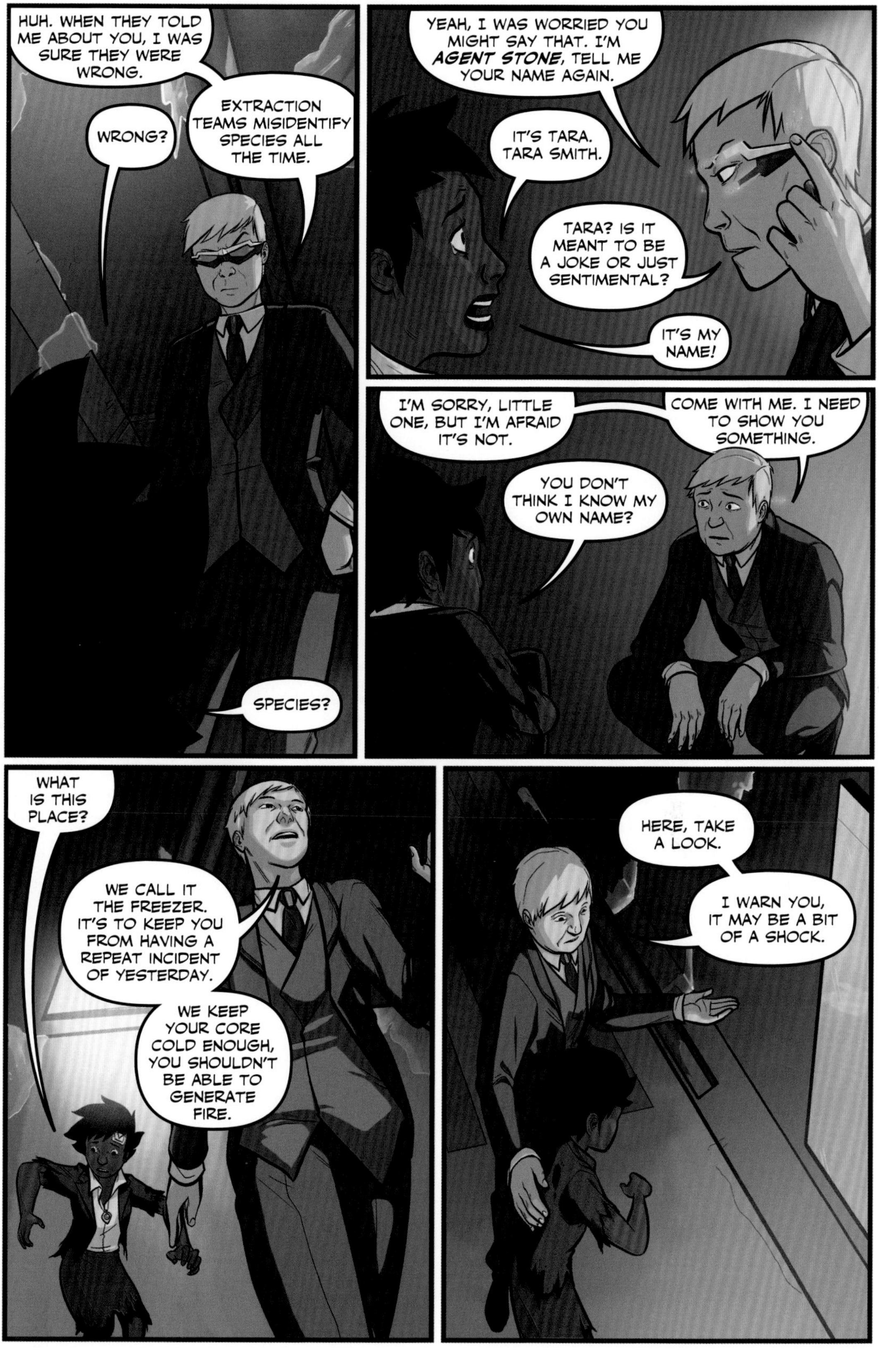
HUH. WHEN THEY TOLD ME ABOUT YOU, I WAS SURE THEY WERE WRONG.
WRONG?
EXTRACTION TEAMS MISIDENTIFY SPECIES ALL THE TIME.
SPECIES?
YEAH, I WAS WORRIED YOU MIGHT SAY THAT. I'M *AGENT STONE*, TELL ME YOUR NAME AGAIN.
IT'S TARA. TARA SMITH.
TARA? IS IT MEANT TO BE A JOKE OR JUST SENTIMENTAL?
IT'S MY NAME!
I'M SORRY, LITTLE ONE, BUT I'M AFRAID IT'S NOT.
COME WITH ME. I NEED TO SHOW YOU SOMETHING.
YOU DON'T THINK I KNOW MY OWN NAME?
WHAT IS THIS PLACE?
WE CALL IT THE FREEZER. IT'S TO KEEP YOU FROM HAVING A REPEAT INCIDENT OF YESTERDAY.
WE KEEP YOUR CORE COLD ENOUGH, YOU SHOULDN'T BE ABLE TO GENERATE FIRE.
HERE, TAKE A LOOK.
I WARN YOU, IT MAY BE A BIT OF A SHOCK.

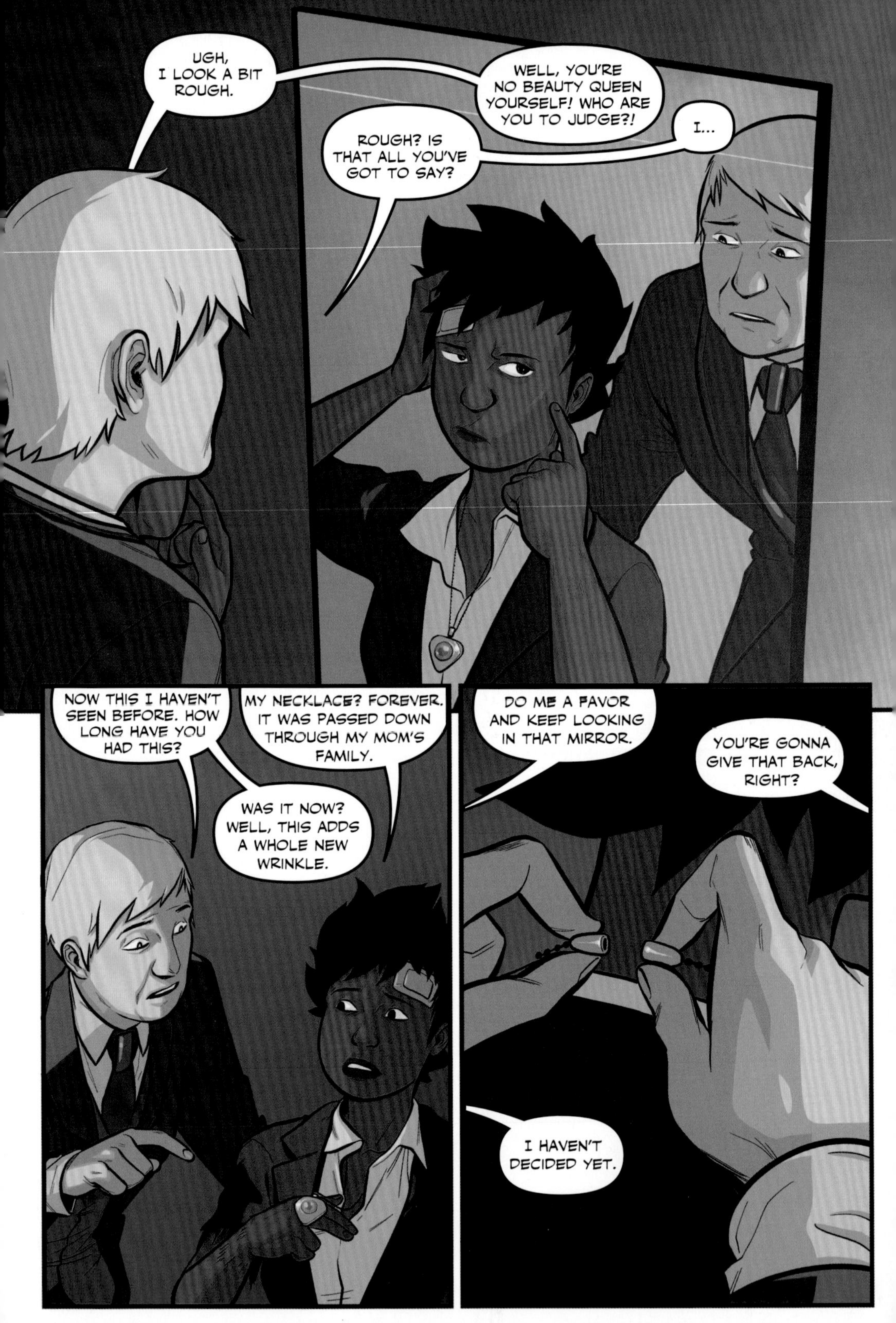

UGH, I LOOK A BIT ROUGH.
WELL, YOU'RE NO BEAUTY QUEEN YOURSELF! WHO ARE YOU TO JUDGE?!
ROUGH? IS THAT ALL YOU'VE GOT TO SAY?
I...
NOW THIS I HAVEN'T SEEN BEFORE. HOW LONG HAVE YOU HAD THIS?
MY NECKLACE? FOREVER. IT WAS PASSED DOWN THROUGH MY MOM'S FAMILY.
WAS IT NOW? WELL, THIS ADDS A WHOLE NEW WRINKLE.
DO ME A FAVOR AND KEEP LOOKING IN THAT MIRROR.
YOU'RE GONNA GIVE THAT BACK, RIGHT?
I HAVEN'T DECIDED YET.

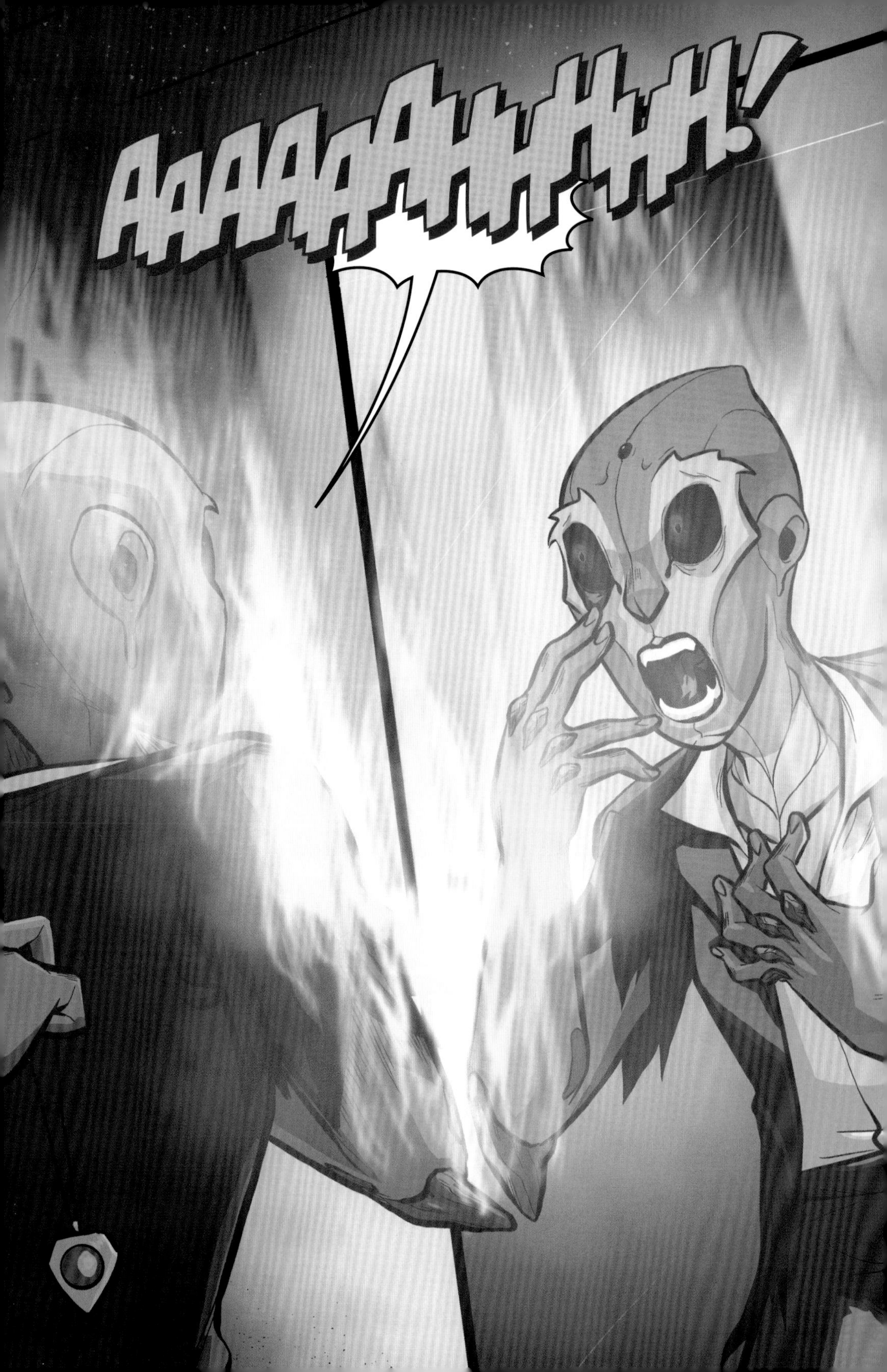
AAAAAHHHH!

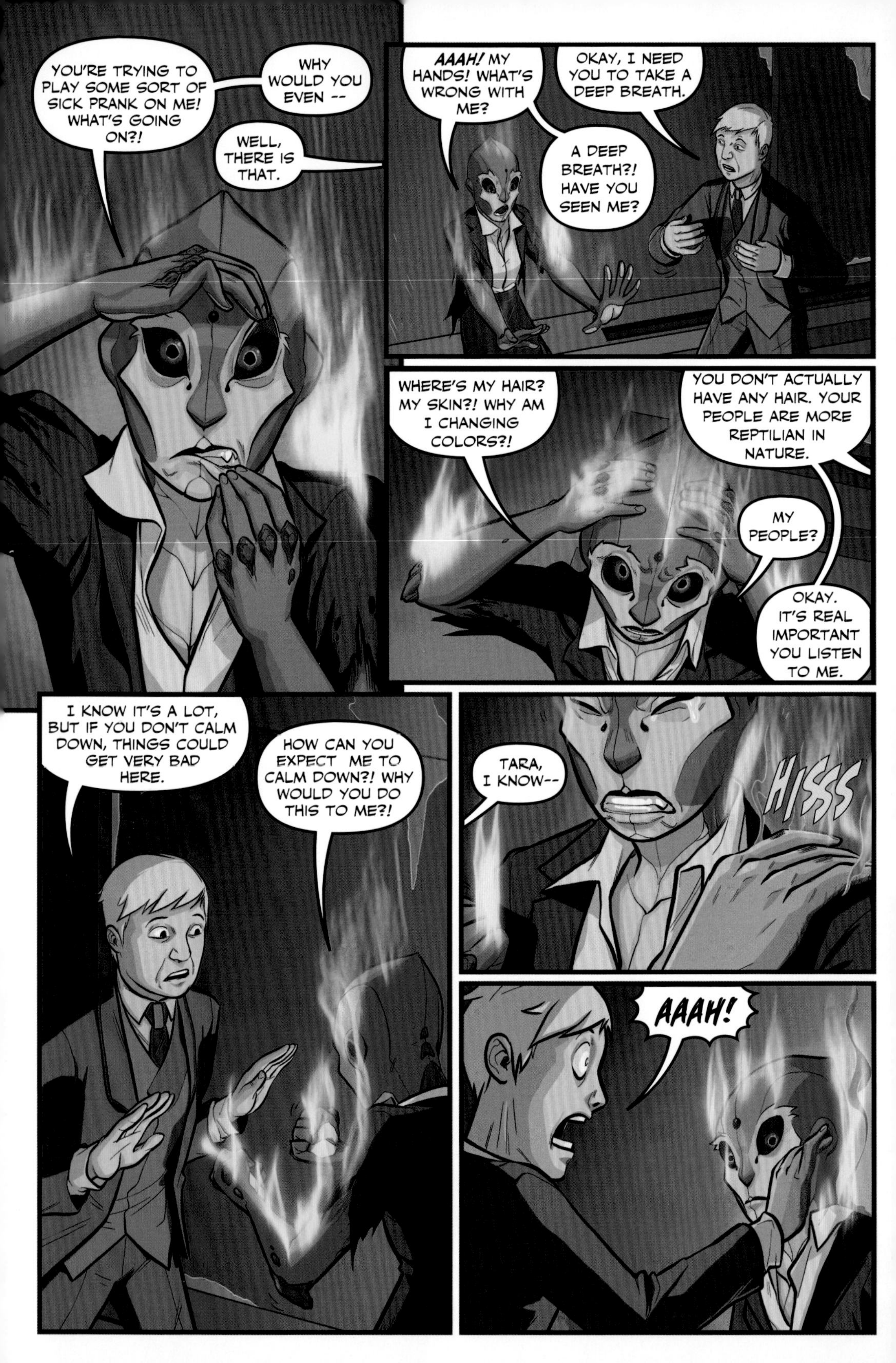
YOU'RE TRYING TO PLAY SOME SORT OF SICK PRANK ON ME! WHAT'S GOING ON?!
WHY WOULD YOU EVEN --
WELL, THERE IS THAT.
AAAH! MY HANDS! WHAT'S WRONG WITH ME?
OKAY, I NEED YOU TO TAKE A DEEP BREATH.
A DEEP BREATH?! HAVE YOU SEEN ME?
WHERE'S MY HAIR? MY SKIN?! WHY AM I CHANGING COLORS?!
YOU DON'T ACTUALLY HAVE ANY HAIR. YOUR PEOPLE ARE MORE REPTILIAN IN NATURE.
MY PEOPLE?
OKAY. IT'S REAL IMPORTANT YOU LISTEN TO ME.
I KNOW IT'S A LOT, BUT IF YOU DON'T CALM DOWN, THINGS COULD GET VERY BAD HERE.
HOW CAN YOU EXPECT ME TO CALM DOWN?! WHY WOULD YOU DO THIS TO ME?!
TARA, I KNOW--
HISSS
AAAH!

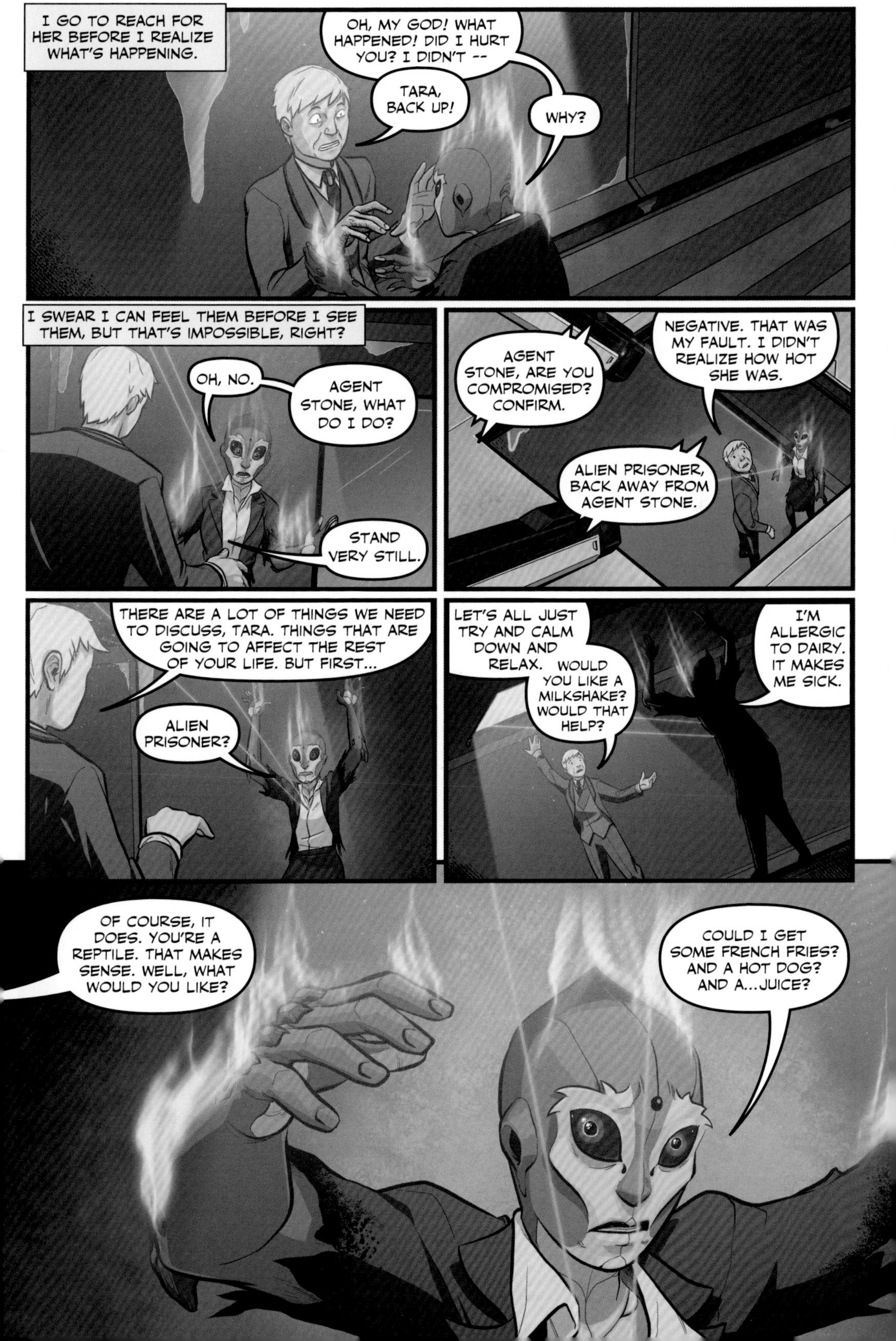
I GO TO REACH FOR HER BEFORE I REALIZE WHAT'S HAPPENING.
OH, MY GOD! WHAT HAPPENED! DID I HURT YOU? I DIDN'T --
TARA, BACK UP!
WHY?
I SWEAR I CAN FEEL THEM BEFORE I SEE THEM, BUT THAT'S IMPOSSIBLE, RIGHT?
OH, NO.
AGENT STONE, WHAT DO I DO?
STAND VERY STILL.
AGENT STONE, ARE YOU COMPROMISED? CONFIRM.
NEGATIVE. THAT WAS MY FAULT. I DIDN'T REALIZE HOW HOT SHE WAS.
ALIEN PRISONER, BACK AWAY FROM AGENT STONE.
THERE ARE A LOT OF THINGS WE NEED TO DISCUSS, TARA. THINGS THAT ARE GOING TO AFFECT THE REST OF YOUR LIFE. BUT FIRST...
ALIEN PRISONER?
LET'S ALL JUST TRY AND CALM DOWN AND RELAX.
WOULD YOU LIKE A MILKSHAKE? WOULD THAT HELP?
I'M ALLERGIC TO DAIRY. IT MAKES ME SICK.
OF COURSE, IT DOES. YOU'RE A REPTILE. THAT MAKES SENSE. WELL, WHAT WOULD YOU LIKE?
COULD I GET SOME FRENCH FRIES? AND A HOT DOG? AND A...JUICE?

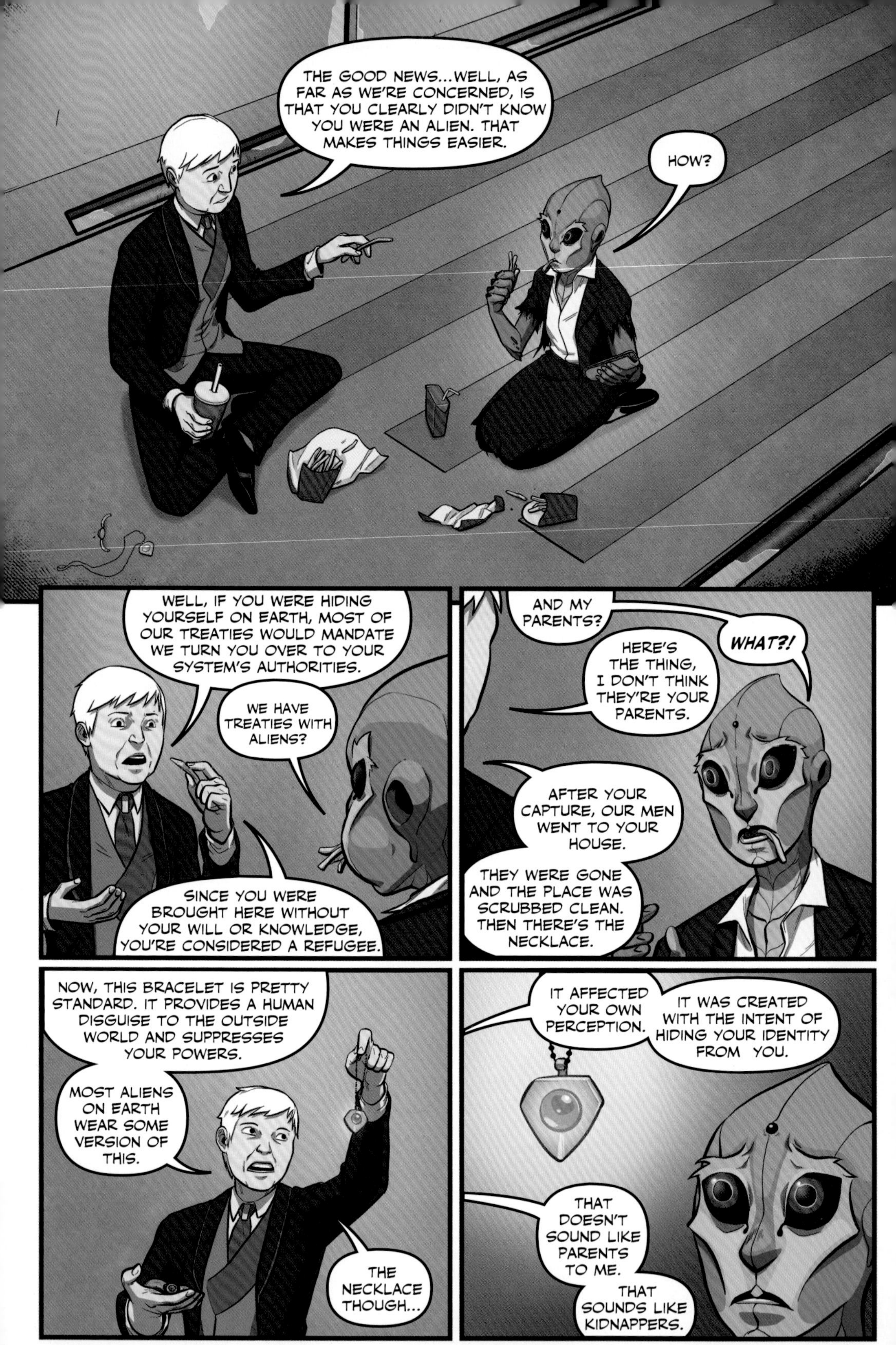
THE GOOD NEWS...WELL, AS FAR AS WE'RE CONCERNED, IS THAT YOU CLEARLY DIDN'T KNOW YOU WERE AN ALIEN. THAT MAKES THINGS EASIER.
HOW?
WELL, IF YOU WERE HIDING YOURSELF ON EARTH, MOST OF OUR TREATIES WOULD MANDATE WE TURN YOU OVER TO YOUR SYSTEM'S AUTHORITIES.
WE HAVE TREATIES WITH ALIENS?
SINCE YOU WERE BROUGHT HERE WITHOUT YOUR WILL OR KNOWLEDGE, YOU'RE CONSIDERED A REFUGEE.
AND MY PARENTS?
WHAT?!
HERE'S THE THING, I DON'T THINK THEY'RE YOUR PARENTS.
AFTER YOUR CAPTURE, OUR MEN WENT TO YOUR HOUSE.
THEY WERE GONE AND THE PLACE WAS SCRUBBED CLEAN. THEN THERE'S THE NECKLACE.
NOW, THIS BRACELET IS PRETTY STANDARD. IT PROVIDES A HUMAN DISGUISE TO THE OUTSIDE WORLD AND SUPPRESSES YOUR POWERS.
MOST ALIENS ON EARTH WEAR SOME VERSION OF THIS.
THE NECKLACE THOUGH...
IT AFFECTED YOUR OWN PERCEPTION.
IT WAS CREATED WITH THE INTENT OF HIDING YOUR IDENTITY FROM YOU.
THAT DOESN'T SOUND LIKE PARENTS TO ME.
THAT SOUNDS LIKE KIDNAPPERS.

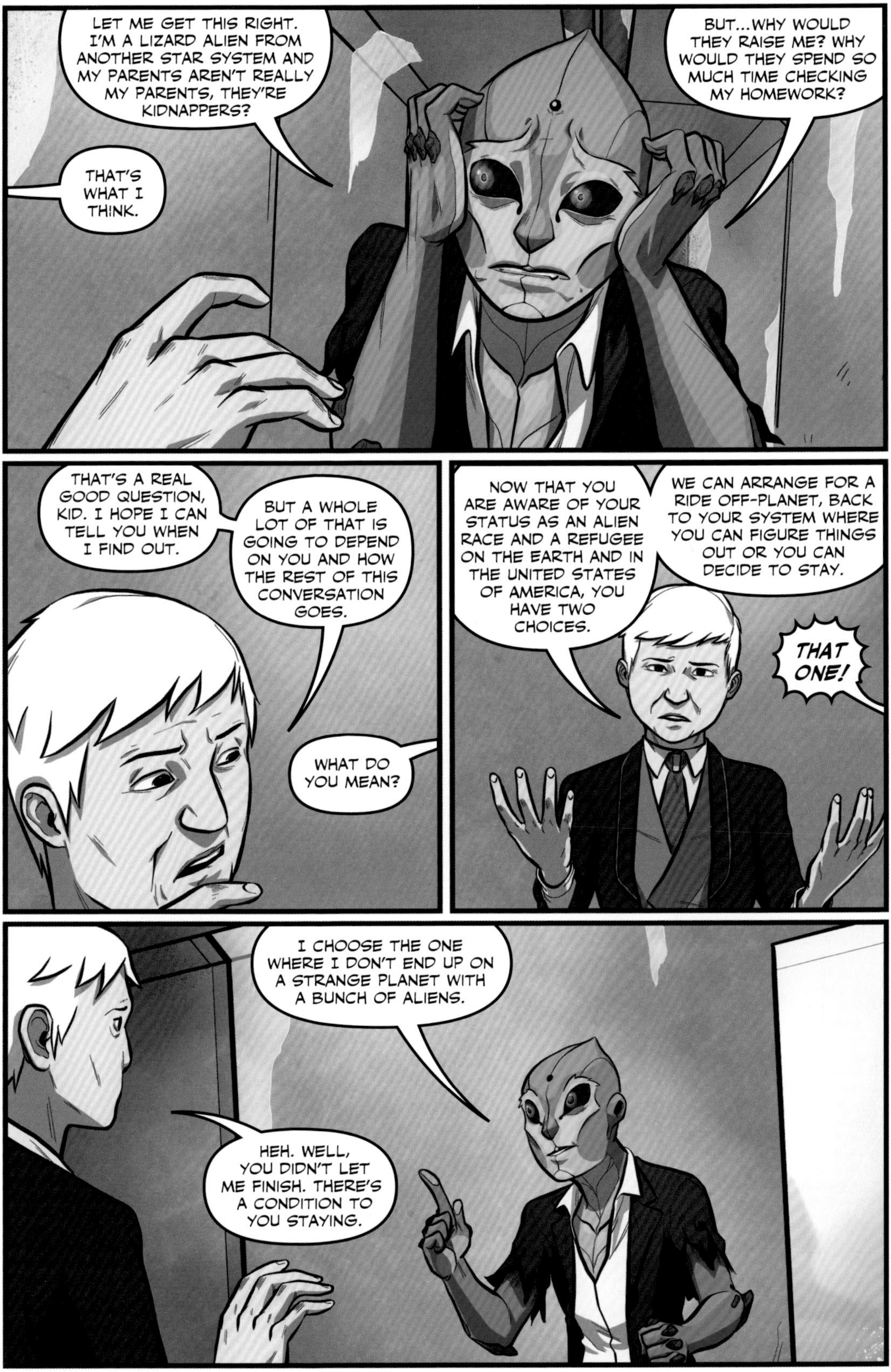
LET ME GET THIS RIGHT. I'M A LIZARD ALIEN FROM ANOTHER STAR SYSTEM AND MY PARENTS AREN'T REALLY MY PARENTS, THEY'RE KIDNAPPERS?
THAT'S WHAT I THINK.
BUT...WHY WOULD THEY RAISE ME? WHY WOULD THEY SPEND SO MUCH TIME CHECKING MY HOMEWORK?
THAT'S A REAL GOOD QUESTION, KID. I HOPE I CAN TELL YOU WHEN I FIND OUT.
BUT A WHOLE LOT OF THAT IS GOING TO DEPEND ON YOU AND HOW THE REST OF THIS CONVERSATION GOES.
WHAT DO YOU MEAN?
NOW THAT YOU ARE AWARE OF YOUR STATUS AS AN ALIEN RACE AND A REFUGEE ON THE EARTH AND IN THE UNITED STATES OF AMERICA, YOU HAVE TWO CHOICES.
WE CAN ARRANGE FOR A RIDE OFF-PLANET, BACK TO YOUR SYSTEM WHERE YOU CAN FIGURE THINGS OUT OR YOU CAN DECIDE TO STAY.
THAT ONE!
I CHOOSE THE ONE WHERE I DON'T END UP ON A STRANGE PLANET WITH A BUNCH OF ALIENS.
HEH. WELL, YOU DIDN'T LET ME FINISH. THERE'S A CONDITION TO YOU STAYING.

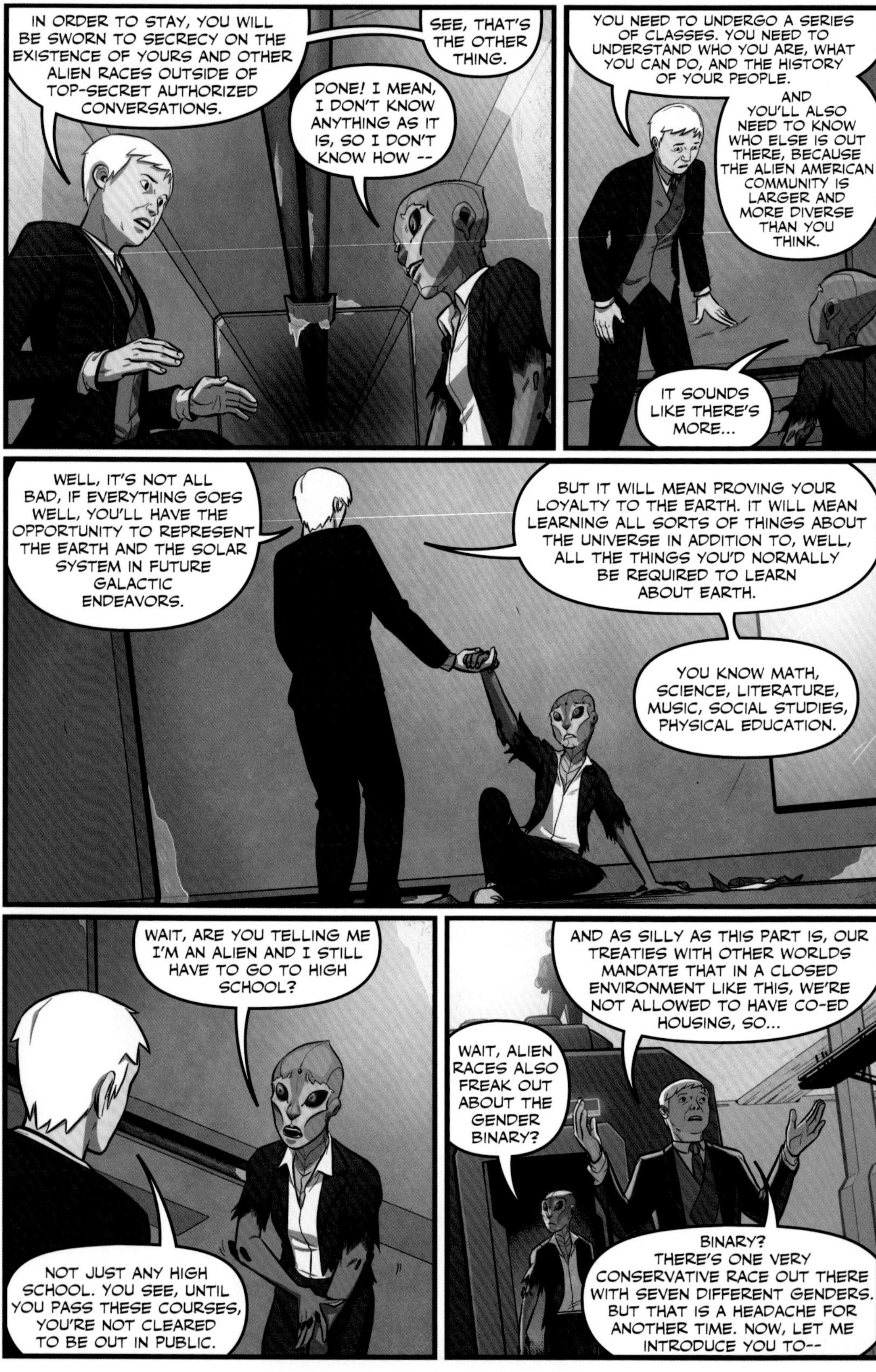
IN ORDER TO STAY, YOU WILL BE SWORN TO SECRECY ON THE EXISTENCE OF YOURS AND OTHER ALIEN RACES OUTSIDE OF TOP-SECRET AUTHORIZED CONVERSATIONS.
DONE! I MEAN, I DON'T KNOW ANYTHING AS IT IS, SO I DON'T KNOW HOW --
SEE, THAT'S THE OTHER THING.
YOU NEED TO UNDERGO A SERIES OF CLASSES. YOU NEED TO UNDERSTAND WHO YOU ARE, WHAT YOU CAN DO, AND THE HISTORY OF YOUR PEOPLE.
AND YOU'LL ALSO NEED TO KNOW WHO ELSE IS OUT THERE, BECAUSE THE ALIEN AMERICAN COMMUNITY IS LARGER AND MORE DIVERSE THAN YOU THINK.
IT SOUNDS LIKE THERE'S MORE...
WELL, IT'S NOT ALL BAD, IF EVERYTHING GOES WELL, YOU'LL HAVE THE OPPORTUNITY TO REPRESENT THE EARTH AND THE SOLAR SYSTEM IN FUTURE GALACTIC ENDEAVORS.
BUT IT WILL MEAN PROVING YOUR LOYALTY TO THE EARTH. IT WILL MEAN LEARNING ALL SORTS OF THINGS ABOUT THE UNIVERSE IN ADDITION TO, WELL, ALL THE THINGS YOU'D NORMALLY BE REQUIRED TO LEARN ABOUT EARTH.
YOU KNOW MATH, SCIENCE, LITERATURE, MUSIC, SOCIAL STUDIES, PHYSICAL EDUCATION.
WAIT, ARE YOU TELLING ME I'M AN ALIEN AND I STILL HAVE TO GO TO HIGH SCHOOL?
NOT JUST ANY HIGH SCHOOL. YOU SEE, UNTIL YOU PASS THESE COURSES, YOU'RE NOT CLEARED TO BE OUT IN PUBLIC.
AND AS SILLY AS THIS PART IS, OUR TREATIES WITH OTHER WORLDS MANDATE THAT IN A CLOSED ENVIRONMENT LIKE THIS, WE'RE NOT ALLOWED TO HAVE CO-ED HOUSING, SO...
WAIT, ALIEN RACES ALSO FREAK OUT ABOUT THE GENDER BINARY?
BINARY? THERE'S ONE VERY CONSERVATIVE RACE OUT THERE WITH SEVEN DIFFERENT GENDERS. BUT THAT IS A HEADACHE FOR ANOTHER TIME. NOW, LET ME INTRODUCE YOU TO--

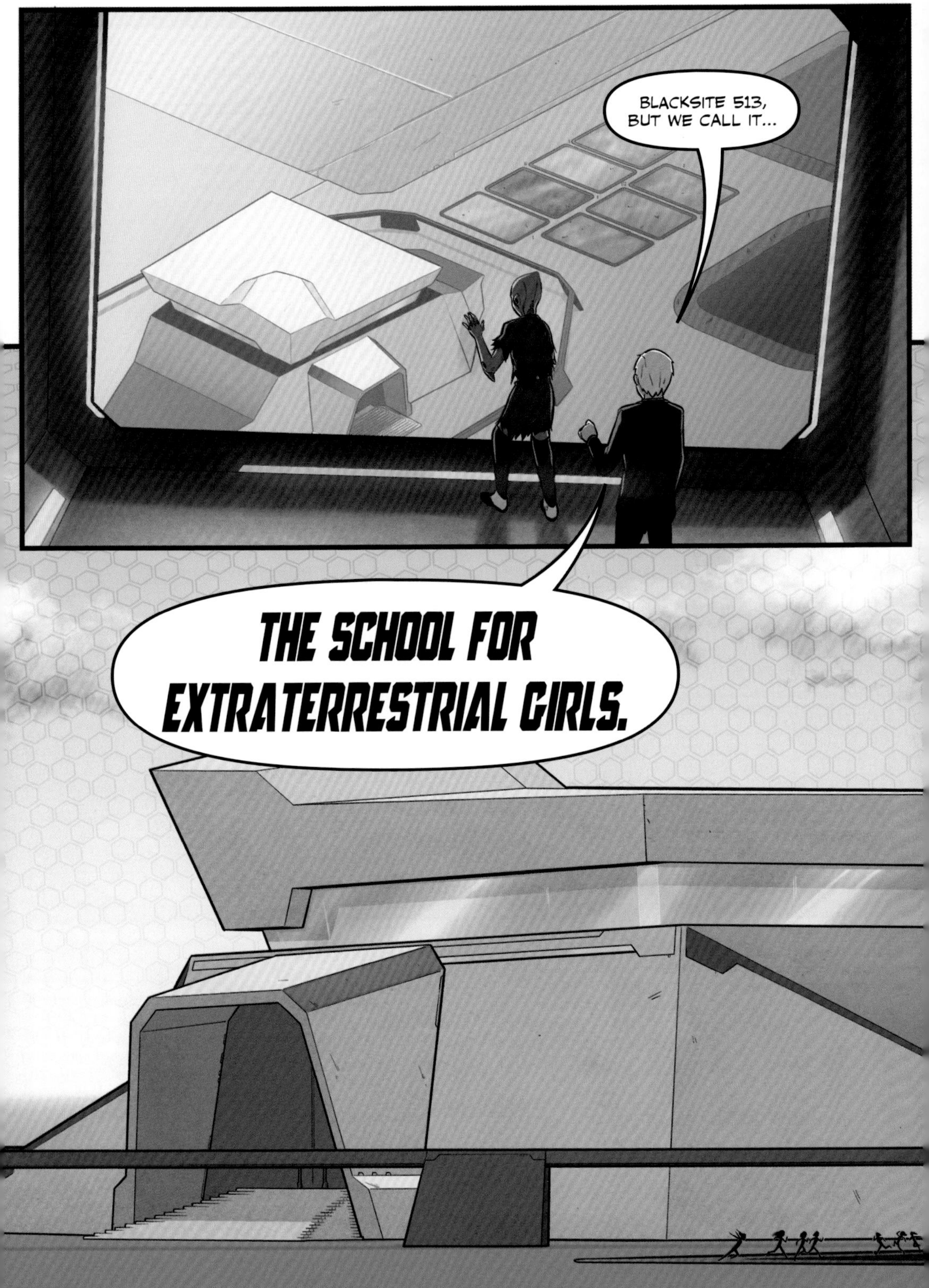
BLACKSITE 513, BUT WE CALL IT...
THE SCHOOL FOR EXTRATERRESTRIAL GIRLS.

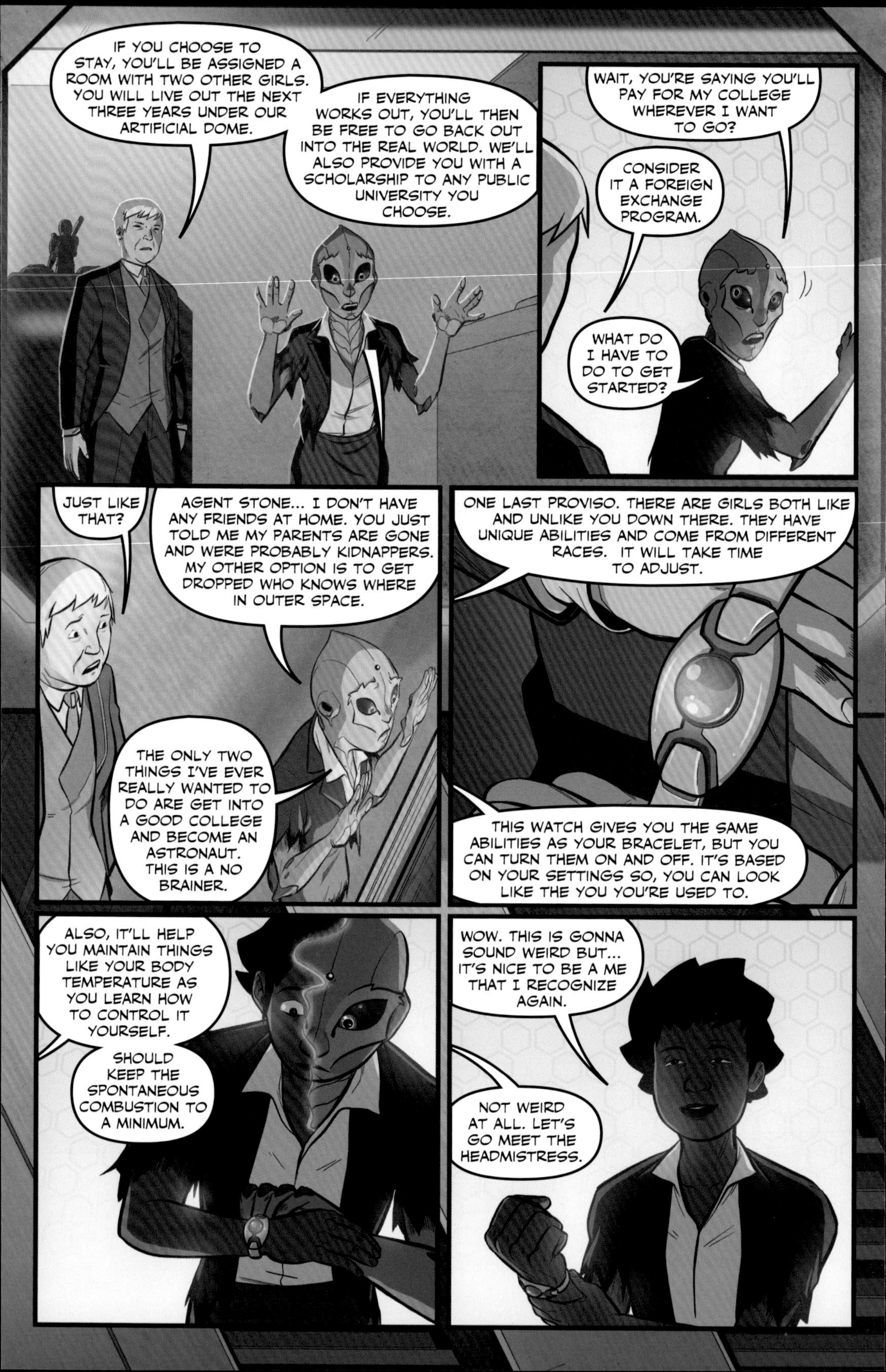
IF YOU CHOOSE TO STAY, YOU'LL BE ASSIGNED A ROOM WITH TWO OTHER GIRLS. YOU WILL LIVE OUT THE NEXT THREE YEARS UNDER OUR ARTIFICIAL DOME.
IF EVERYTHING WORKS OUT, YOU'LL THEN BE FREE TO GO BACK OUT INTO THE REAL WORLD. WE'LL ALSO PROVIDE YOU WITH A SCHOLARSHIP TO ANY PUBLIC UNIVERSITY YOU CHOOSE.
WAIT, YOU'RE SAYING YOU'LL PAY FOR MY COLLEGE WHEREVER I WANT TO GO?
CONSIDER IT A FOREIGN EXCHANGE PROGRAM.
WHAT DO I HAVE TO DO TO GET STARTED?
JUST LIKE THAT?
AGENT STONE... I DON'T HAVE ANY FRIENDS AT HOME. YOU JUST TOLD ME MY PARENTS ARE GONE AND WERE PROBABLY KIDNAPPERS. MY OTHER OPTION IS TO GET DROPPED WHO KNOWS WHERE IN OUTER SPACE.
THE ONLY TWO THINGS I'VE EVER REALLY WANTED TO DO ARE GET INTO A GOOD COLLEGE AND BECOME AN ASTRONAUT. THIS IS A NO BRAINER.
ONE LAST PROVISO. THERE ARE GIRLS BOTH LIKE AND UNLIKE YOU DOWN THERE. THEY HAVE UNIQUE ABILITIES AND COME FROM DIFFERENT RACES. IT WILL TAKE TIME TO ADJUST.
THIS WATCH GIVES YOU THE SAME ABILITIES AS YOUR BRACELET, BUT YOU CAN TURN THEM ON AND OFF. IT'S BASED ON YOUR SETTINGS SO, YOU CAN LOOK LIKE THE YOU YOU'RE USED TO.
ALSO, IT'LL HELP YOU MAINTAIN THINGS LIKE YOUR BODY TEMPERATURE AS YOU LEARN HOW TO CONTROL IT YOURSELF.
SHOULD KEEP THE SPONTANEOUS COMBUSTION TO A MINIMUM.
WOW. THIS IS GONNA SOUND WEIRD BUT... IT'S NICE TO BE A ME THAT I RECOGNIZE AGAIN.
NOT WEIRD AT ALL. LET'S GO MEET THE HEADMISTRESS.

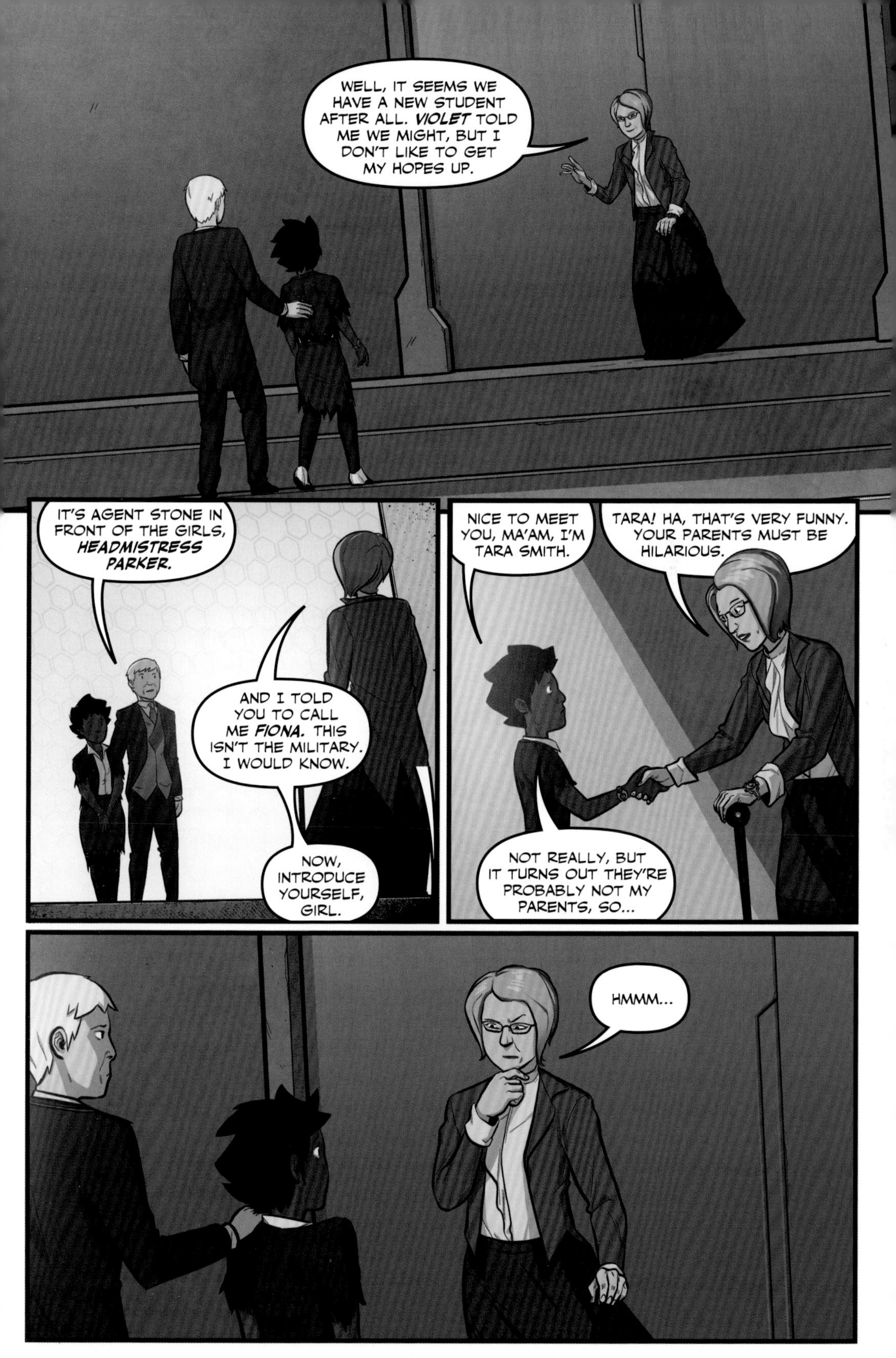
WELL, IT SEEMS WE HAVE A NEW STUDENT AFTER ALL. VIOLET TOLD ME WE MIGHT, BUT I DON'T LIKE TO GET MY HOPES UP.
IT'S AGENT STONE IN FRONT OF THE GIRLS, HEADMISTRESS PARKER.
AND I TOLD YOU TO CALL ME FIONA. THIS ISN'T THE MILITARY. I WOULD KNOW.
NOW, INTRODUCE YOURSELF, GIRL.
NICE TO MEET YOU, MA'AM, I'M TARA SMITH.
TARA! HA, THAT'S VERY FUNNY. YOUR PARENTS MUST BE HILARIOUS.
NOT REALLY, BUT IT TURNS OUT THEY'RE PROBABLY NOT MY PARENTS, SO...
HMMM...

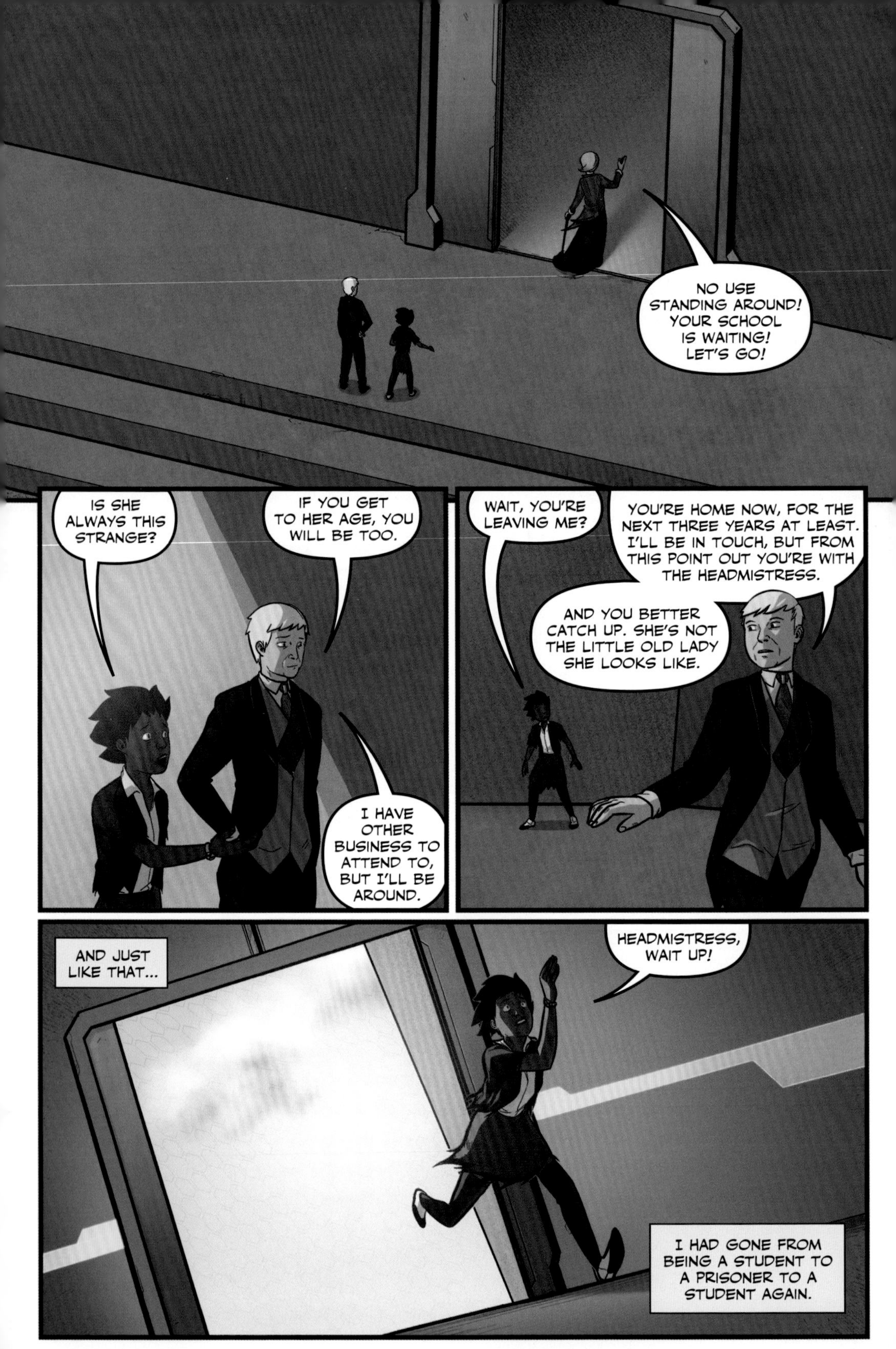
NO USE STANDING AROUND! YOUR SCHOOL IS WAITING! LET'S GO!
IS SHE ALWAYS THIS STRANGE?
IF YOU GET TO HER AGE, YOU WILL BE TOO.
I HAVE OTHER BUSINESS TO ATTEND TO, BUT I'LL BE AROUND.
WAIT, YOU'RE LEAVING ME?
YOU'RE HOME NOW, FOR THE NEXT THREE YEARS AT LEAST. I'LL BE IN TOUCH, BUT FROM THIS POINT OUT YOU'RE WITH THE HEADMISTRESS.
AND YOU BETTER CATCH UP. SHE'S NOT THE LITTLE OLD LADY SHE LOOKS LIKE.
AND JUST LIKE THAT...
HEADMISTRESS, WAIT UP!
I HAD GONE FROM BEING A STUDENT TO A PRISONER TO A STUDENT AGAIN.

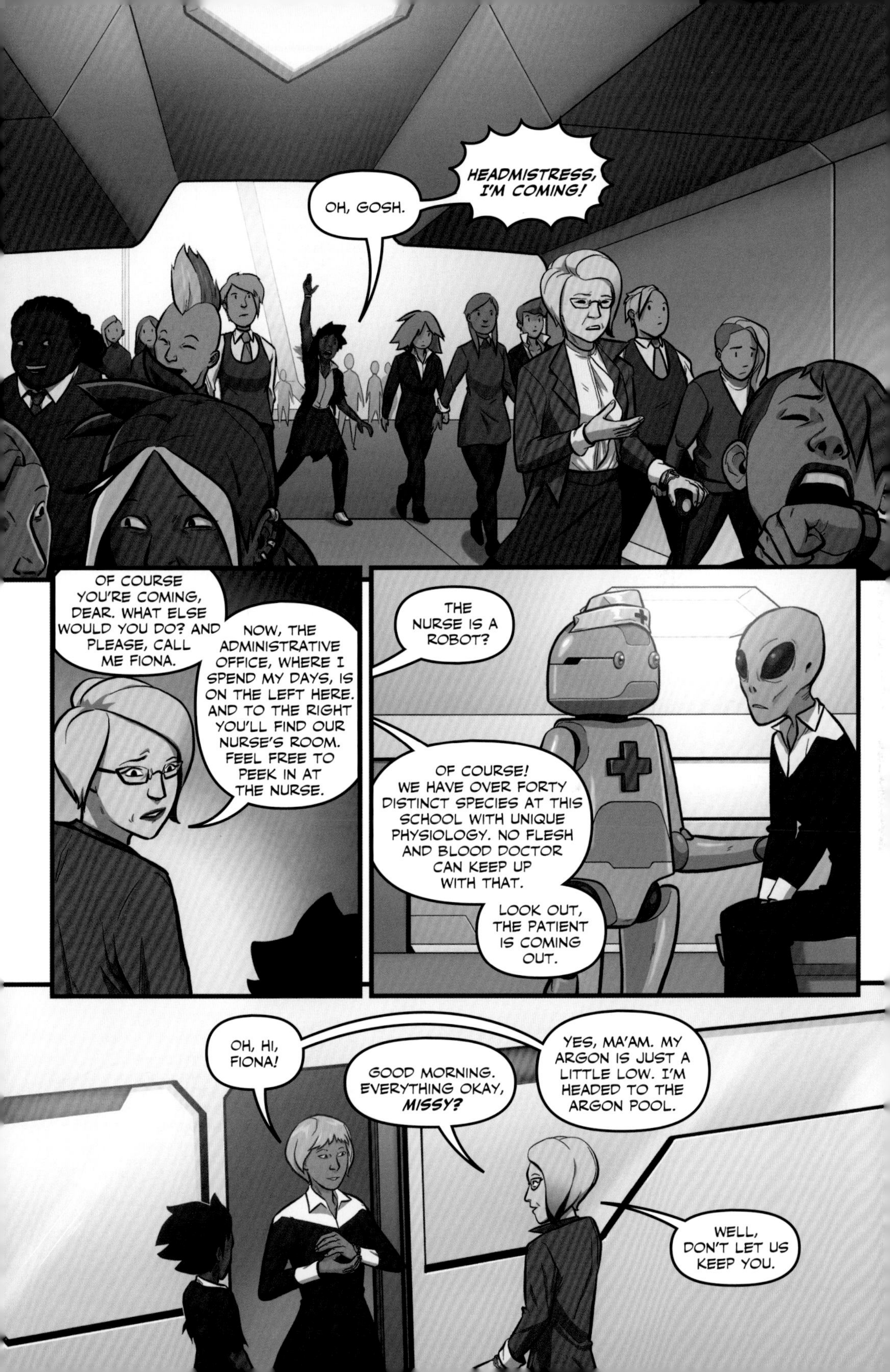

OH, GOSH.
HEADMISTRESS, I'M COMING!
OF COURSE YOU'RE COMING, DEAR. WHAT ELSE WOULD YOU DO? AND PLEASE, CALL ME FIONA.
NOW, THE ADMINISTRATIVE OFFICE, WHERE I SPEND MY DAYS, IS ON THE LEFT HERE. AND TO THE RIGHT YOU'LL FIND OUR NURSE'S ROOM. FEEL FREE TO PEEK IN AT THE NURSE.
THE NURSE IS A ROBOT?
OF COURSE! WE HAVE OVER FORTY DISTINCT SPECIES AT THIS SCHOOL WITH UNIQUE PHYSIOLOGY. NO FLESH AND BLOOD DOCTOR CAN KEEP UP WITH THAT.
LOOK OUT, THE PATIENT IS COMING OUT.
OH, HI, FIONA!
GOOD MORNING. EVERYTHING OKAY, MISSY?
YES, MA'AM. MY ARGON IS JUST A LITTLE LOW. I'M HEADED TO THE ARGON POOL.
WELL, DON'T LET US KEEP YOU.

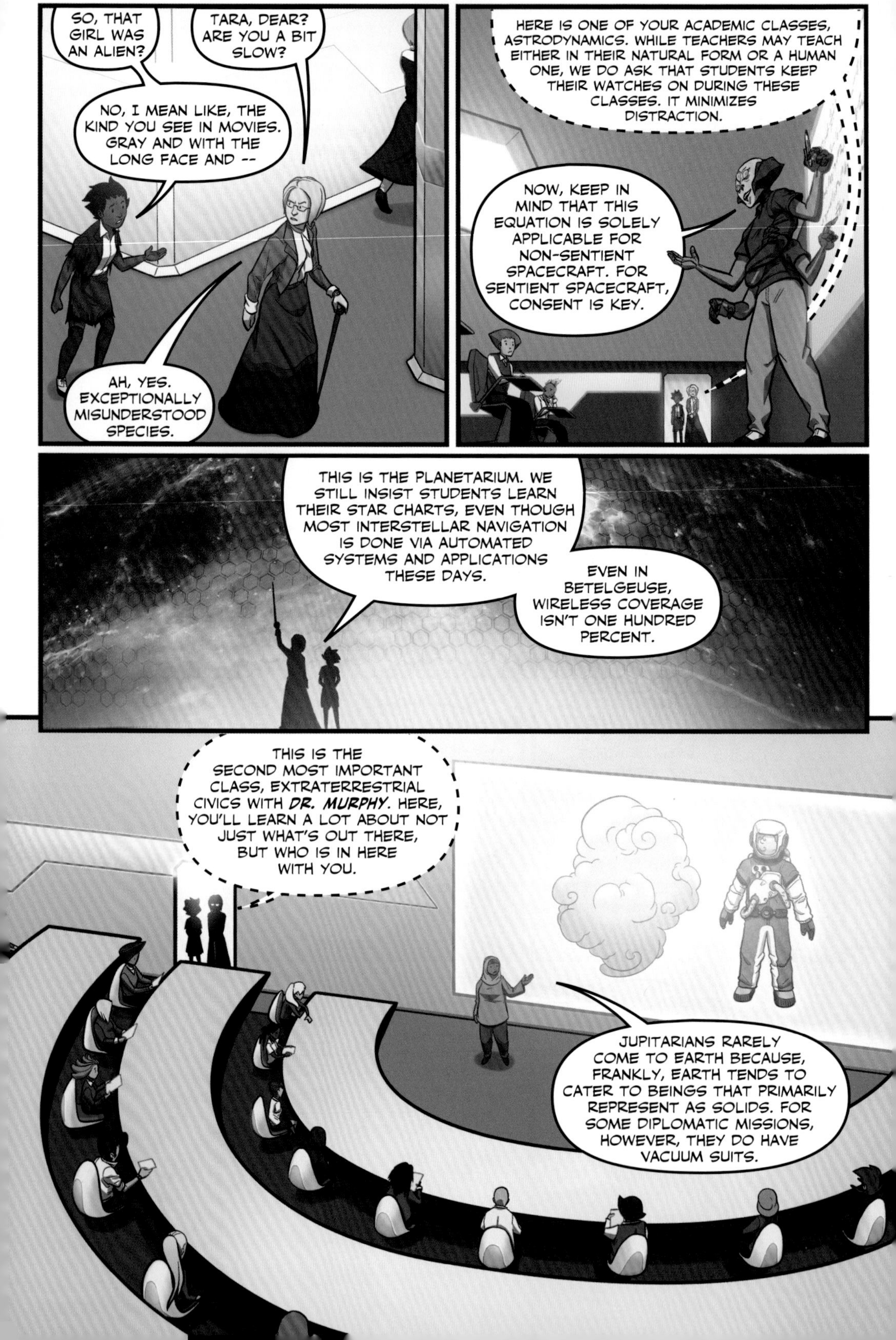

SO, THAT GIRL WAS AN ALIEN?
TARA, DEAR? ARE YOU A BIT SLOW?
NO, I MEAN LIKE, THE KIND YOU SEE IN MOVIES. GRAY AND WITH THE LONG FACE AND --
AH, YES. EXCEPTIONALLY MISUNDERSTOOD SPECIES.
HERE IS ONE OF YOUR ACADEMIC CLASSES, ASTRODYNAMICS. WHILE TEACHERS MAY TEACH EITHER IN THEIR NATURAL FORM OR A HUMAN ONE, WE DO ASK THAT STUDENTS KEEP THEIR WATCHES ON DURING THESE CLASSES. IT MINIMIZES DISTRACTION.
NOW, KEEP IN MIND THAT THIS EQUATION IS SOLELY APPLICABLE FOR NON-SENTIENT SPACECRAFT. FOR SENTIENT SPACECRAFT, CONSENT IS KEY.
THIS IS THE PLANETARIUM. WE STILL INSIST STUDENTS LEARN THEIR STAR CHARTS, EVEN THOUGH MOST INTERSTELLAR NAVIGATION IS DONE VIA AUTOMATED SYSTEMS AND APPLICATIONS THESE DAYS.
EVEN IN BETELGEUSE, WIRELESS COVERAGE ISN'T ONE HUNDRED PERCENT.
THIS IS THE SECOND MOST IMPORTANT CLASS, EXTRATERRESTRIAL CIVICS WITH DR. MURPHY. HERE, YOU'LL LEARN A LOT ABOUT NOT JUST WHAT'S OUT THERE, BUT WHO IS IN HERE WITH YOU.
JUPITARIANS RARELY COME TO EARTH BECAUSE, FRANKLY, EARTH TENDS TO CATER TO BEINGS THAT PRIMARILY REPRESENT AS SOLIDS. FOR SOME DIPLOMATIC MISSIONS, HOWEVER, THEY DO HAVE VACUUM SUITS.

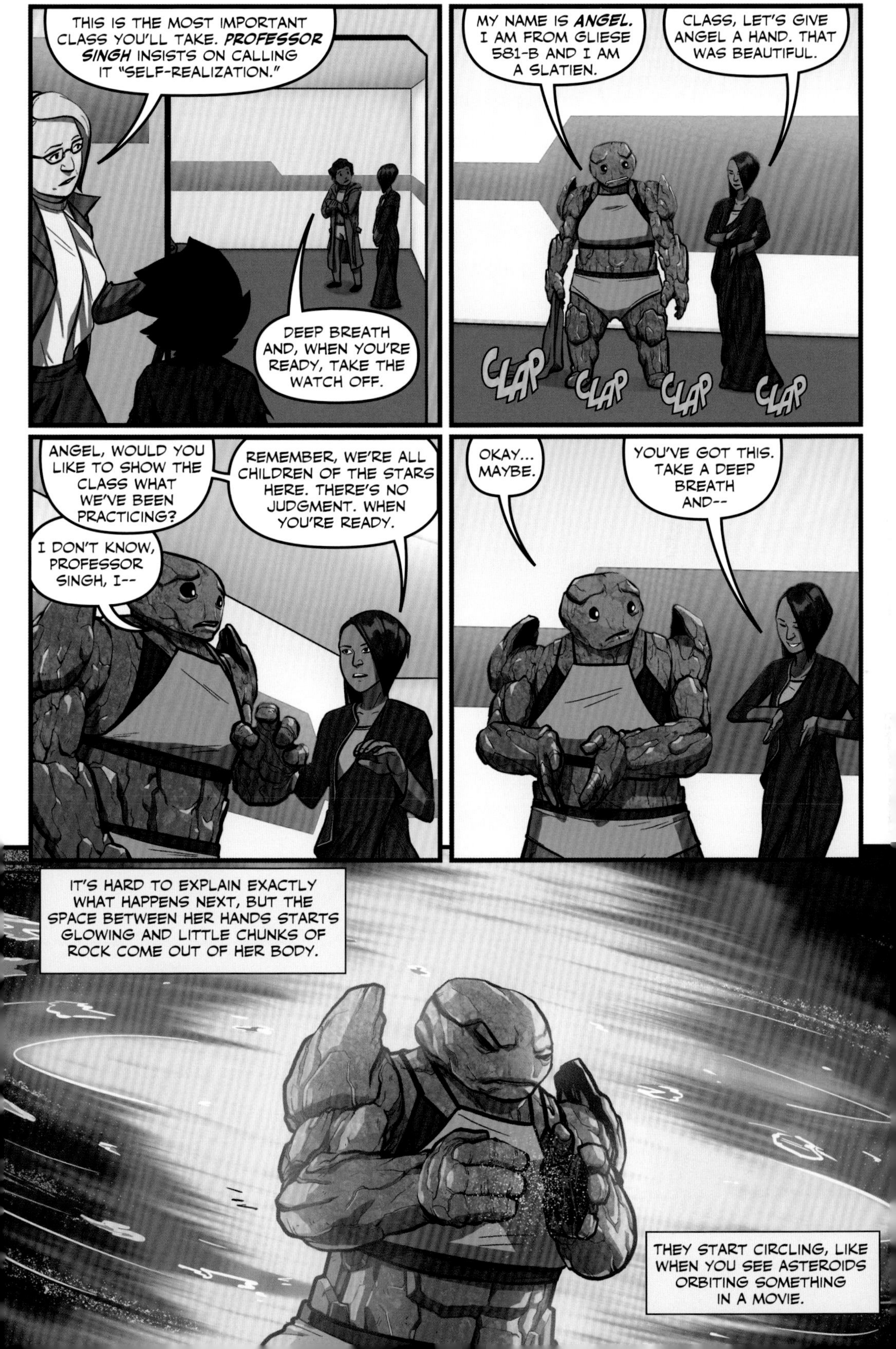
THIS IS THE MOST IMPORTANT CLASS YOU'LL TAKE. PROFESSOR SINGH INSISTS ON CALLING IT "SELF-REALIZATION."
DEEP BREATH AND, WHEN YOU'RE READY, TAKE THE WATCH OFF.
MY NAME IS ANGEL. I AM FROM GLIESE 581-B AND I AM A SLATIEN.
CLASS, LET'S GIVE ANGEL A HAND. THAT WAS BEAUTIFUL.
CLAP
CLAP
CLAP
CLAP
ANGEL, WOULD YOU LIKE TO SHOW THE CLASS WHAT WE'VE BEEN PRACTICING?
I DON'T KNOW, PROFESSOR SINGH, I--
REMEMBER, WE'RE ALL CHILDREN OF THE STARS HERE. THERE'S NO JUDGMENT. WHEN YOU'RE READY.
OKAY... MAYBE.
YOU'VE GOT THIS. TAKE A DEEP BREATH AND--
IT'S HARD TO EXPLAIN EXACTLY WHAT HAPPENS NEXT, BUT THE SPACE BETWEEN HER HANDS STARTS GLOWING AND LITTLE CHUNKS OF ROCK COME OUT OF HER BODY.
THEY START CIRCLING, LIKE WHEN YOU SEE ASTEROIDS ORBITING SOMETHING IN A MOVIE.

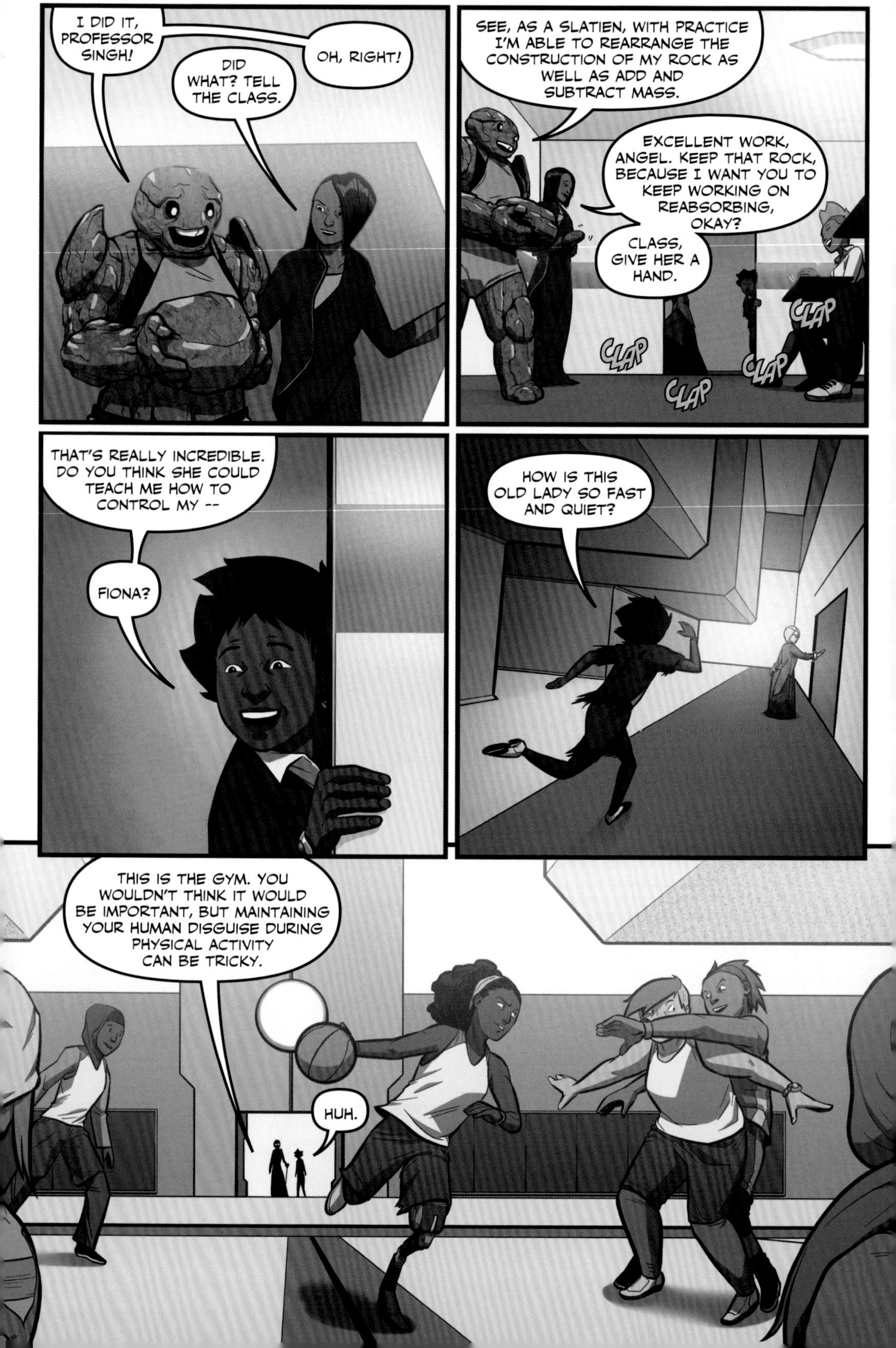
I DID IT, PROFESSOR SINGH!
DID WHAT? TELL THE CLASS.
OH, RIGHT!
SEE, AS A SLATIEN, WITH PRACTICE I'M ABLE TO REARRANGE THE CONSTRUCTION OF MY ROCK AS WELL AS ADD AND SUBTRACT MASS.
EXCELLENT WORK, ANGEL. KEEP THAT ROCK, BECAUSE I WANT YOU TO KEEP WORKING ON REABSORBING, OKAY?
CLASS, GIVE HER A HAND.
CLAP
CLAP
CLAP
CLAP
THAT'S REALLY INCREDIBLE. DO YOU THINK SHE COULD TEACH ME HOW TO CONTROL MY --
FIONA?
HOW IS THIS OLD LADY SO FAST AND QUIET?
THIS IS THE GYM. YOU WOULDN'T THINK IT WOULD BE IMPORTANT, BUT MAINTAINING YOUR HUMAN DISGUISE DURING PHYSICAL ACTIVITY CAN BE TRICKY.
HUH.

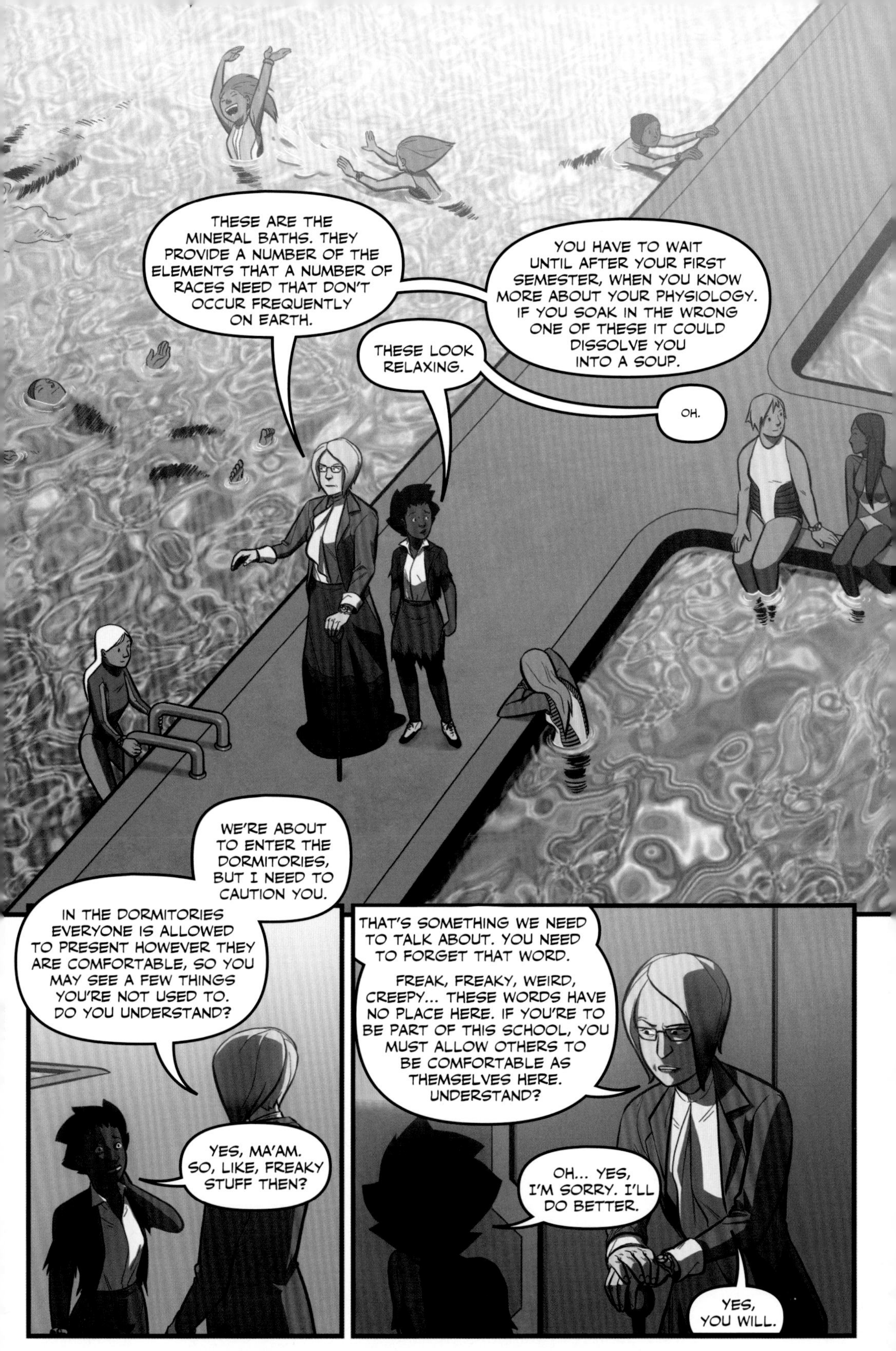

THESE ARE THE MINERAL BATHS. THEY PROVIDE A NUMBER OF THE ELEMENTS THAT A NUMBER OF RACES NEED THAT DON'T OCCUR FREQUENTLY ON EARTH.
THESE LOOK RELAXING.
YOU HAVE TO WAIT UNTIL AFTER YOUR FIRST SEMESTER, WHEN YOU KNOW MORE ABOUT YOUR PHYSIOLOGY. IF YOU SOAK IN THE WRONG ONE OF THESE IT COULD DISSOLVE YOU INTO A SOUP.
OH.
WE'RE ABOUT TO ENTER THE DORMITORIES, BUT I NEED TO CAUTION YOU.
IN THE DORMITORIES EVERYONE IS ALLOWED TO PRESENT HOWEVER THEY ARE COMFORTABLE, SO YOU MAY SEE A FEW THINGS YOU'RE NOT USED TO. DO YOU UNDERSTAND?
YES, MA'AM. SO, LIKE, FREAKY STUFF THEN?
THAT'S SOMETHING WE NEED TO TALK ABOUT. YOU NEED TO FORGET THAT WORD.
FREAK, FREAKY, WEIRD, CREEPY... THESE WORDS HAVE NO PLACE HERE. IF YOU'RE TO BE PART OF THIS SCHOOL, YOU MUST ALLOW OTHERS TO BE COMFORTABLE AS THEMSELVES HERE. UNDERSTAND?
OH... YES, I'M SORRY. I'LL DO BETTER.
YES, YOU WILL.

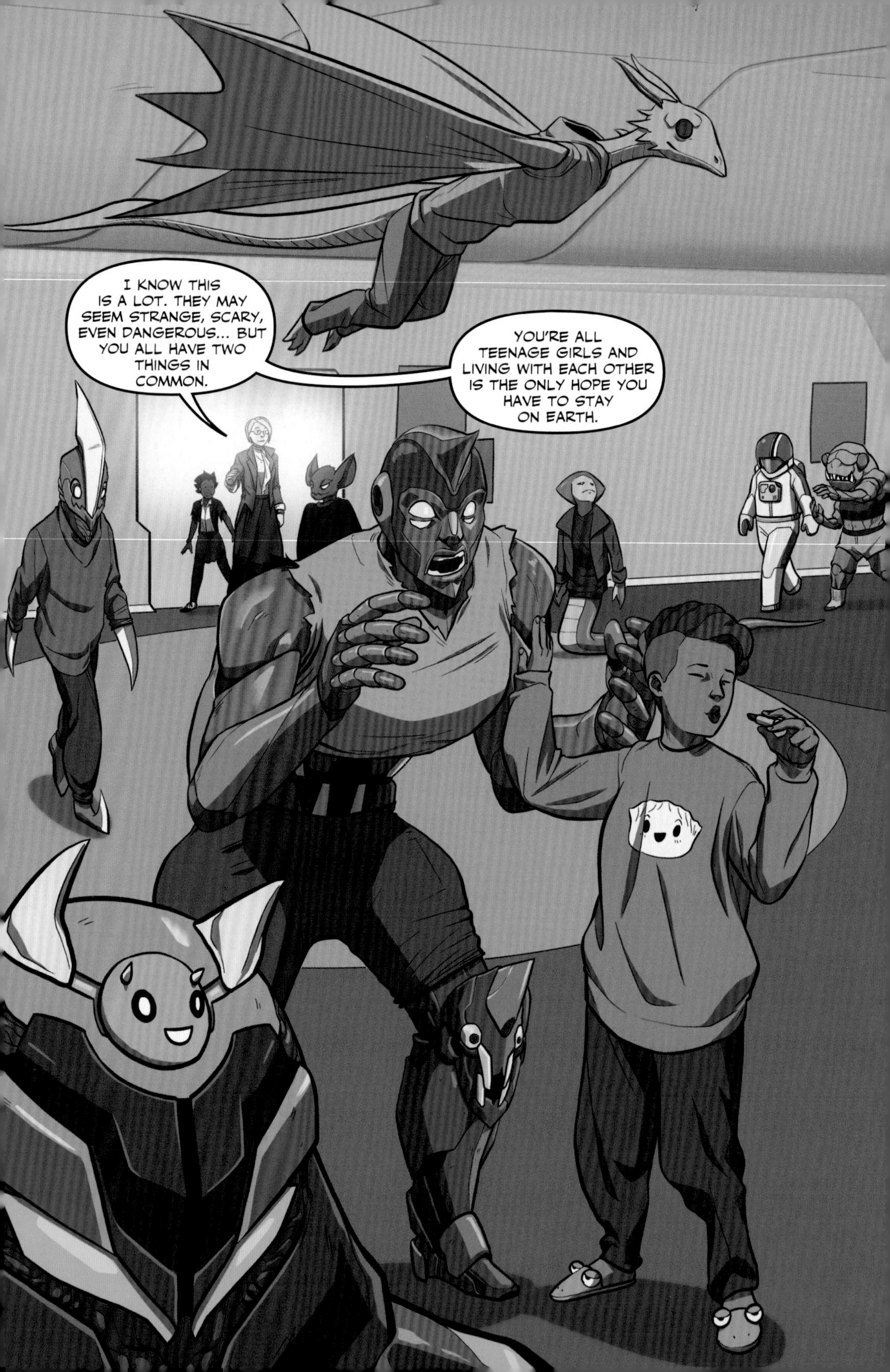
I KNOW THIS IS A LOT. THEY MAY SEEM STRANGE, SCARY, EVEN DANGEROUS... BUT YOU ALL HAVE TWO THINGS IN COMMON.
YOU'RE ALL TEENAGE GIRLS AND LIVING WITH EACH OTHER IS THE ONLY HOPE YOU HAVE TO STAY ON EARTH.

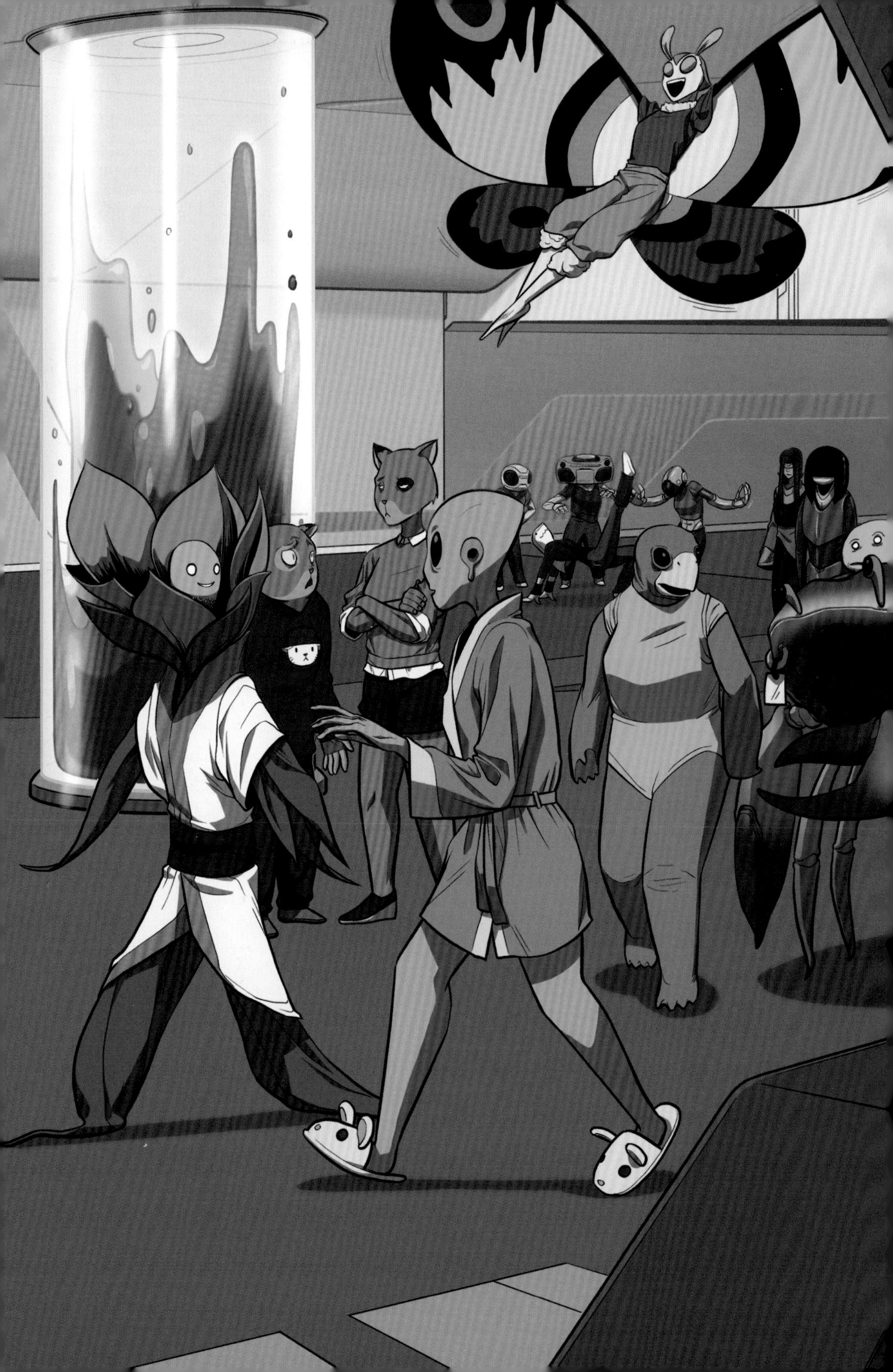

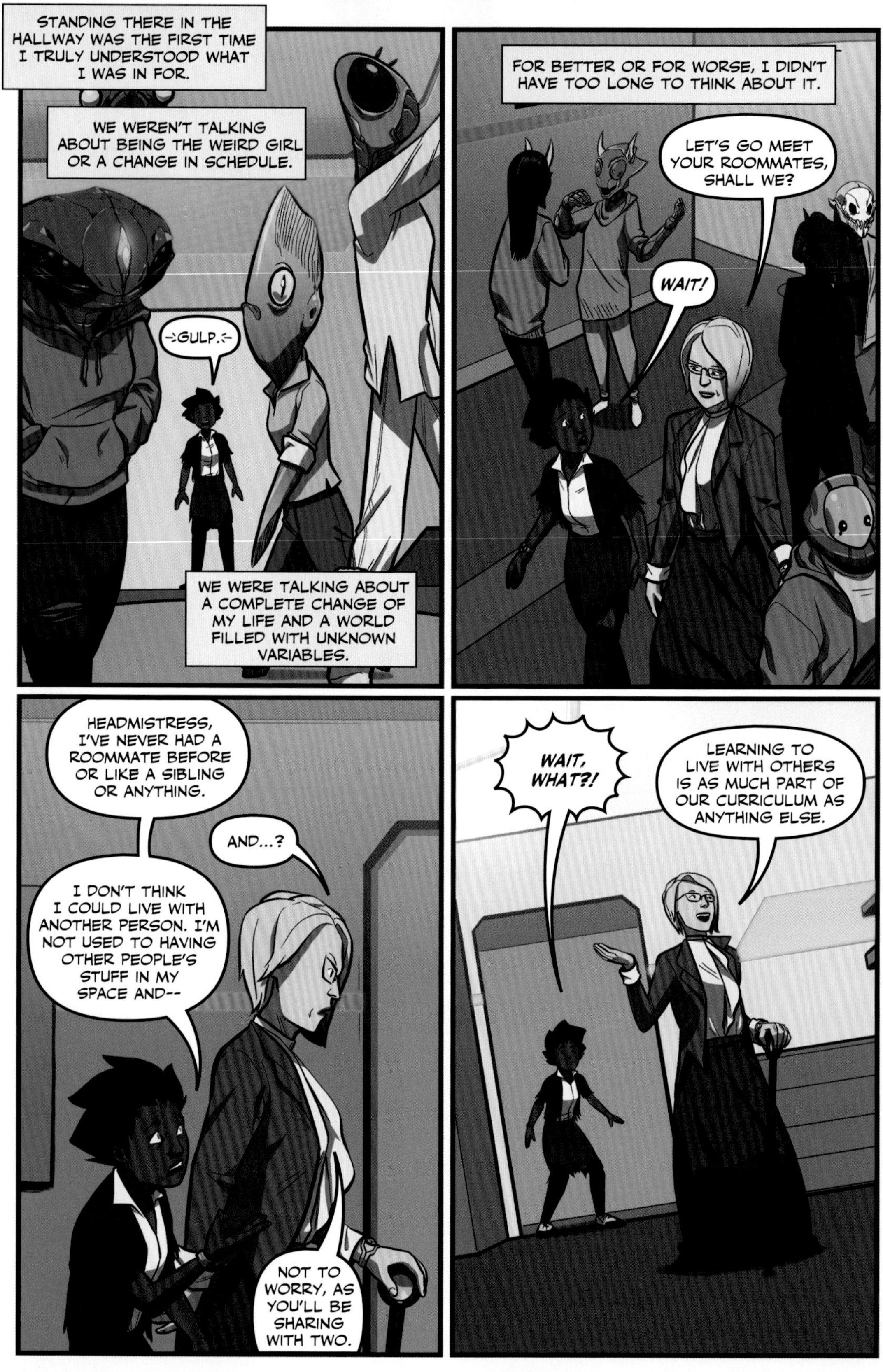
STANDING THERE IN THE HALLWAY WAS THE FIRST TIME I TRULY UNDERSTOOD WHAT I WAS IN FOR.
WE WEREN'T TALKING ABOUT BEING THE WEIRD GIRL OR A CHANGE IN SCHEDULE.
GULP.
WE WERE TALKING ABOUT A COMPLETE CHANGE OF MY LIFE AND A WORLD FILLED WITH UNKNOWN VARIABLES.
FOR BETTER OR FOR WORSE, I DIDN'T HAVE TOO LONG TO THINK ABOUT IT.
LET'S GO MEET YOUR ROOMMATES, SHALL WE?
WAIT!
HEADMISTRESS, I'VE NEVER HAD A ROOMMATE BEFORE OR LIKE A SIBLING OR ANYTHING.
AND...?
I DON'T THINK I COULD LIVE WITH ANOTHER PERSON. I'M NOT USED TO HAVING OTHER PEOPLE'S STUFF IN MY SPACE AND--
NOT TO WORRY, AS YOU'LL BE SHARING WITH TWO.
WAIT, WHAT?!
LEARNING TO LIVE WITH OTHERS IS AS MUCH PART OF OUR CURRICULUM AS ANYTHING ELSE.

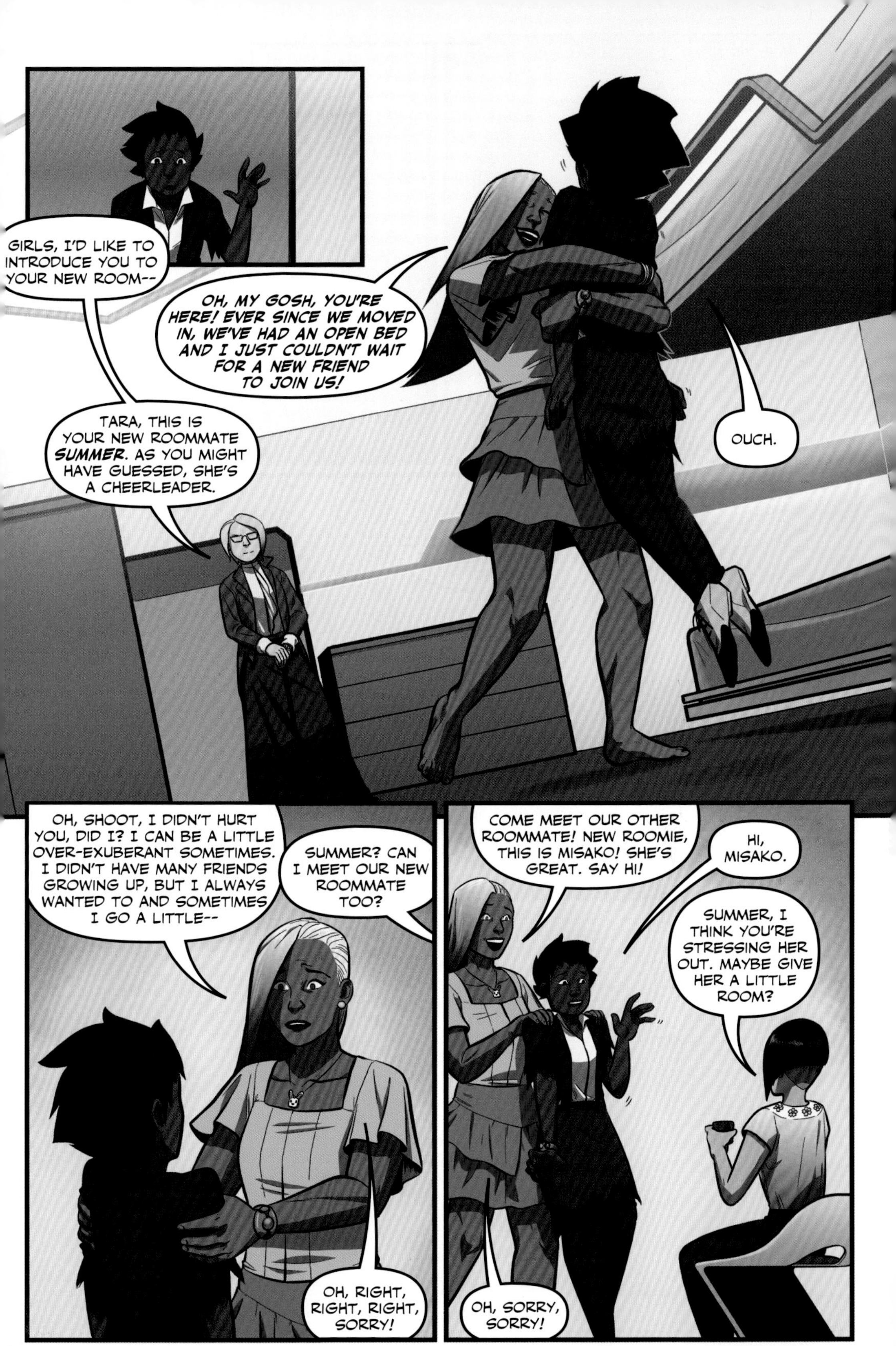
GIRLS, I'D LIKE TO INTRODUCE YOU TO YOUR NEW ROOM--
OH, MY GOSH, YOU'RE HERE! EVER SINCE WE MOVED IN, WE'VE HAD AN OPEN BED AND I JUST COULDN'T WAIT FOR A NEW FRIEND TO JOIN US!
TARA, THIS IS YOUR NEW ROOMMATE *SUMMER*. AS YOU MIGHT HAVE GUESSED, SHE'S A CHEERLEADER.
OUCH.
OH, SHOOT, I DIDN'T HURT YOU, DID I? I CAN BE A LITTLE OVER-EXUBERANT SOMETIMES. I DIDN'T HAVE MANY FRIENDS GROWING UP, BUT I ALWAYS WANTED TO AND SOMETIMES I GO A LITTLE--
SUMMER? CAN I MEET OUR NEW ROOMMATE TOO?
OH, RIGHT, RIGHT, RIGHT, SORRY!
COME MEET OUR OTHER ROOMMATE! NEW ROOMIE, THIS IS MISAKO! SHE'S GREAT. SAY HI!
HI, MISAKO.
SUMMER, I THINK YOU'RE STRESSING HER OUT. MAYBE GIVE HER A LITTLE ROOM?
OH, SORRY, SORRY!

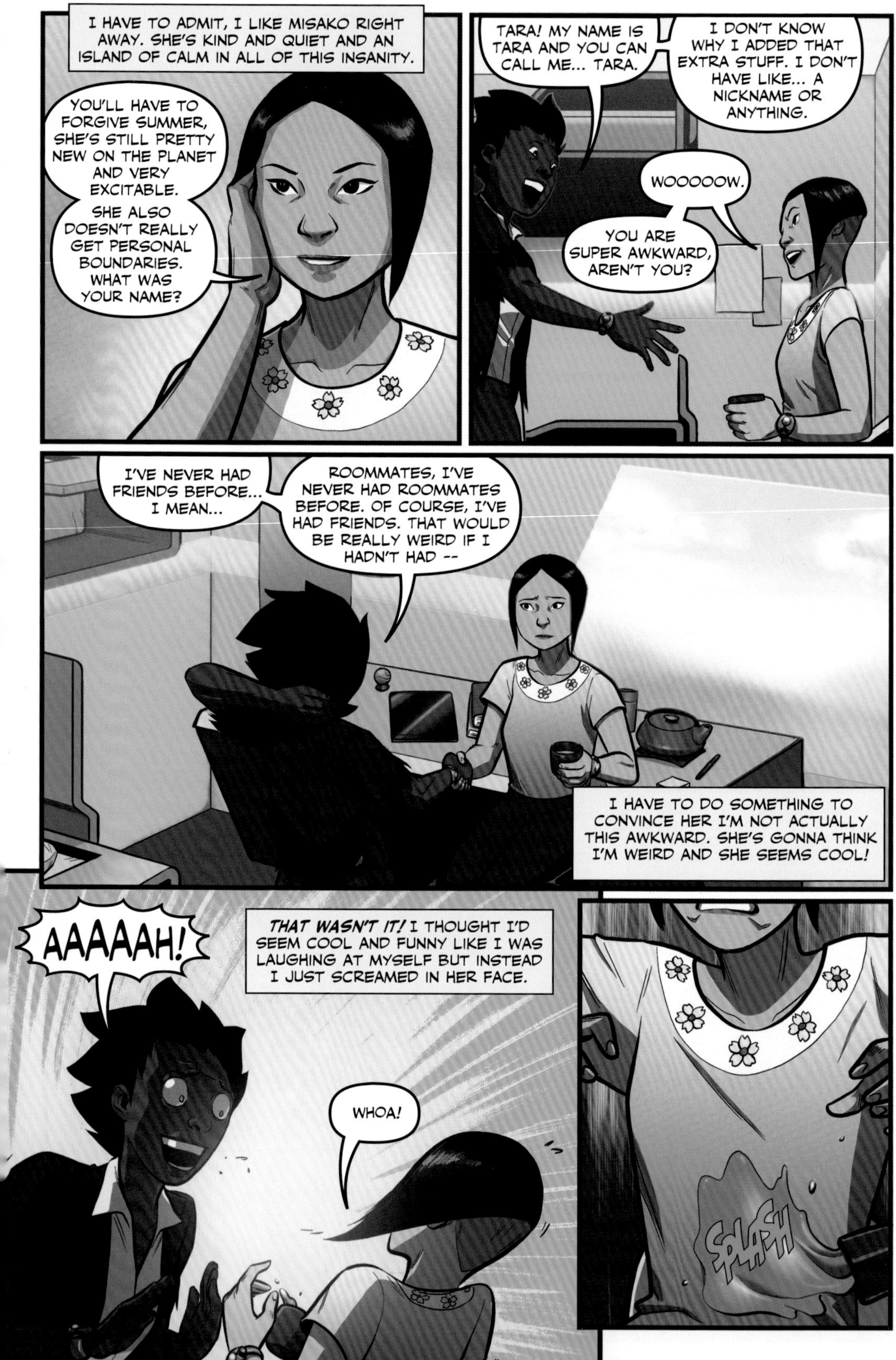
I HAVE TO ADMIT, I LIKE MISAKO RIGHT AWAY. SHE'S KIND AND QUIET AND AN ISLAND OF CALM IN ALL OF THIS INSANITY.
YOU'LL HAVE TO FORGIVE SUMMER, SHE'S STILL PRETTY NEW ON THE PLANET AND VERY EXCITABLE.
SHE ALSO DOESN'T REALLY GET PERSONAL BOUNDARIES. WHAT WAS YOUR NAME?
TARA! MY NAME IS TARA AND YOU CAN CALL ME... TARA.
I DON'T KNOW WHY I ADDED THAT EXTRA STUFF. I DON'T HAVE LIKE... A NICKNAME OR ANYTHING.
WOOOOOW.
YOU ARE SUPER AWKWARD, AREN'T YOU?
I'VE NEVER HAD FRIENDS BEFORE... I MEAN...
ROOMMATES, I'VE NEVER HAD ROOMMATES BEFORE. OF COURSE, I'VE HAD FRIENDS. THAT WOULD BE REALLY WEIRD IF I HADN'T HAD --
I HAVE TO DO SOMETHING TO CONVINCE HER I'M NOT ACTUALLY THIS AWKWARD. SHE'S GONNA THINK I'M WEIRD AND SHE SEEMS COOL!
AAAAAH!
THAT WASN'T IT! I THOUGHT I'D SEEM COOL AND FUNNY LIKE I WAS LAUGHING AT MYSELF BUT INSTEAD I JUST SCREAMED IN HER FACE.
WHOA!
SPLASH

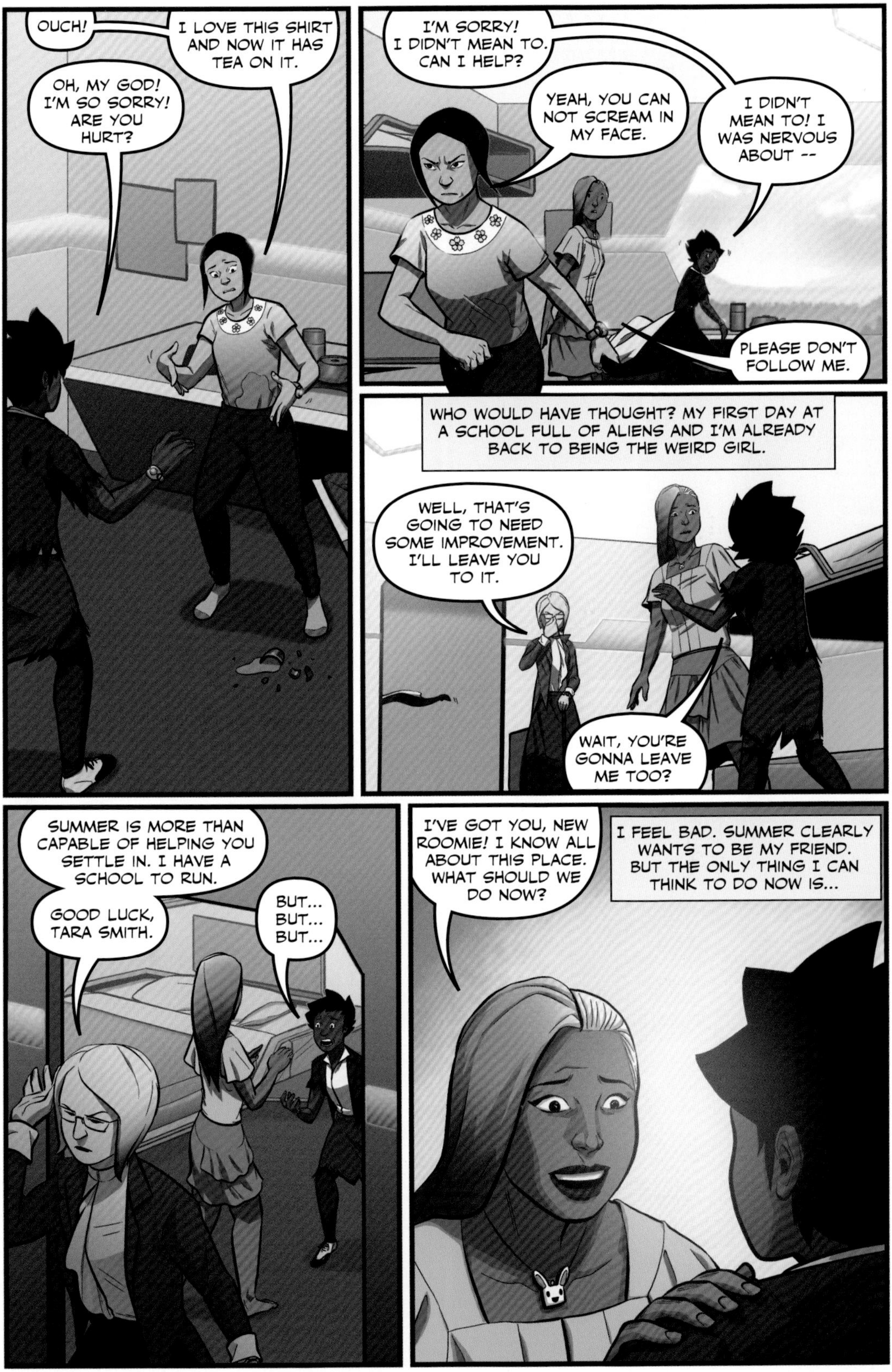
OUCH!
I LOVE THIS SHIRT AND NOW IT HAS TEA ON IT.
OH, MY GOD! I'M SO SORRY! ARE YOU HURT?
I'M SORRY! I DIDN'T MEAN TO. CAN I HELP?
YEAH, YOU CAN NOT SCREAM IN MY FACE.
I DIDN'T MEAN TO! I WAS NERVOUS ABOUT --
PLEASE DON'T FOLLOW ME.
WHO WOULD HAVE THOUGHT? MY FIRST DAY AT A SCHOOL FULL OF ALIENS AND I'M ALREADY BACK TO BEING THE WEIRD GIRL.
WELL, THAT'S GOING TO NEED SOME IMPROVEMENT. I'LL LEAVE YOU TO IT.
WAIT, YOU'RE GONNA LEAVE ME TOO?
SUMMER IS MORE THAN CAPABLE OF HELPING YOU SETTLE IN. I HAVE A SCHOOL TO RUN.
GOOD LUCK, TARA SMITH.
BUT... BUT... BUT...
I'VE GOT YOU, NEW ROOMIE! I KNOW ALL ABOUT THIS PLACE. WHAT SHOULD WE DO NOW?
I FEEL BAD. SUMMER CLEARLY WANTS TO BE MY FRIEND. BUT THE ONLY THING I CAN THINK TO DO NOW IS...

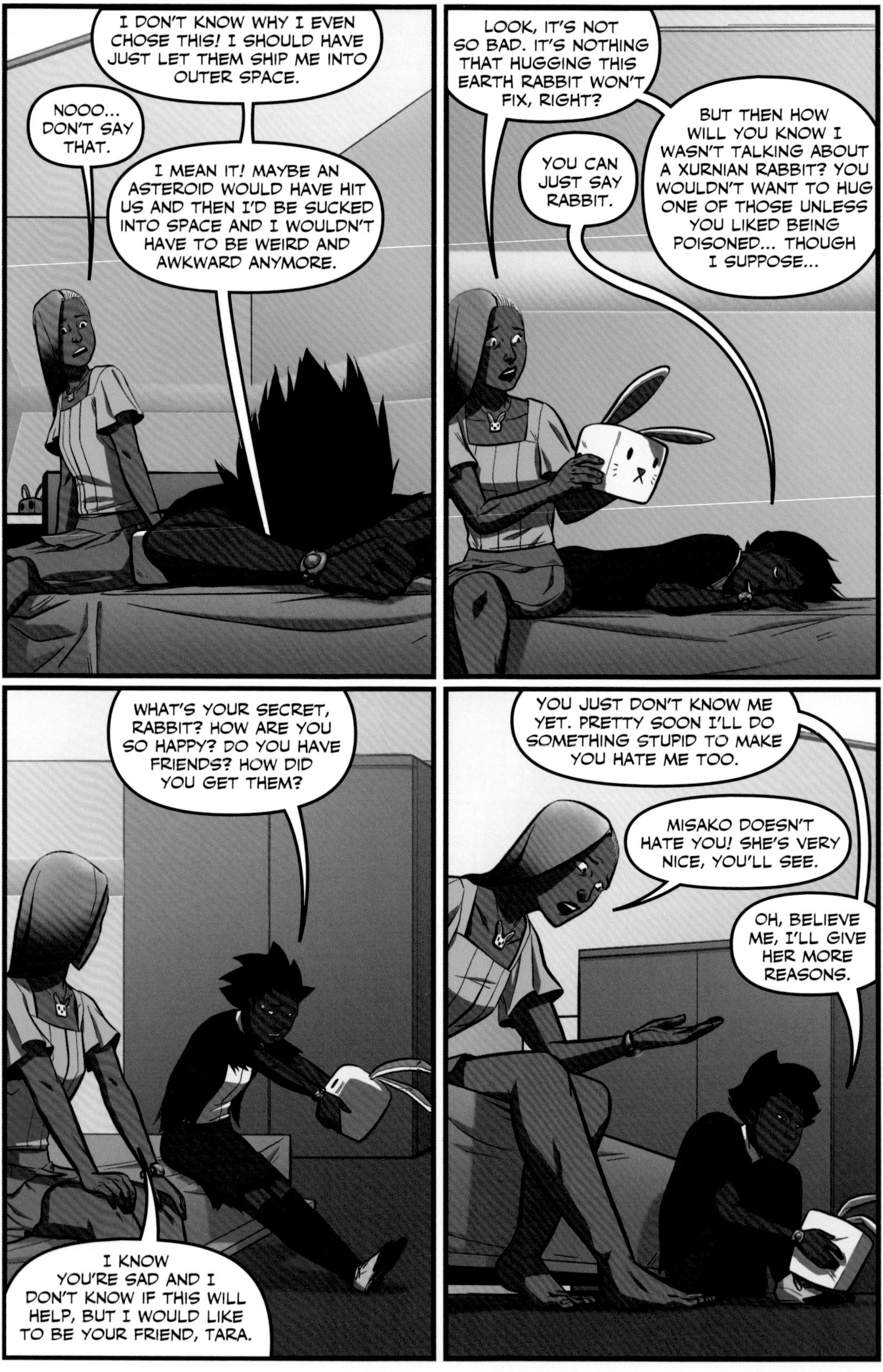
I DON'T KNOW WHY I EVEN CHOSE THIS! I SHOULD HAVE JUST LET THEM SHIP ME INTO OUTER SPACE.
NOOO... DON'T SAY THAT.
I MEAN IT! MAYBE AN ASTEROID WOULD HAVE HIT US AND THEN I'D BE SUCKED INTO SPACE AND I WOULDN'T HAVE TO BE WEIRD AND AWKWARD ANYMORE.
LOOK, IT'S NOT SO BAD. IT'S NOTHING THAT HUGGING THIS EARTH RABBIT WON'T FIX, RIGHT?
YOU CAN JUST SAY RABBIT.
BUT THEN HOW WILL YOU KNOW I WASN'T TALKING ABOUT A XURNIAN RABBIT? YOU WOULDN'T WANT TO HUG ONE OF THOSE UNLESS YOU LIKED BEING POISONED... THOUGH I SUPPOSE...
WHAT'S YOUR SECRET, RABBIT? HOW ARE YOU SO HAPPY? DO YOU HAVE FRIENDS? HOW DID YOU GET THEM?
I KNOW YOU'RE SAD AND I DON'T KNOW IF THIS WILL HELP, BUT I WOULD LIKE TO BE YOUR FRIEND, TARA.
YOU JUST DON'T KNOW ME YET. PRETTY SOON I'LL DO SOMETHING STUPID TO MAKE YOU HATE ME TOO.
MISAKO DOESN'T HATE YOU! SHE'S VERY NICE, YOU'LL SEE.
OH, BELIEVE ME, I'LL GIVE HER MORE REASONS.

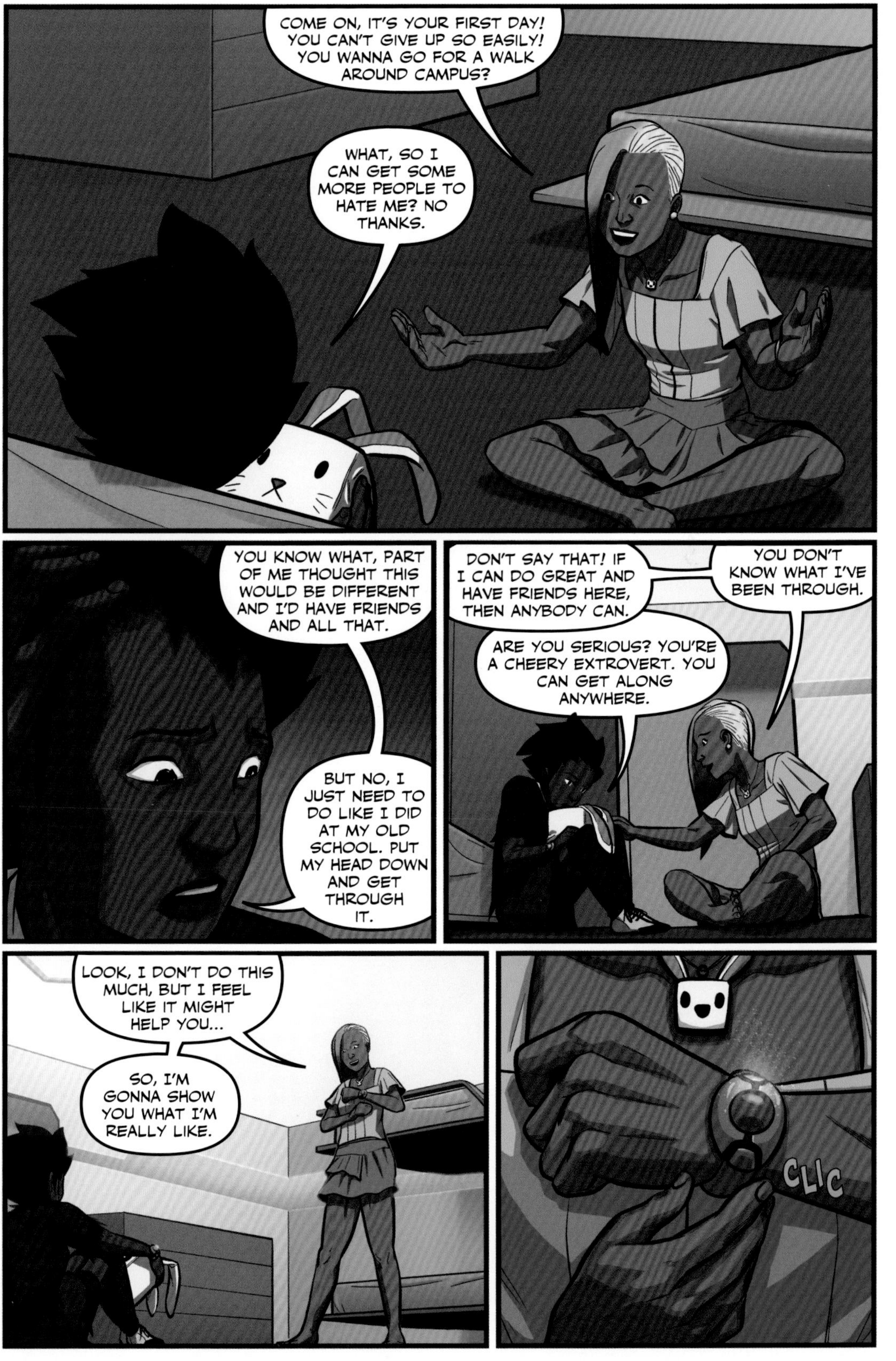
COME ON, IT'S YOUR FIRST DAY! YOU CAN'T GIVE UP SO EASILY! YOU WANNA GO FOR A WALK AROUND CAMPUS?
WHAT, SO I CAN GET SOME MORE PEOPLE TO HATE ME? NO THANKS.
YOU KNOW WHAT, PART OF ME THOUGHT THIS WOULD BE DIFFERENT AND I'D HAVE FRIENDS AND ALL THAT.
BUT NO, I JUST NEED TO DO LIKE I DID AT MY OLD SCHOOL. PUT MY HEAD DOWN AND GET THROUGH IT.
DON'T SAY THAT! IF I CAN DO GREAT AND HAVE FRIENDS HERE, THEN ANYBODY CAN.
YOU DON'T KNOW WHAT I'VE BEEN THROUGH.
ARE YOU SERIOUS? YOU'RE A CHEERY EXTROVERT. YOU CAN GET ALONG ANYWHERE.
LOOK, I DON'T DO THIS MUCH, BUT I FEEL LIKE IT MIGHT HELP YOU...
SO, I'M GONNA SHOW YOU WHAT I'M REALLY LIKE.
CLIC

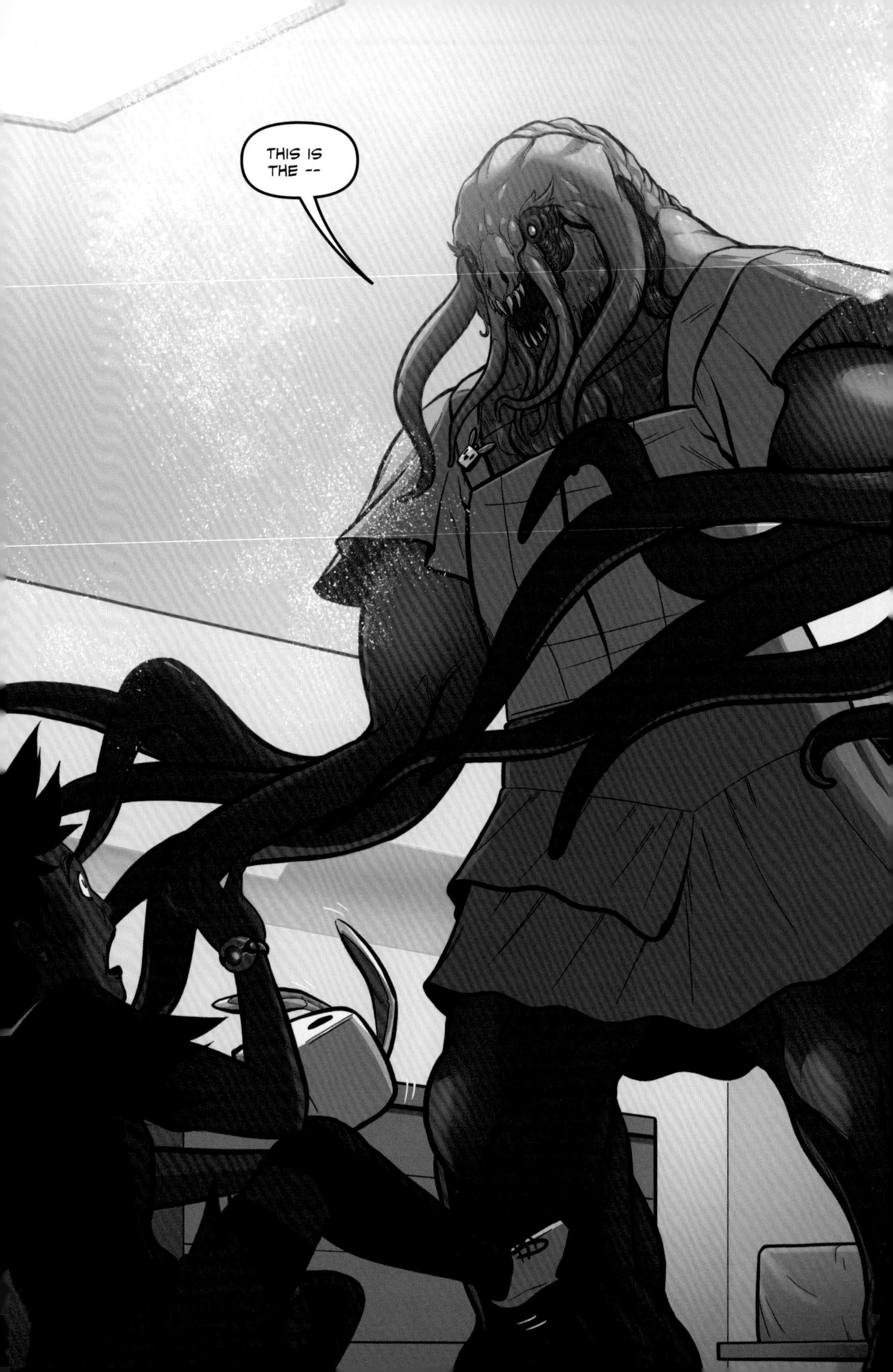
THIS IS THE --

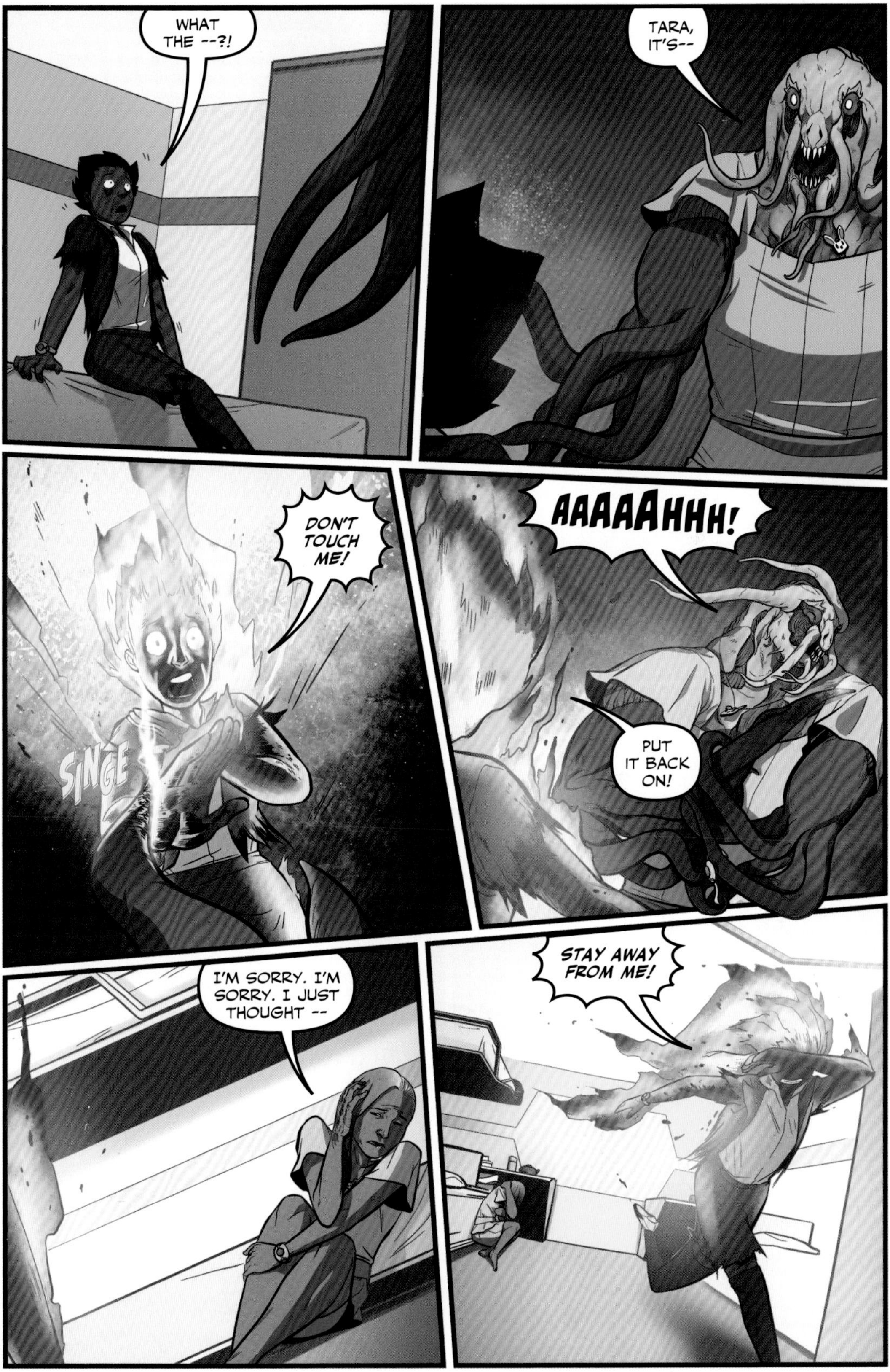
WHAT THE --?!
TARA, IT'S--
DON'T TOUCH ME!
SINGE
AAAAAHHH!
PUT IT BACK ON!
I'M SORRY. I'M SORRY. I JUST THOUGHT --
STAY AWAY FROM ME!

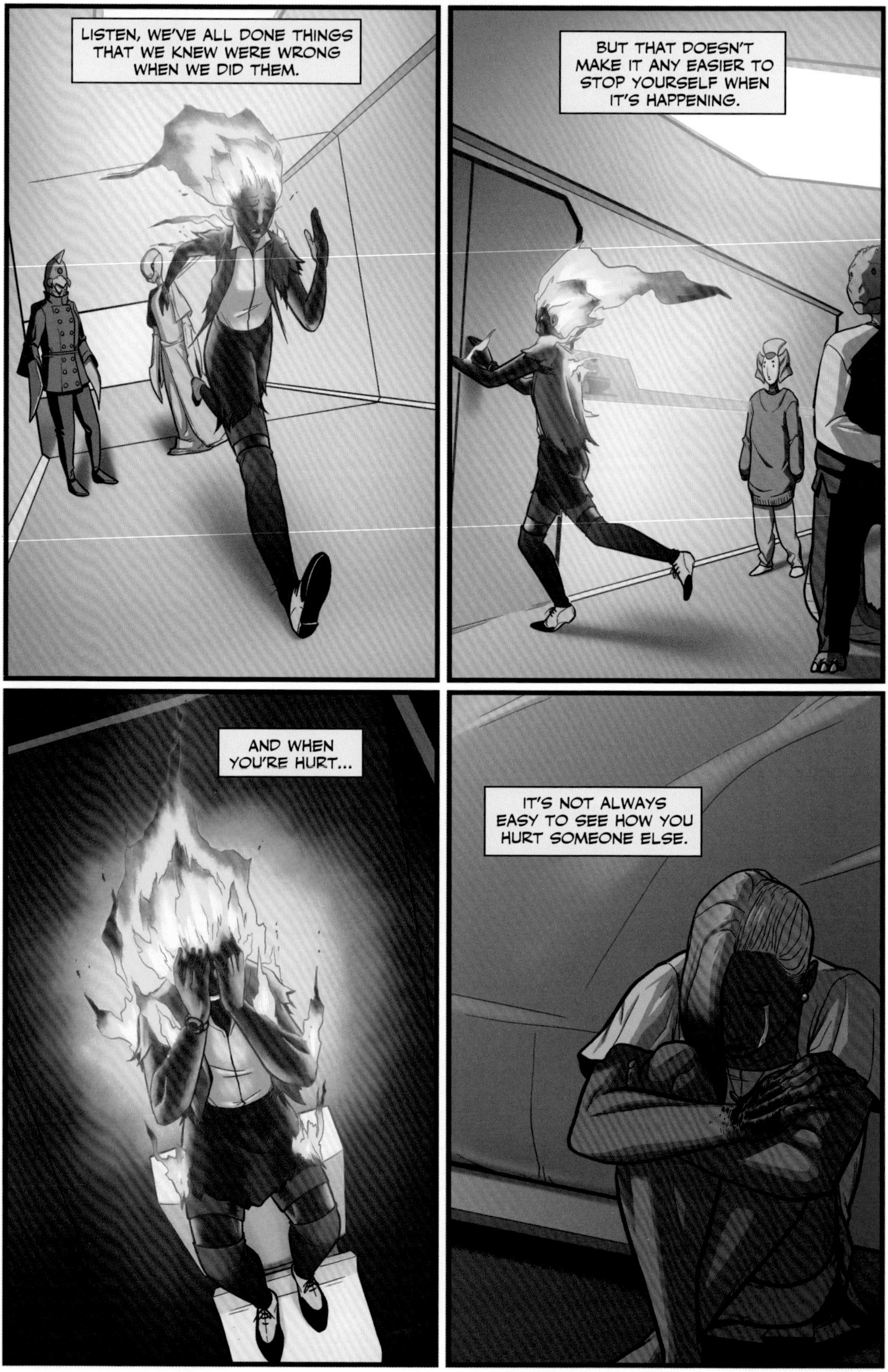
LISTEN, WE'VE ALL DONE THINGS THAT WE KNEW WERE WRONG WHEN WE DID THEM.
BUT THAT DOESN'T MAKE IT ANY EASIER TO STOP YOURSELF WHEN IT'S HAPPENING.
AND WHEN YOU'RE HURT...
IT'S NOT ALWAYS EASY TO SEE HOW YOU HURT SOMEONE ELSE.

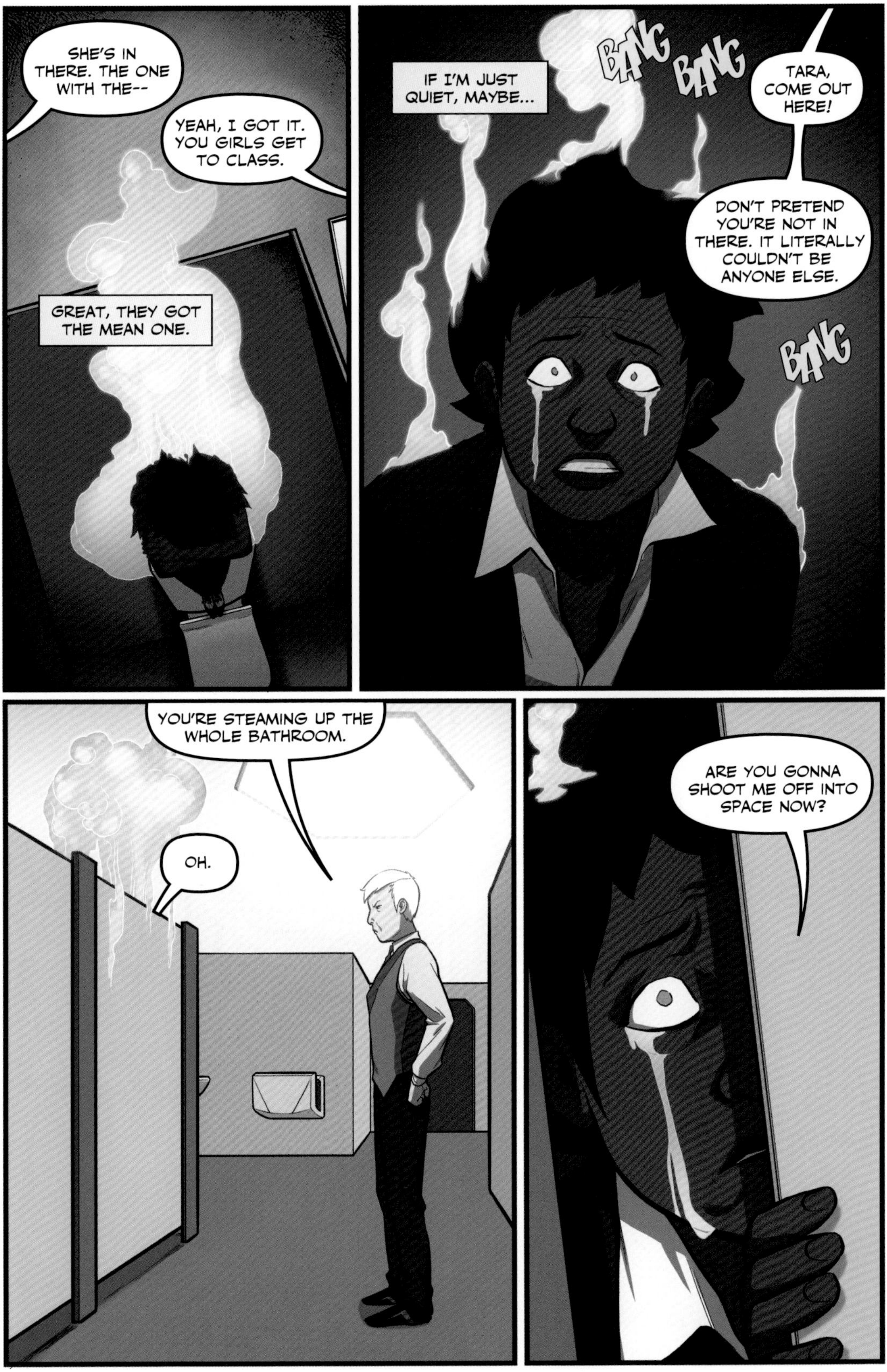
SHE'S IN THERE. THE ONE WITH THE--
YEAH, I GOT IT. YOU GIRLS GET TO CLASS.
GREAT, THEY GOT THE MEAN ONE.
IF I'M JUST QUIET, MAYBE...
BANG
BANG
TARA, COME OUT HERE!
DON'T PRETEND YOU'RE NOT IN THERE. IT LITERALLY COULDN'T BE ANYONE ELSE.
BANG
YOU'RE STEAMING UP THE WHOLE BATHROOM.
OH.
ARE YOU GONNA SHOOT ME OFF INTO SPACE NOW?

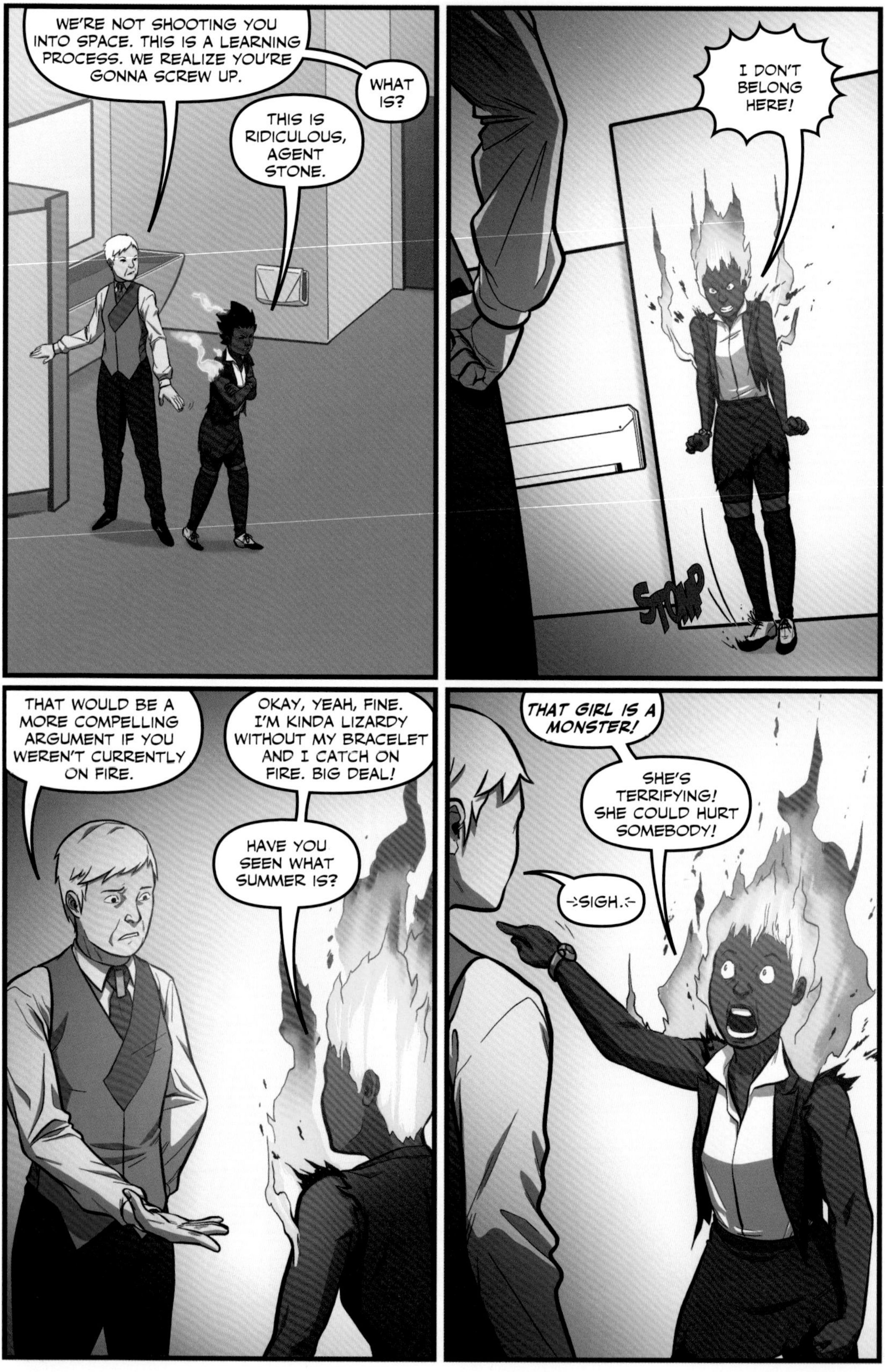
WE'RE NOT SHOOTING YOU INTO SPACE. THIS IS A LEARNING PROCESS. WE REALIZE YOU'RE GONNA SCREW UP.
WHAT IS?
THIS IS RIDICULOUS, AGENT STONE.
I DON'T BELONG HERE!
STOMP
THAT WOULD BE A MORE COMPELLING ARGUMENT IF YOU WEREN'T CURRENTLY ON FIRE.
OKAY, YEAH, FINE. I'M KINDA LIZARDY WITHOUT MY BRACELET AND I CATCH ON FIRE. BIG DEAL!
HAVE YOU SEEN WHAT SUMMER IS?
THAT GIRL IS A MONSTER!
SHE'S TERRIFYING! SHE COULD HURT SOMEBODY!
SIGH.

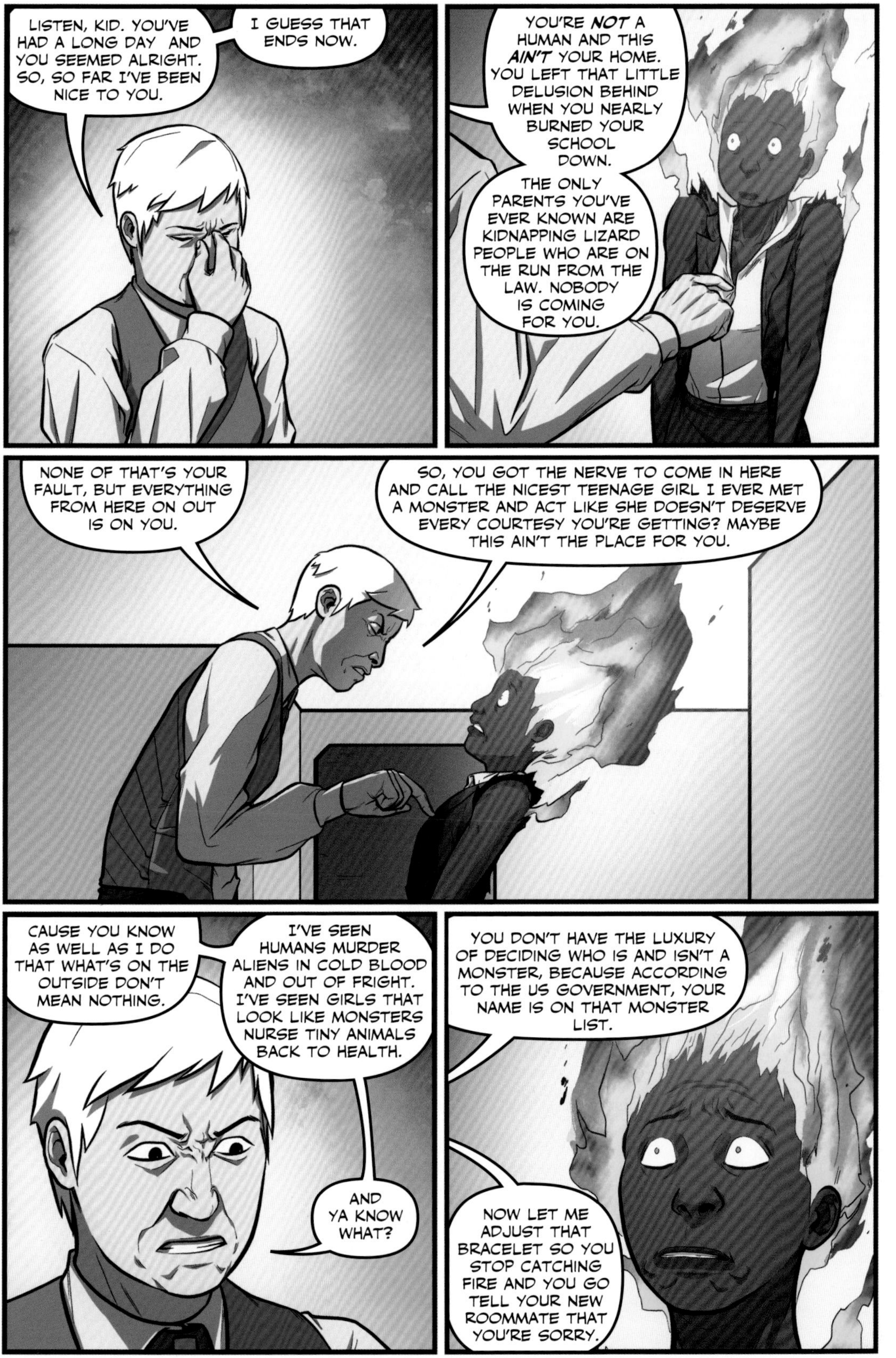
LISTEN, KID. YOU'VE HAD A LONG DAY AND YOU SEEMED ALRIGHT. SO, SO FAR I'VE BEEN NICE TO YOU.
I GUESS THAT ENDS NOW.
YOU'RE *NOT* A HUMAN AND THIS *AIN'T* YOUR HOME. YOU LEFT THAT LITTLE DELUSION BEHIND WHEN YOU NEARLY BURNED YOUR SCHOOL DOWN.
THE ONLY PARENTS YOU'VE EVER KNOWN ARE KIDNAPPING LIZARD PEOPLE WHO ARE ON THE RUN FROM THE LAW. NOBODY IS COMING FOR YOU.
NONE OF THAT'S YOUR FAULT, BUT EVERYTHING FROM HERE ON OUT IS ON YOU.
SO, YOU GOT THE NERVE TO COME IN HERE AND CALL THE NICEST TEENAGE GIRL I EVER MET A MONSTER AND ACT LIKE SHE DOESN'T DESERVE EVERY COURTESY YOU'RE GETTING? MAYBE THIS AIN'T THE PLACE FOR YOU.
CAUSE YOU KNOW AS WELL AS I DO THAT WHAT'S ON THE OUTSIDE DON'T MEAN NOTHING.
I'VE SEEN HUMANS MURDER ALIENS IN COLD BLOOD AND OUT OF FRIGHT. I'VE SEEN GIRLS THAT LOOK LIKE MONSTERS NURSE TINY ANIMALS BACK TO HEALTH.
AND YA KNOW WHAT?
YOU DON'T HAVE THE LUXURY OF DECIDING WHO IS AND ISN'T A MONSTER, BECAUSE ACCORDING TO THE US GOVERNMENT, YOUR NAME IS ON THAT MONSTER LIST.
NOW LET ME ADJUST THAT BRACELET SO YOU STOP CATCHING FIRE AND YOU GO TELL YOUR NEW ROOMMATE THAT YOU'RE SORRY.

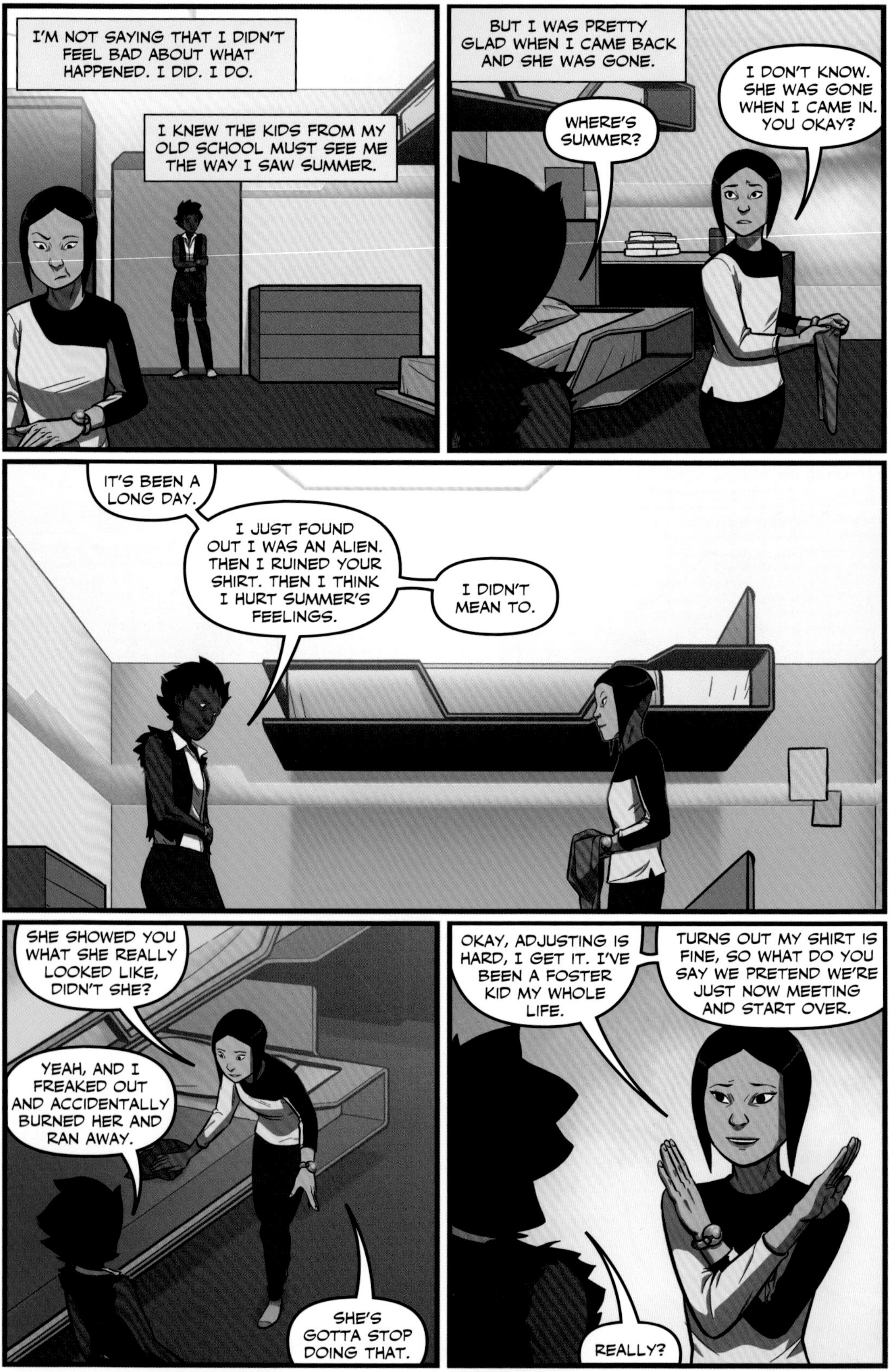
I'M NOT SAYING THAT I DIDN'T FEEL BAD ABOUT WHAT HAPPENED. I DID. I DO.
I KNEW THE KIDS FROM MY OLD SCHOOL MUST SEE ME THE WAY I SAW SUMMER.
BUT I WAS PRETTY GLAD WHEN I CAME BACK AND SHE WAS GONE.
WHERE'S SUMMER?
I DON'T KNOW. SHE WAS GONE WHEN I CAME IN. YOU OKAY?
IT'S BEEN A LONG DAY.
I JUST FOUND OUT I WAS AN ALIEN. THEN I RUINED YOUR SHIRT. THEN I THINK I HURT SUMMER'S FEELINGS.
I DIDN'T MEAN TO.
SHE SHOWED YOU WHAT SHE REALLY LOOKED LIKE, DIDN'T SHE?
YEAH, AND I FREAKED OUT AND ACCIDENTALLY BURNED HER AND RAN AWAY.
SHE'S GOTTA STOP DOING THAT.
OKAY, ADJUSTING IS HARD, I GET IT. I'VE BEEN A FOSTER KID MY WHOLE LIFE.
TURNS OUT MY SHIRT IS FINE, SO WHAT DO YOU SAY WE PRETEND WE'RE JUST NOW MEETING AND START OVER.
REALLY?

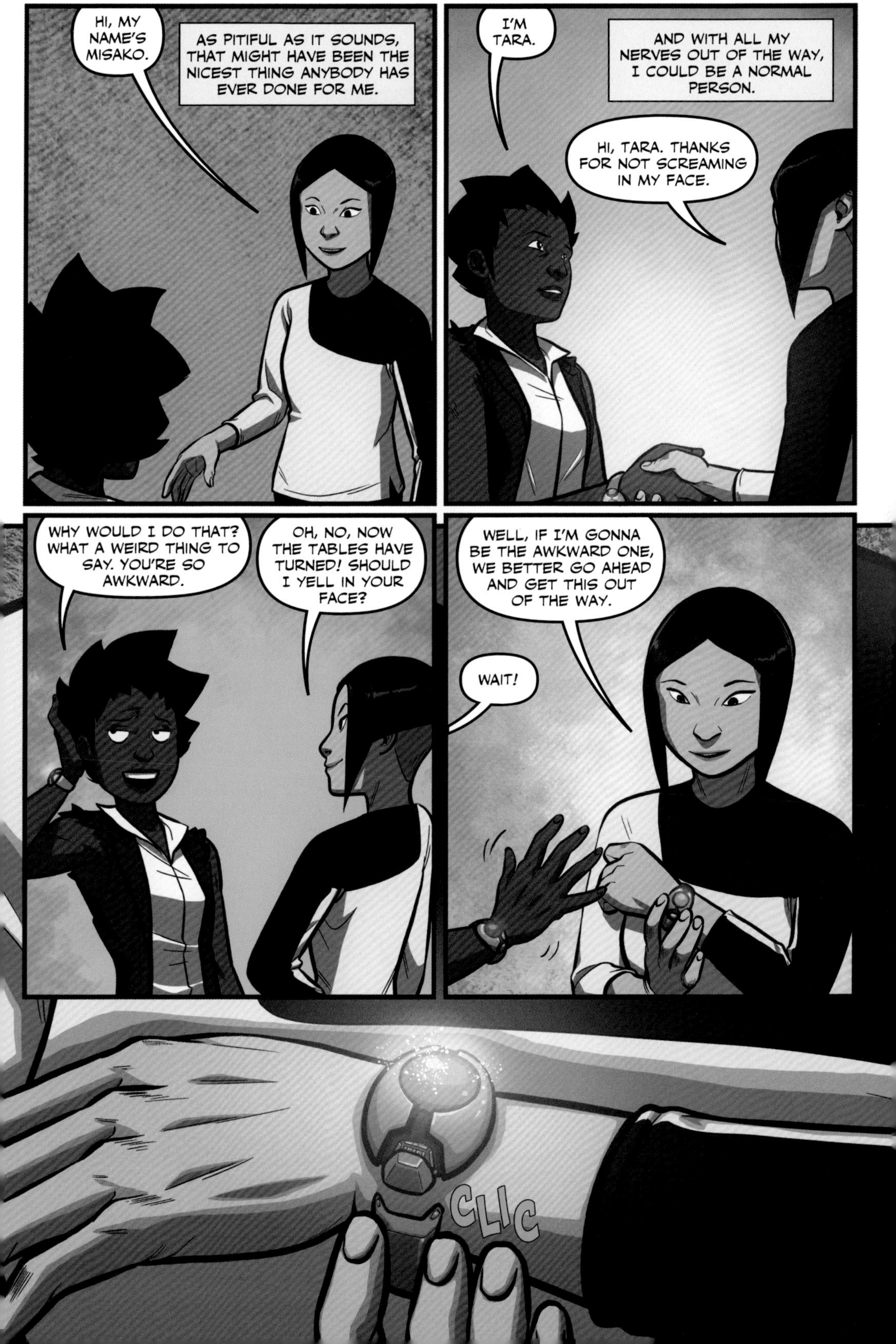
HI, MY NAME'S MISAKO.
AS PITIFUL AS IT SOUNDS, THAT MIGHT HAVE BEEN THE NICEST THING ANYBODY HAS EVER DONE FOR ME.
I'M TARA.
AND WITH ALL MY NERVES OUT OF THE WAY, I COULD BE A NORMAL PERSON.
HI, TARA. THANKS FOR NOT SCREAMING IN MY FACE.
WHY WOULD I DO THAT? WHAT A WEIRD THING TO SAY. YOU'RE SO AWKWARD.
OH, NO, NOW THE TABLES HAVE TURNED! SHOULD I YELL IN YOUR FACE?
WELL, IF I'M GONNA BE THE AWKWARD ONE, WE BETTER GO AHEAD AND GET THIS OUT OF THE WAY.
WAIT!
CLIC

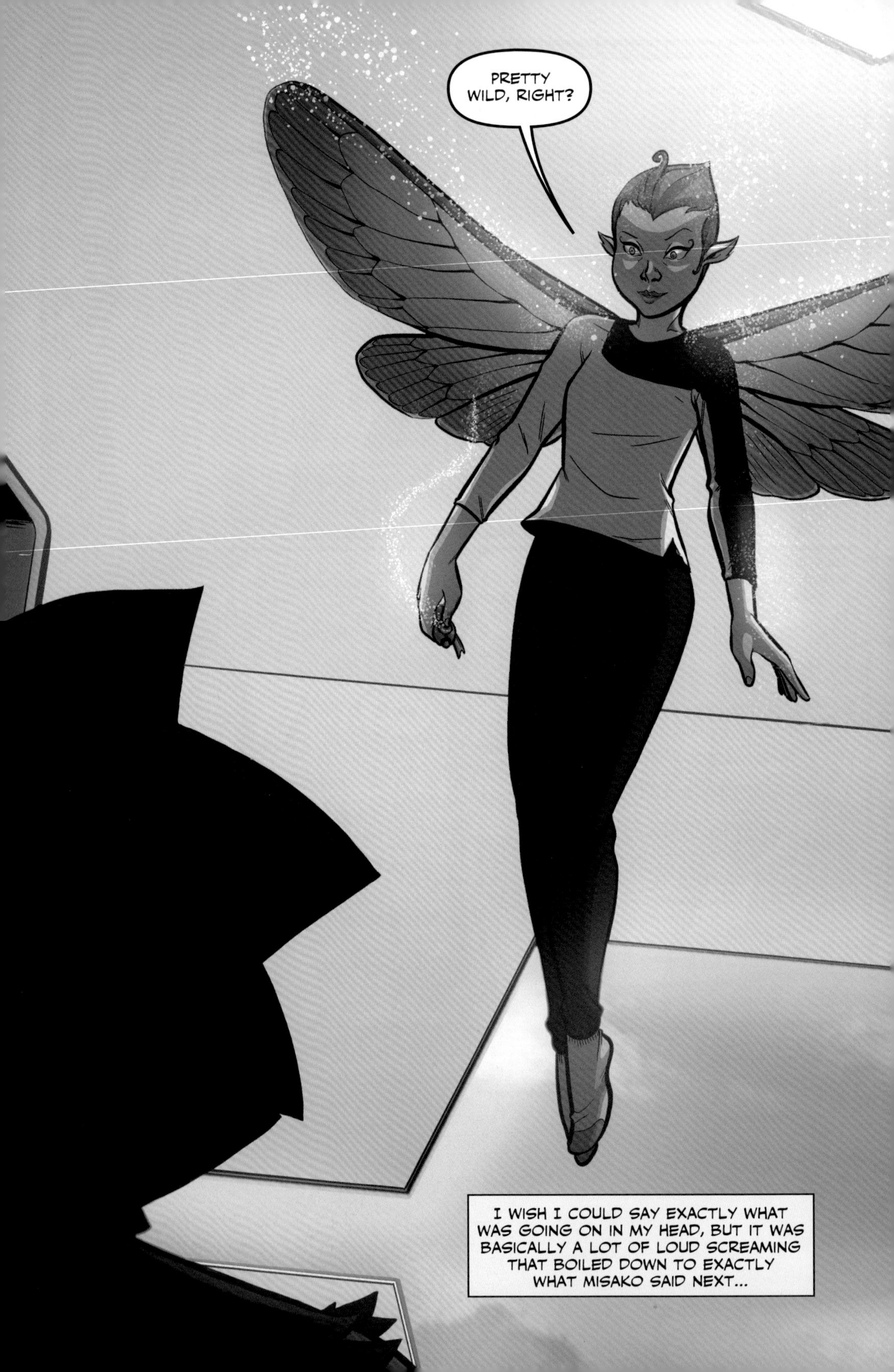
PRETTY WILD, RIGHT?
I WISH I COULD SAY EXACTLY WHAT WAS GOING ON IN MY HEAD, BUT IT WAS BASICALLY A LOT OF LOUD SCREAMING THAT BOILED DOWN TO EXACTLY WHAT MISAKO SAID NEXT...

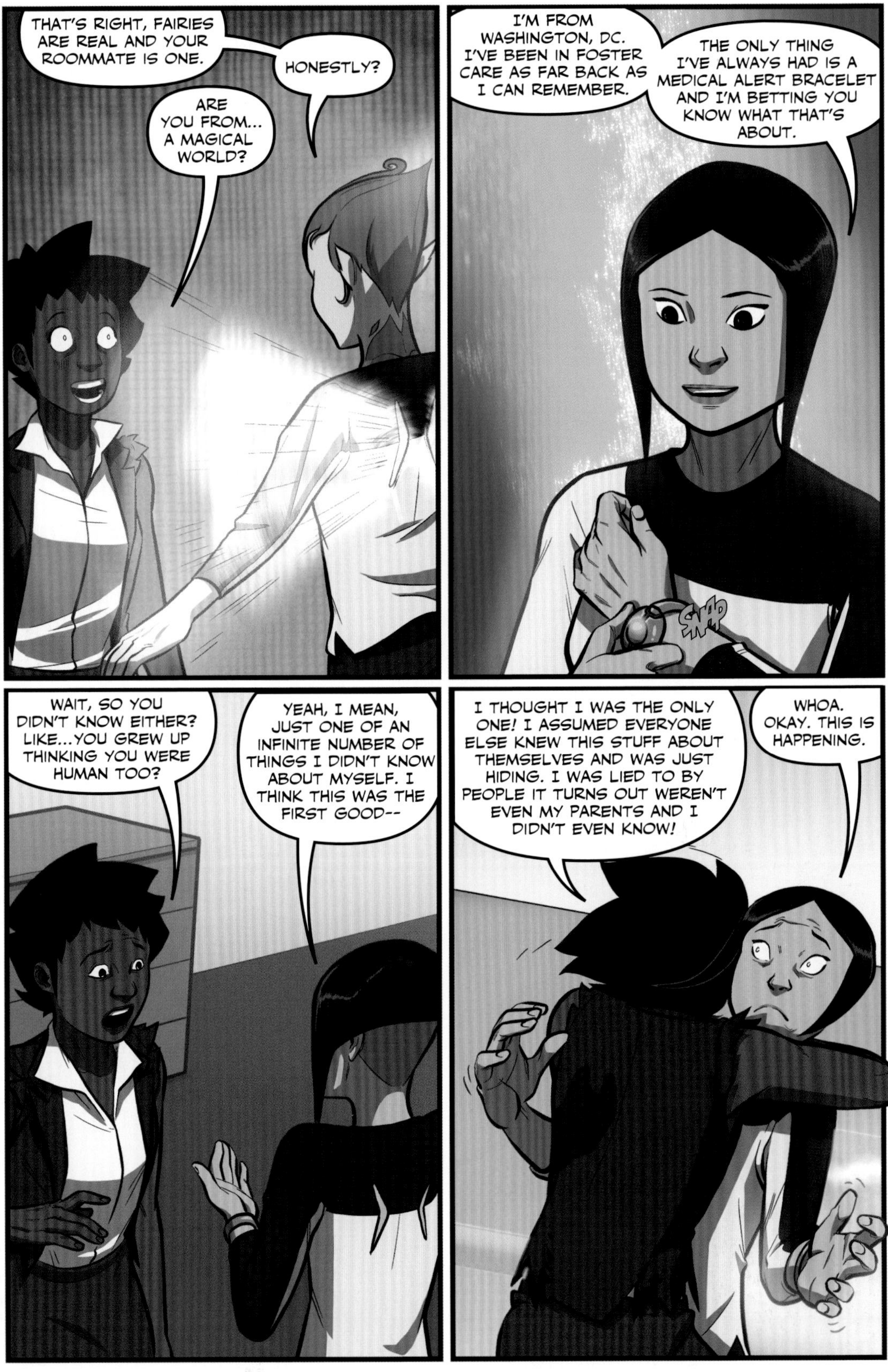
THAT'S RIGHT, FAIRIES ARE REAL AND YOUR ROOMMATE IS ONE.
HONESTLY?
ARE YOU FROM... A MAGICAL WORLD?
I'M FROM WASHINGTON, DC. I'VE BEEN IN FOSTER CARE AS FAR BACK AS I CAN REMEMBER.
THE ONLY THING I'VE ALWAYS HAD IS A MEDICAL ALERT BRACELET AND I'M BETTING YOU KNOW WHAT THAT'S ABOUT.
SNAP
WAIT, SO YOU DIDN'T KNOW EITHER? LIKE...YOU GREW UP THINKING YOU WERE HUMAN TOO?
YEAH, I MEAN, JUST ONE OF AN INFINITE NUMBER OF THINGS I DIDN'T KNOW ABOUT MYSELF. I THINK THIS WAS THE FIRST GOOD--
I THOUGHT I WAS THE ONLY ONE! I ASSUMED EVERYONE ELSE KNEW THIS STUFF ABOUT THEMSELVES AND WAS JUST HIDING. I WAS LIED TO BY PEOPLE IT TURNS OUT WEREN'T EVEN MY PARENTS AND I DIDN'T EVEN KNOW!
WHOA. OKAY. THIS IS HAPPENING.

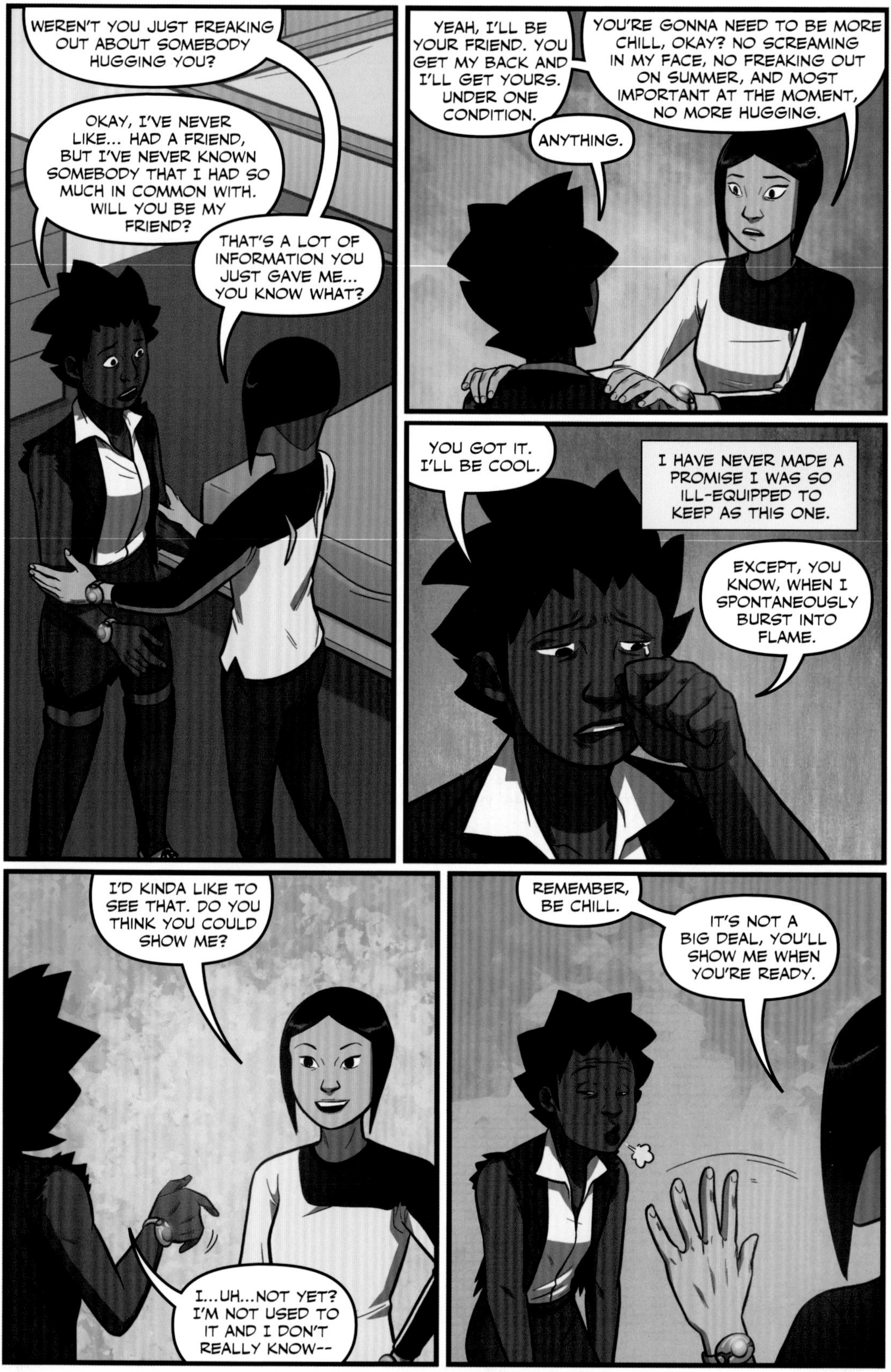
WEREN'T YOU JUST FREAKING OUT ABOUT SOMEBODY HUGGING YOU?
OKAY, I'VE NEVER LIKE... HAD A FRIEND, BUT I'VE NEVER KNOWN SOMEBODY THAT I HAD SO MUCH IN COMMON WITH. WILL YOU BE MY FRIEND?
THAT'S A LOT OF INFORMATION YOU JUST GAVE ME... YOU KNOW WHAT?
YEAH, I'LL BE YOUR FRIEND. YOU GET MY BACK AND I'LL GET YOURS. UNDER ONE CONDITION.
YOU'RE GONNA NEED TO BE MORE CHILL, OKAY? NO SCREAMING IN MY FACE, NO FREAKING OUT ON SUMMER, AND MOST IMPORTANT AT THE MOMENT, NO MORE HUGGING.
ANYTHING.
YOU GOT IT. I'LL BE COOL.
I HAVE NEVER MADE A PROMISE I WAS SO ILL-EQUIPPED TO KEEP AS THIS ONE.
EXCEPT, YOU KNOW, WHEN I SPONTANEOUSLY BURST INTO FLAME.
I'D KINDA LIKE TO SEE THAT. DO YOU THINK YOU COULD SHOW ME?
I...UH...NOT YET? I'M NOT USED TO IT AND I DON'T REALLY KNOW--
REMEMBER, BE CHILL.
IT'S NOT A BIG DEAL, YOU'LL SHOW ME WHEN YOU'RE READY.

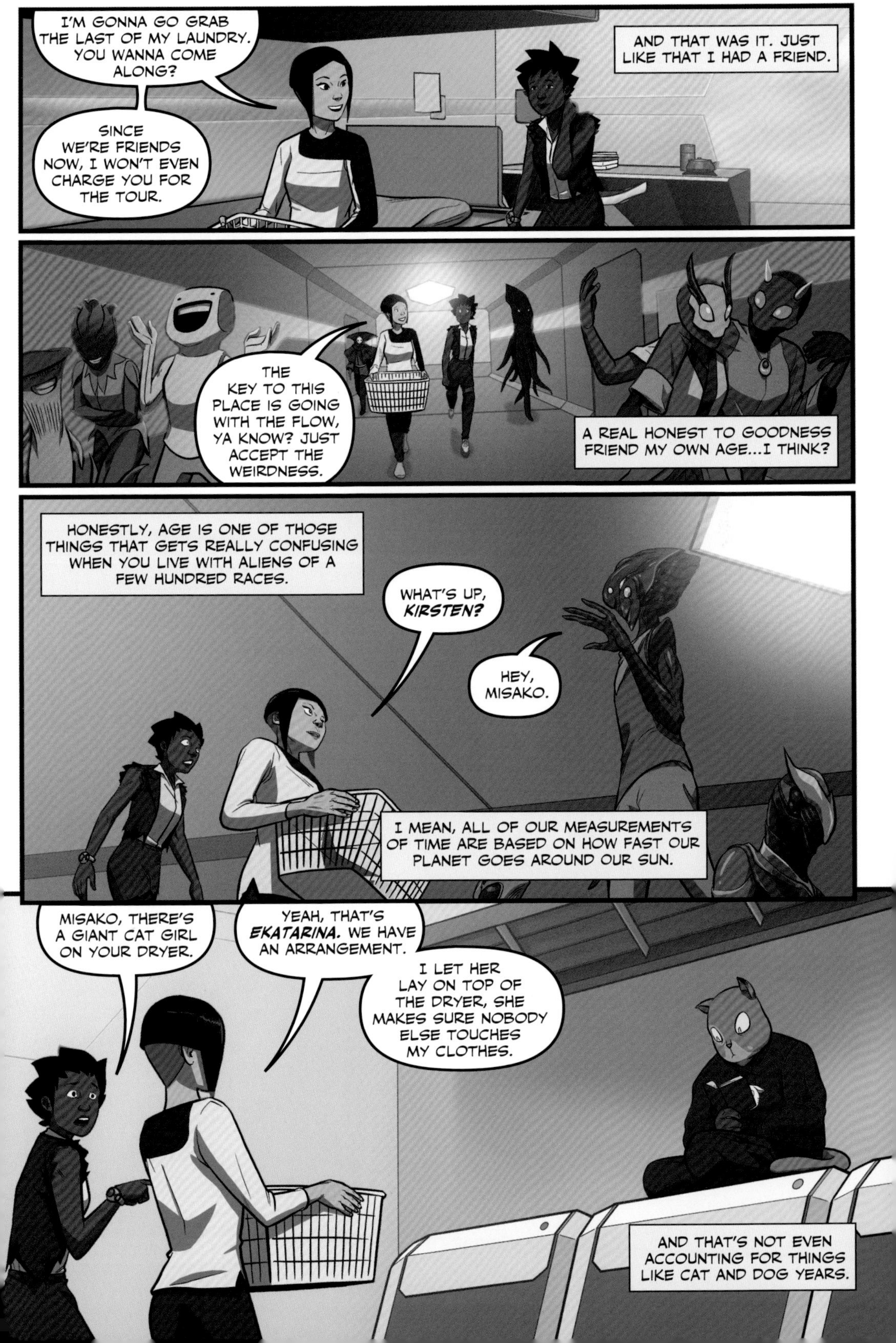

I'M GONNA GO GRAB THE LAST OF MY LAUNDRY. YOU WANNA COME ALONG?
SINCE WE'RE FRIENDS NOW, I WON'T EVEN CHARGE YOU FOR THE TOUR.
AND THAT WAS IT. JUST LIKE THAT I HAD A FRIEND.
THE KEY TO THIS PLACE IS GOING WITH THE FLOW, YA KNOW? JUST ACCEPT THE WEIRDNESS.
A REAL HONEST TO GOODNESS FRIEND MY OWN AGE...I THINK?
HONESTLY, AGE IS ONE OF THOSE THINGS THAT GETS REALLY CONFUSING WHEN YOU LIVE WITH ALIENS OF A FEW HUNDRED RACES.
WHAT'S UP, ***KIRSTEN?***
HEY, MISAKO.
I MEAN, ALL OF OUR MEASUREMENTS OF TIME ARE BASED ON HOW FAST OUR PLANET GOES AROUND OUR SUN.
MISAKO, THERE'S A GIANT CAT GIRL ON YOUR DRYER.
YEAH, THAT'S ***EKATARINA.*** WE HAVE AN ARRANGEMENT.
I LET HER LAY ON TOP OF THE DRYER, SHE MAKES SURE NOBODY ELSE TOUCHES MY CLOTHES.
AND THAT'S NOT EVEN ACCOUNTING FOR THINGS LIKE CAT AND DOG YEARS.

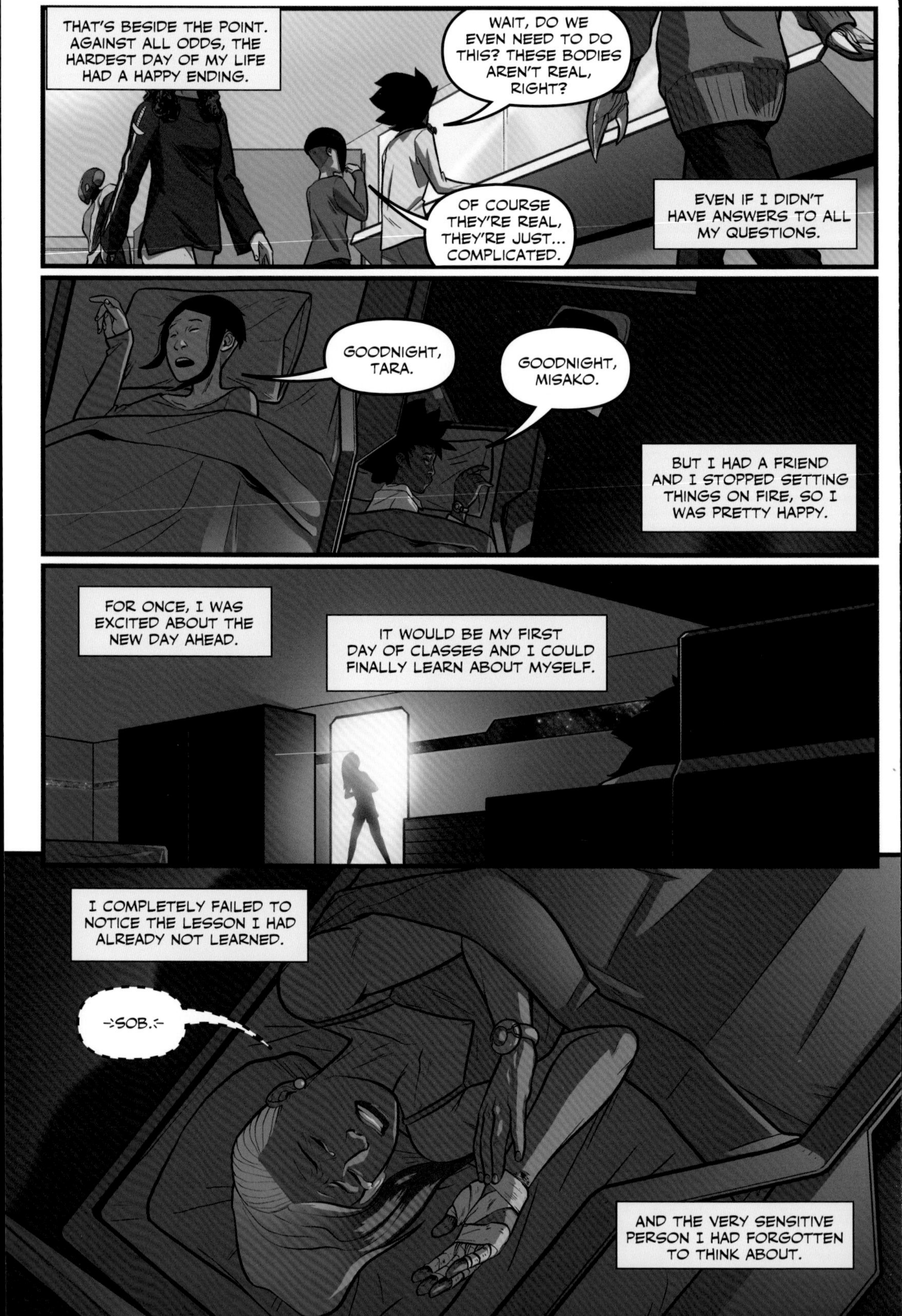
THAT'S BESIDE THE POINT. AGAINST ALL ODDS, THE HARDEST DAY OF MY LIFE HAD A HAPPY ENDING.
WAIT, DO WE EVEN NEED TO DO THIS? THESE BODIES AREN'T REAL, RIGHT?
OF COURSE THEY'RE REAL, THEY'RE JUST... COMPLICATED.
EVEN IF I DIDN'T HAVE ANSWERS TO ALL MY QUESTIONS.
GOODNIGHT, TARA.
GOODNIGHT, MISAKO.
BUT I HAD A FRIEND AND I STOPPED SETTING THINGS ON FIRE, SO I WAS PRETTY HAPPY.
FOR ONCE, I WAS EXCITED ABOUT THE NEW DAY AHEAD.
IT WOULD BE MY FIRST DAY OF CLASSES AND I COULD FINALLY LEARN ABOUT MYSELF.
I COMPLETELY FAILED TO NOTICE THE LESSON I HAD ALREADY NOT LEARNED.
-:SOB.:-
AND THE VERY SENSITIVE PERSON I HAD FORGOTTEN TO THINK ABOUT.

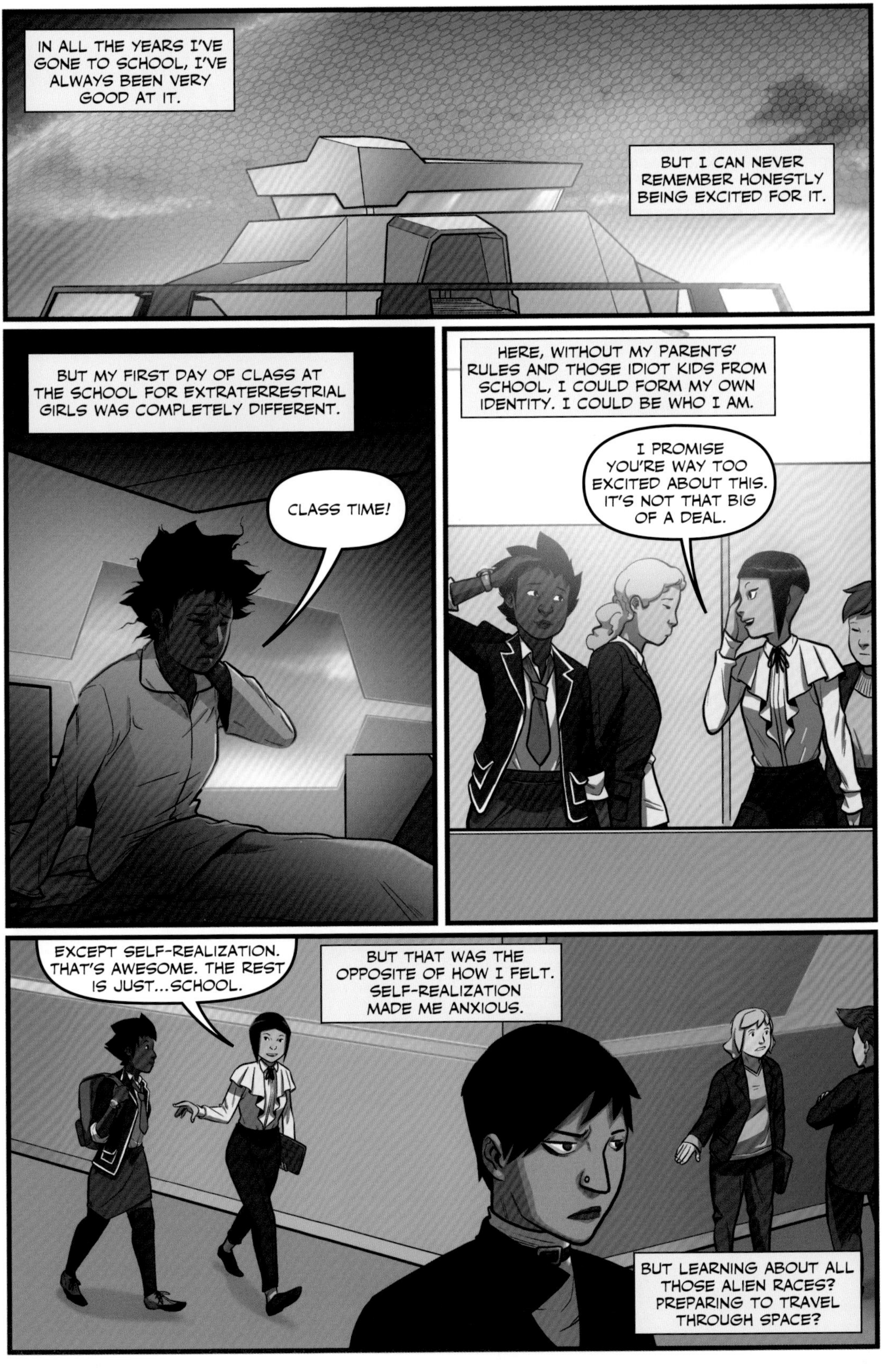
IN ALL THE YEARS I'VE GONE TO SCHOOL, I'VE ALWAYS BEEN VERY GOOD AT IT.
BUT I CAN NEVER REMEMBER HONESTLY BEING EXCITED FOR IT.
BUT MY FIRST DAY OF CLASS AT THE SCHOOL FOR EXTRATERRESTRIAL GIRLS WAS COMPLETELY DIFFERENT.
CLASS TIME!
HERE, WITHOUT MY PARENTS' RULES AND THOSE IDIOT KIDS FROM SCHOOL, I COULD FORM MY OWN IDENTITY. I COULD BE WHO I AM.
I PROMISE YOU'RE WAY TOO EXCITED ABOUT THIS. IT'S NOT THAT BIG OF A DEAL.
EXCEPT SELF-REALIZATION. THAT'S AWESOME. THE REST IS JUST...SCHOOL.
BUT THAT WAS THE OPPOSITE OF HOW I FELT. SELF-REALIZATION MADE ME ANXIOUS.
BUT LEARNING ABOUT ALL THOSE ALIEN RACES? PREPARING TO TRAVEL THROUGH SPACE?

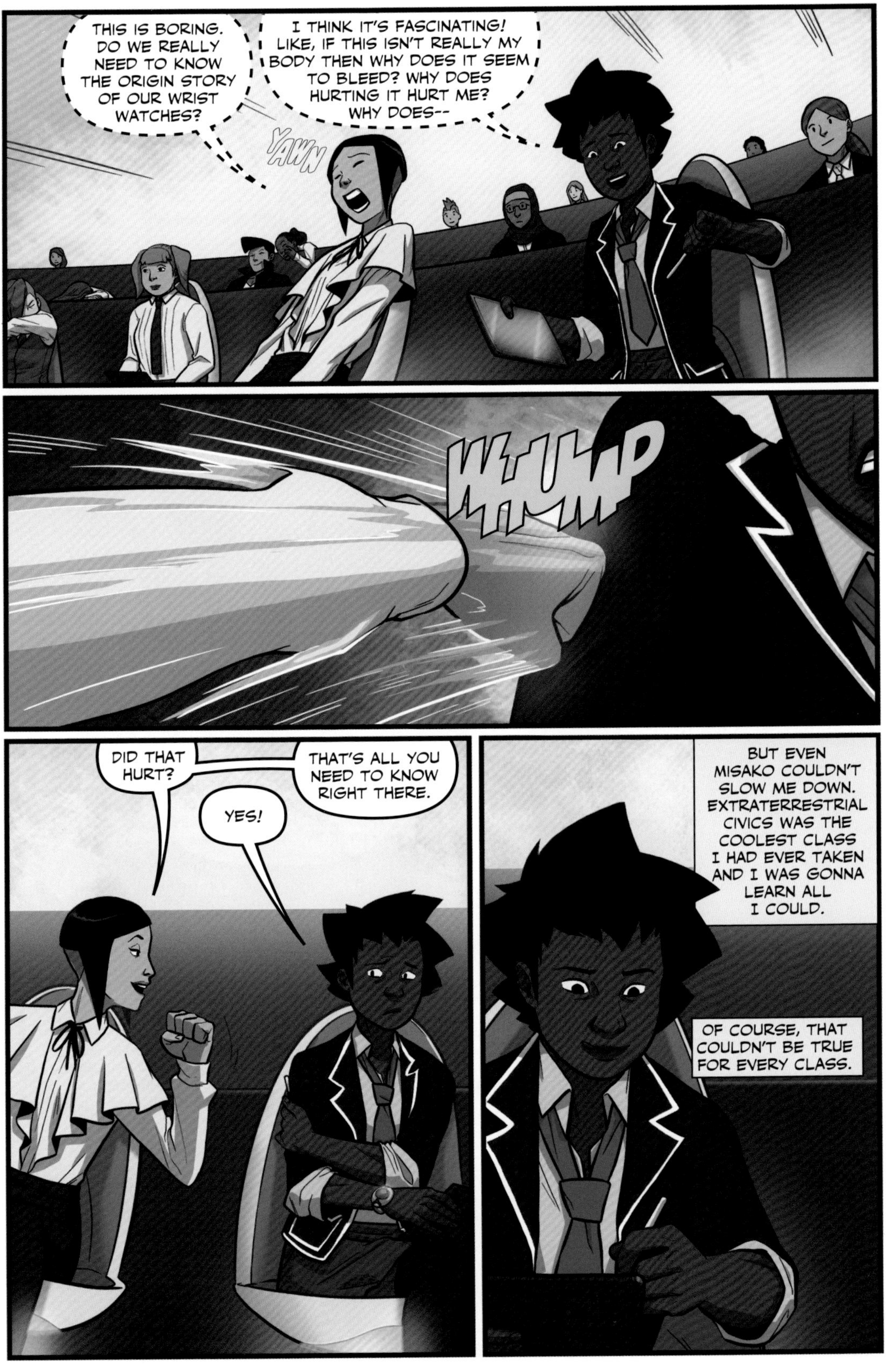
THIS IS BORING. DO WE REALLY NEED TO KNOW THE ORIGIN STORY OF OUR WRIST WATCHES?
I THINK IT'S FASCINATING! LIKE, IF THIS ISN'T REALLY MY BODY THEN WHY DOES IT SEEM TO BLEED? WHY DOES HURTING IT HURT ME? WHY DOES--
YAWN
WHUMP
DID THAT HURT?
YES!
THAT'S ALL YOU NEED TO KNOW RIGHT THERE.
BUT EVEN MISAKO COULDN'T SLOW ME DOWN. EXTRATERRESTRIAL CIVICS WAS THE COOLEST CLASS I HAD EVER TAKEN AND I WAS GONNA LEARN ALL I COULD.
OF COURSE, THAT COULDN'T BE TRUE FOR EVERY CLASS.

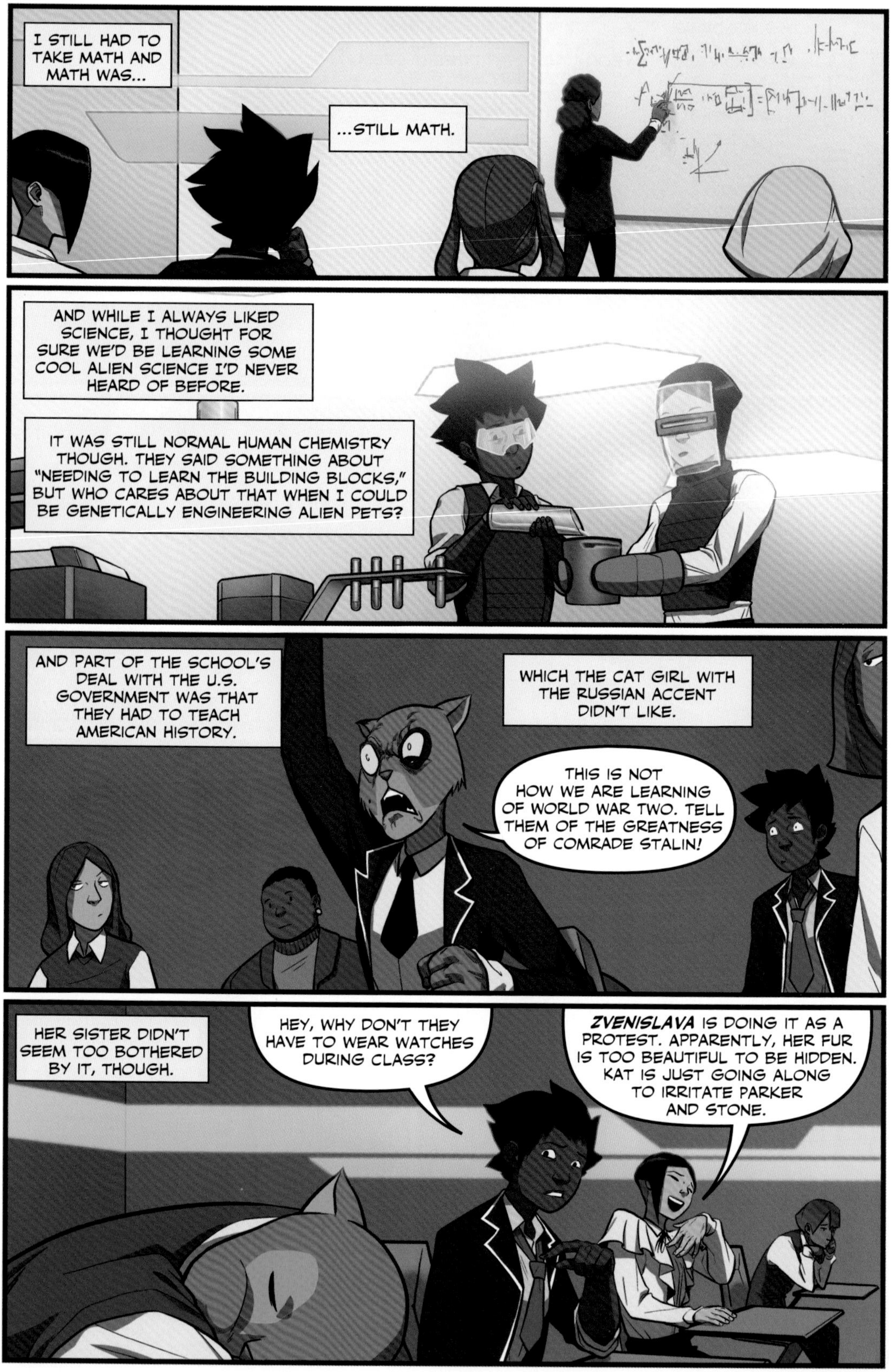
I STILL HAD TO TAKE MATH AND MATH WAS...
...STILL MATH.
AND WHILE I ALWAYS LIKED SCIENCE, I THOUGHT FOR SURE WE'D BE LEARNING SOME COOL ALIEN SCIENCE I'D NEVER HEARD OF BEFORE.
IT WAS STILL NORMAL HUMAN CHEMISTRY THOUGH. THEY SAID SOMETHING ABOUT "NEEDING TO LEARN THE BUILDING BLOCKS," BUT WHO CARES ABOUT THAT WHEN I COULD BE GENETICALLY ENGINEERING ALIEN PETS?
AND PART OF THE SCHOOL'S DEAL WITH THE U.S. GOVERNMENT WAS THAT THEY HAD TO TEACH AMERICAN HISTORY.
WHICH THE CAT GIRL WITH THE RUSSIAN ACCENT DIDN'T LIKE.
THIS IS NOT HOW WE ARE LEARNING OF WORLD WAR TWO. TELL THEM OF THE GREATNESS OF COMRADE STALIN!
HER SISTER DIDN'T SEEM TOO BOTHERED BY IT, THOUGH.
HEY, WHY DON'T THEY HAVE TO WEAR WATCHES DURING CLASS?
ZVENISLAVA IS DOING IT AS A PROTEST. APPARENTLY, HER FUR IS TOO BEAUTIFUL TO BE HIDDEN. KAT IS JUST GOING ALONG TO IRRITATE PARKER AND STONE.

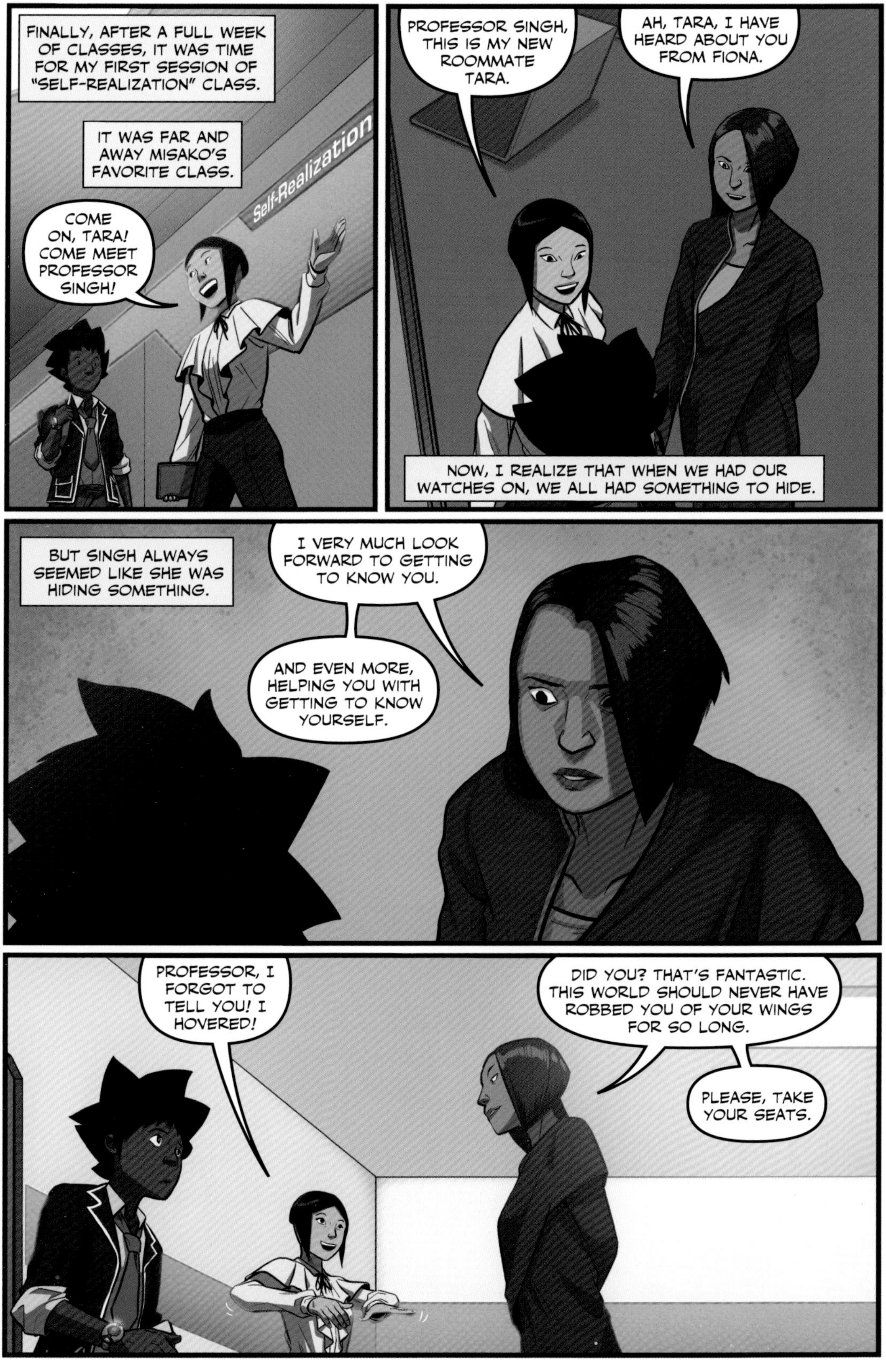
FINALLY, AFTER A FULL WEEK OF CLASSES, IT WAS TIME FOR MY FIRST SESSION OF "SELF-REALIZATION" CLASS.
IT WAS FAR AND AWAY MISAKO'S FAVORITE CLASS.
Self-Realization
COME ON, TARA! COME MEET PROFESSOR SINGH!
PROFESSOR SINGH, THIS IS MY NEW ROOMMATE TARA.
AH, TARA, I HAVE HEARD ABOUT YOU FROM FIONA.
NOW, I REALIZE THAT WHEN WE HAD OUR WATCHES ON, WE ALL HAD SOMETHING TO HIDE.
BUT SINGH ALWAYS SEEMED LIKE SHE WAS HIDING SOMETHING.
I VERY MUCH LOOK FORWARD TO GETTING TO KNOW YOU.
AND EVEN MORE, HELPING YOU WITH GETTING TO KNOW YOURSELF.
PROFESSOR, I FORGOT TO TELL YOU! I HOVERED!
DID YOU? THAT'S FANTASTIC. THIS WORLD SHOULD NEVER HAVE ROBBED YOU OF YOUR WINGS FOR SO LONG.
PLEASE, TAKE YOUR SEATS.

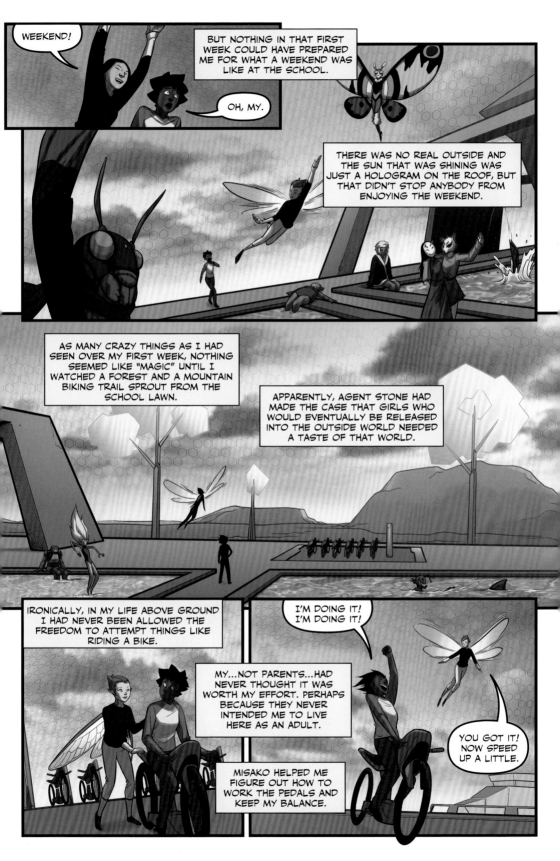

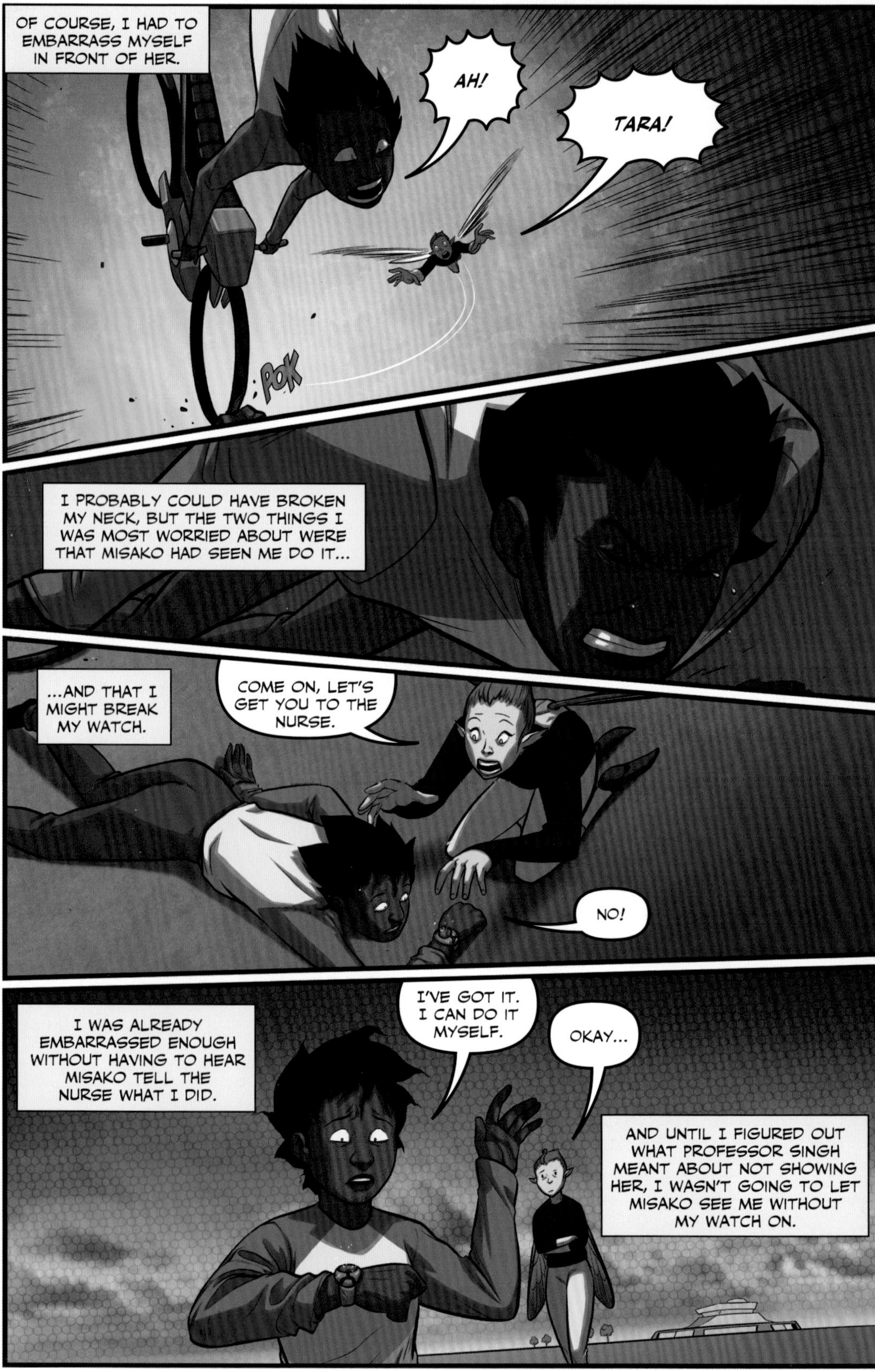
OF COURSE, I HAD TO EMBARRASS MYSELF IN FRONT OF HER.
AH!
TARA!
POK
I PROBABLY COULD HAVE BROKEN MY NECK, BUT THE TWO THINGS I WAS MOST WORRIED ABOUT WERE THAT MISAKO HAD SEEN ME DO IT...
...AND THAT I MIGHT BREAK MY WATCH.
COME ON, LET'S GET YOU TO THE NURSE.
NO!
I WAS ALREADY EMBARRASSED ENOUGH WITHOUT HAVING TO HEAR MISAKO TELL THE NURSE WHAT I DID.
I'VE GOT IT. I CAN DO IT MYSELF.
OKAY...
AND UNTIL I FIGURED OUT WHAT PROFESSOR SINGH MEANT ABOUT NOT SHOWING HER, I WASN'T GOING TO LET MISAKO SEE ME WITHOUT MY WATCH ON.

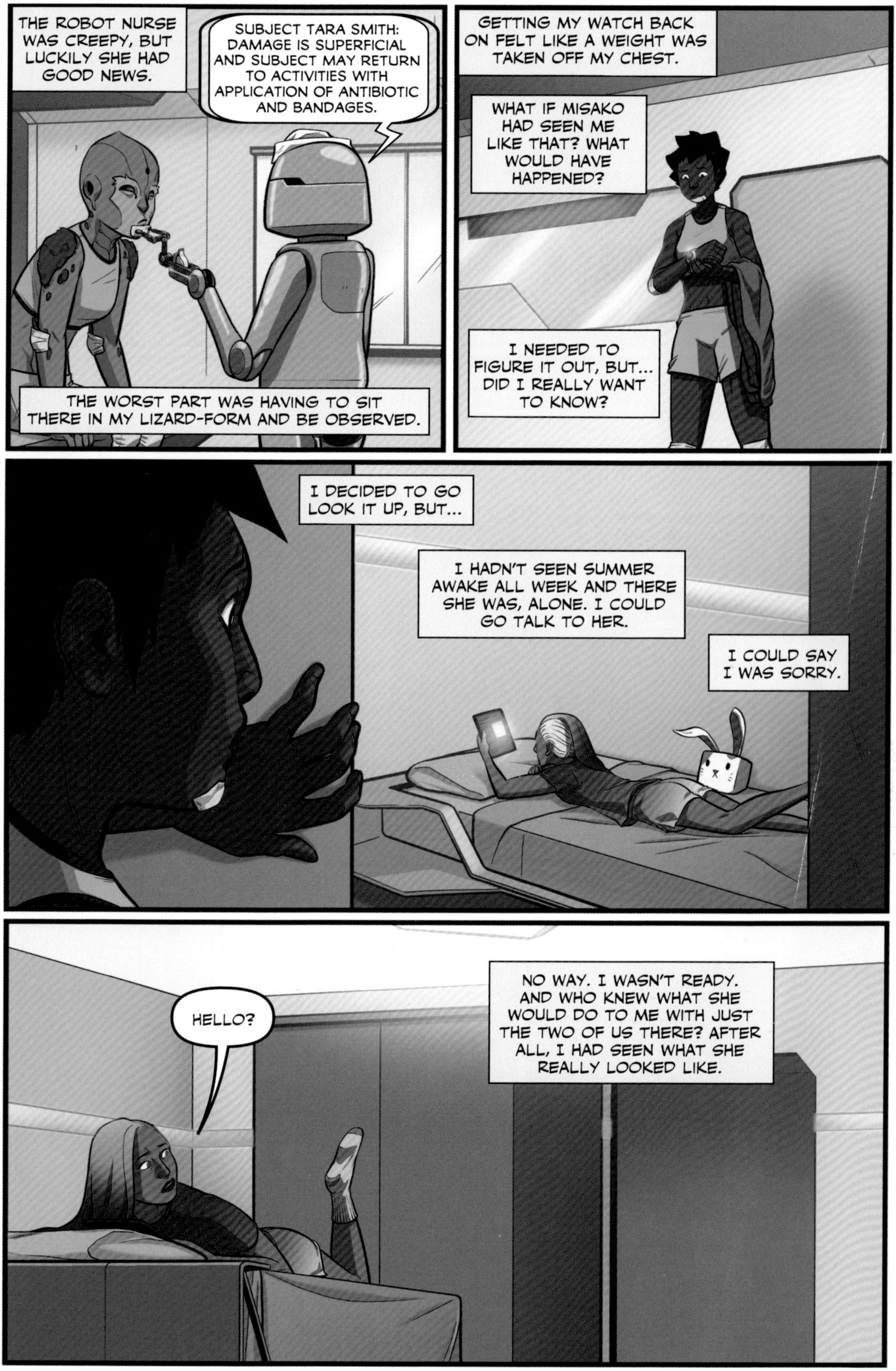
THE ROBOT NURSE WAS CREEPY, BUT LUCKILY SHE HAD GOOD NEWS.
SUBJECT TARA SMITH: DAMAGE IS SUPERFICIAL AND SUBJECT MAY RETURN TO ACTIVITIES WITH APPLICATION OF ANTIBIOTIC AND BANDAGES.
THE WORST PART WAS HAVING TO SIT THERE IN MY LIZARD-FORM AND BE OBSERVED.
GETTING MY WATCH BACK ON FELT LIKE A WEIGHT WAS TAKEN OFF MY CHEST.
WHAT IF MISAKO HAD SEEN ME LIKE THAT? WHAT WOULD HAVE HAPPENED?
I NEEDED TO FIGURE IT OUT, BUT... DID I REALLY WANT TO KNOW?
I DECIDED TO GO LOOK IT UP, BUT...
I HADN'T SEEN SUMMER AWAKE ALL WEEK AND THERE SHE WAS, ALONE. I COULD GO TALK TO HER.
I COULD SAY I WAS SORRY.
HELLO?
NO WAY. I WASN'T READY. AND WHO KNEW WHAT SHE WOULD DO TO ME WITH JUST THE TWO OF US THERE? AFTER ALL, I HAD SEEN WHAT SHE REALLY LOOKED LIKE.

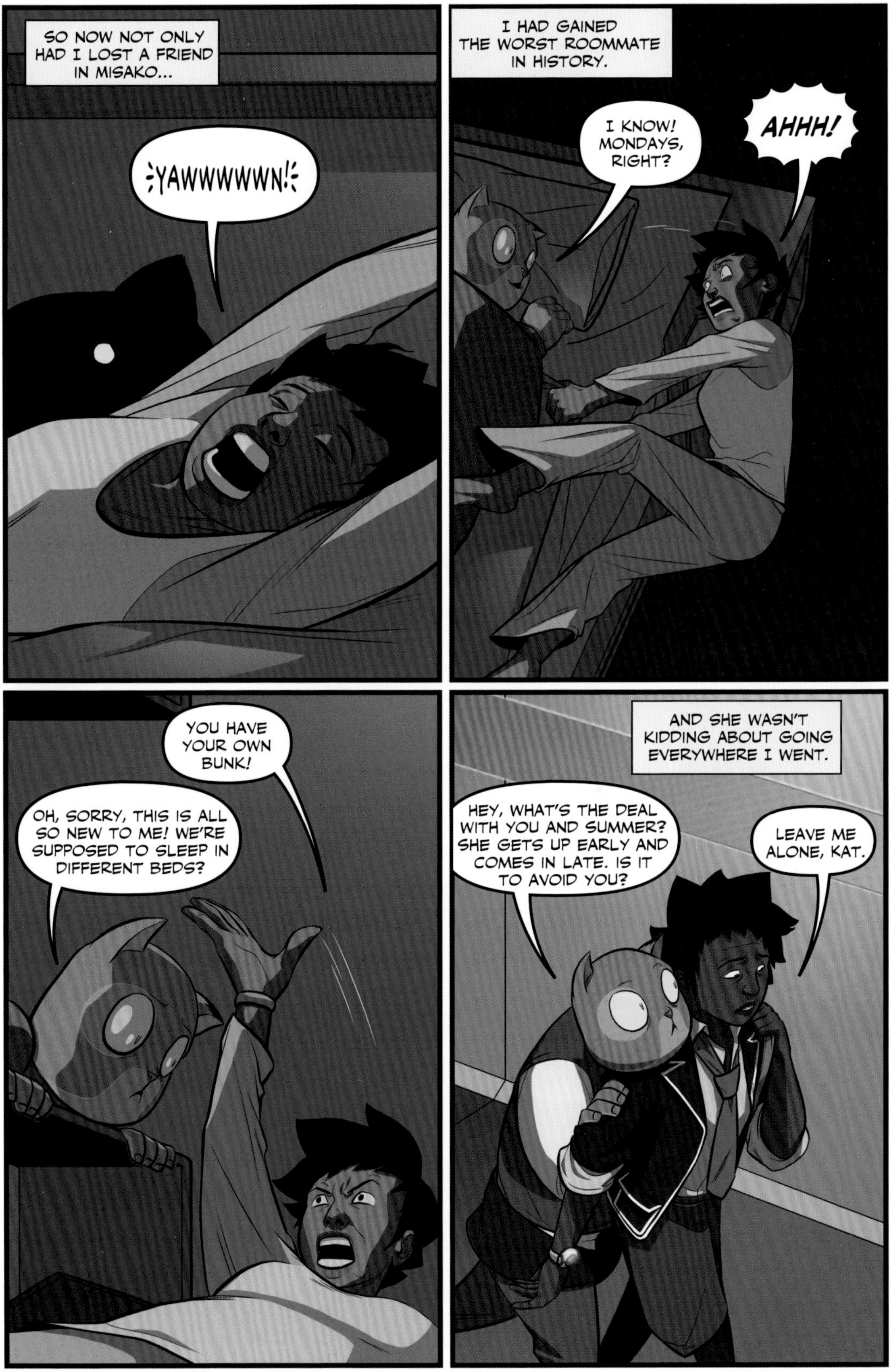

SO NOW NOT ONLY HAD I LOST A FRIEND IN MISAKO...
YAWWWWWN!
I HAD GAINED THE WORST ROOMMATE IN HISTORY.
I KNOW! MONDAYS, RIGHT?
AHHH!
YOU HAVE YOUR OWN BUNK!
OH, SORRY, THIS IS ALL SO NEW TO ME! WE'RE SUPPOSED TO SLEEP IN DIFFERENT BEDS?
AND SHE WASN'T KIDDING ABOUT GOING EVERYWHERE I WENT.
HEY, WHAT'S THE DEAL WITH YOU AND SUMMER? SHE GETS UP EARLY AND COMES IN LATE. IS IT TO AVOID YOU?
LEAVE ME ALONE, KAT.

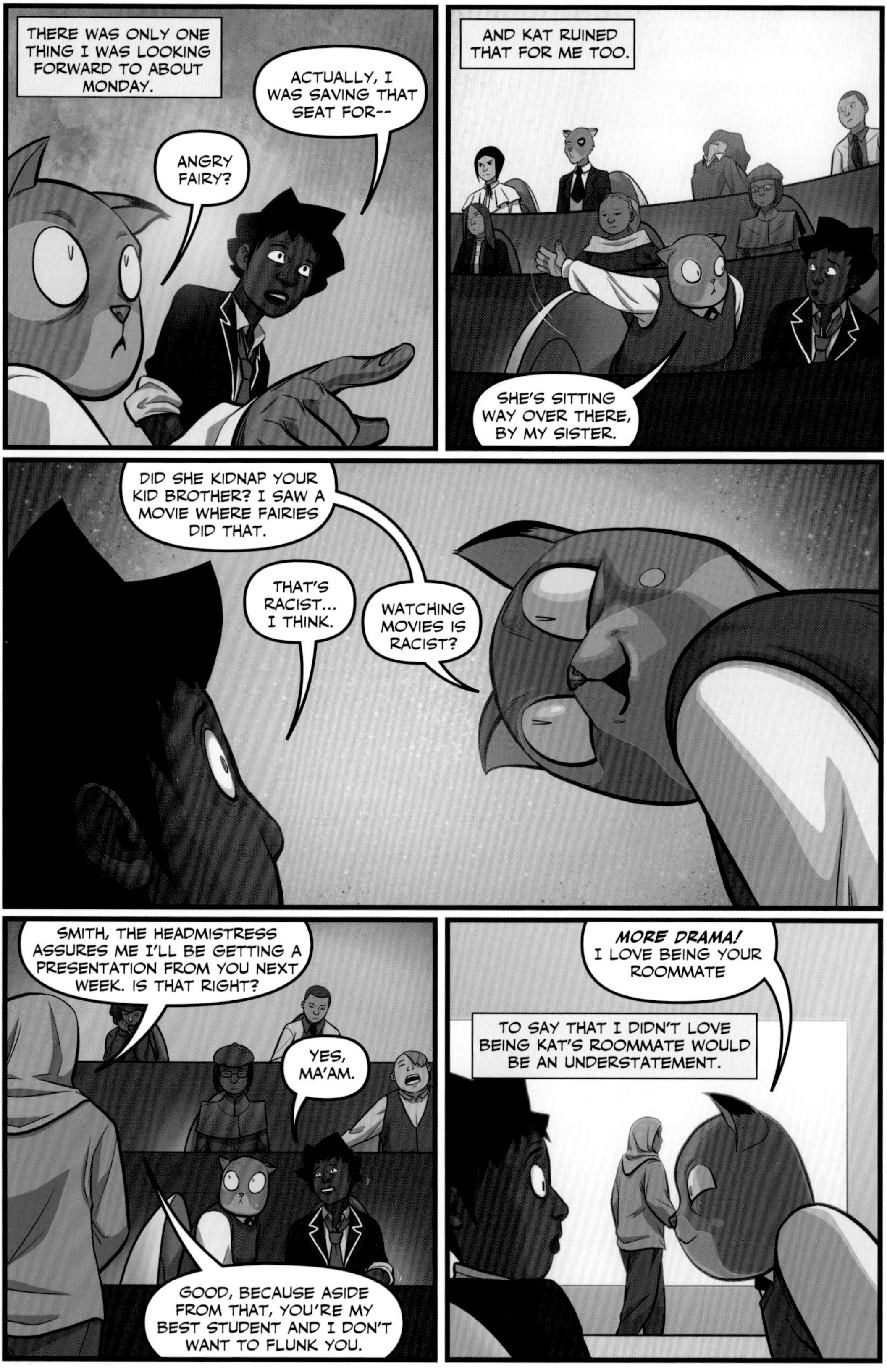
THERE WAS ONLY ONE THING I WAS LOOKING FORWARD TO ABOUT MONDAY.
ACTUALLY, I WAS SAVING THAT SEAT FOR--
ANGRY FAIRY?
AND KAT RUINED THAT FOR ME TOO.
SHE'S SITTING WAY OVER THERE, BY MY SISTER.
DID SHE KIDNAP YOUR KID BROTHER? I SAW A MOVIE WHERE FAIRIES DID THAT.
THAT'S RACIST... I THINK.
WATCHING MOVIES IS RACIST?
SMITH, THE HEADMISTRESS ASSURES ME I'LL BE GETTING A PRESENTATION FROM YOU NEXT WEEK. IS THAT RIGHT?
YES, MA'AM.
GOOD, BECAUSE ASIDE FROM THAT, YOU'RE MY BEST STUDENT AND I DON'T WANT TO FLUNK YOU.
MORE DRAMA! I LOVE BEING YOUR ROOMMATE
TO SAY THAT I DIDN'T LOVE BEING KAT'S ROOMMATE WOULD BE AN UNDERSTATEMENT.

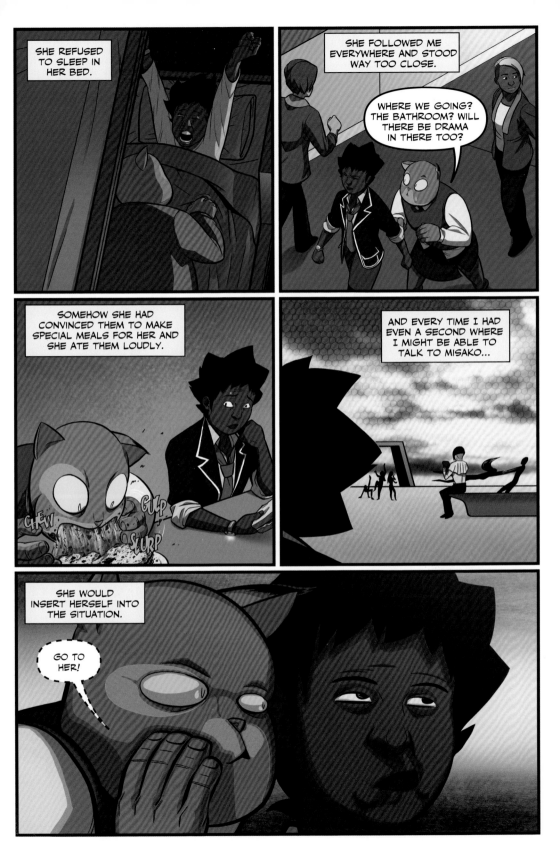

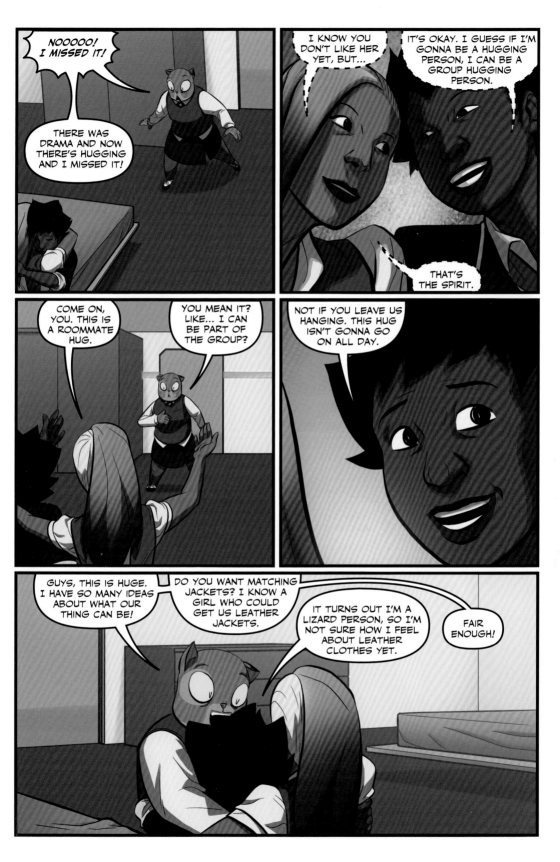

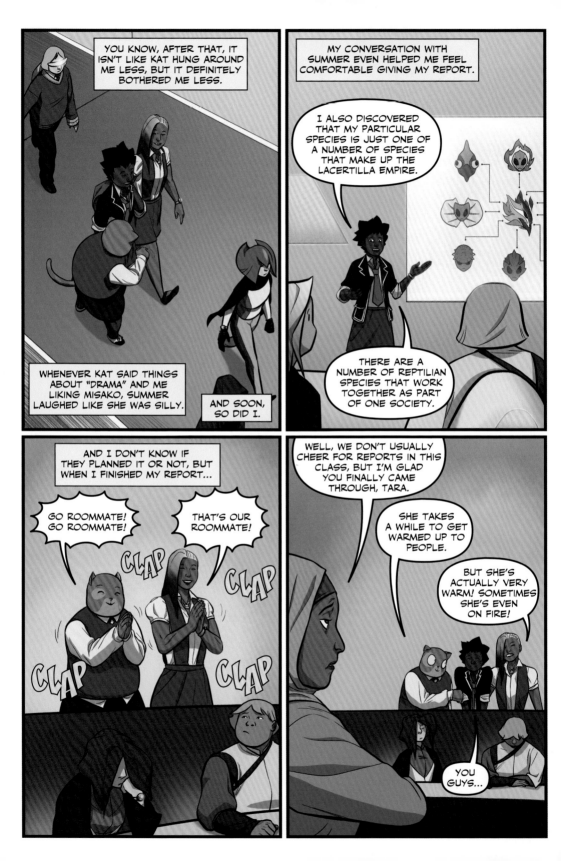

YOU KNOW, AFTER THAT, IT ISN'T LIKE KAT HUNG AROUND ME LESS, BUT IT DEFINITELY BOTHERED ME LESS.

WHENEVER KAT SAID THINGS ABOUT "DRAMA" AND ME LIKING MISAKO, SUMMER LAUGHED LIKE SHE WAS SILLY.

AND SOON, SO DID I.

MY CONVERSATION WITH SUMMER EVEN HELPED ME FEEL COMFORTABLE GIVING MY REPORT.

I ALSO DISCOVERED THAT MY PARTICULAR SPECIES IS JUST ONE OF A NUMBER OF SPECIES THAT MAKE UP THE LACERTILLA EMPIRE.

THERE ARE A NUMBER OF REPTILIAN SPECIES THAT WORK TOGETHER AS PART OF ONE SOCIETY.

AND I DON'T KNOW IF THEY PLANNED IT OR NOT, BUT WHEN I FINISHED MY REPORT...

GO ROOMMATE! GO ROOMMATE!

THAT'S OUR ROOMMATE!

CLAP

CLAP

CLAP

CLAP

WELL, WE DON'T USUALLY CHEER FOR REPORTS IN THIS CLASS, BUT I'M GLAD YOU FINALLY CAME THROUGH, TARA.

SHE TAKES A WHILE TO GET WARMED UP TO PEOPLE.

BUT SHE'S ACTUALLY VERY WARM! SOMETIMES SHE'S EVEN ON FIRE!

YOU GUYS...

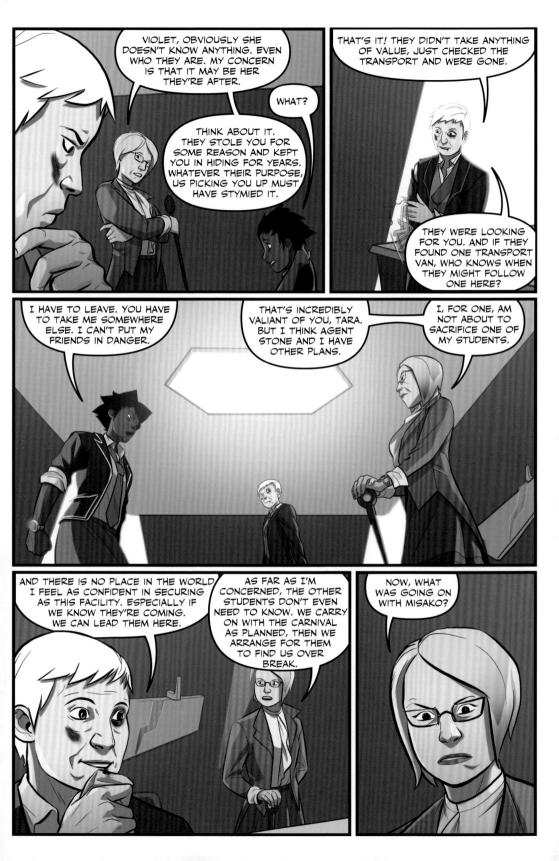

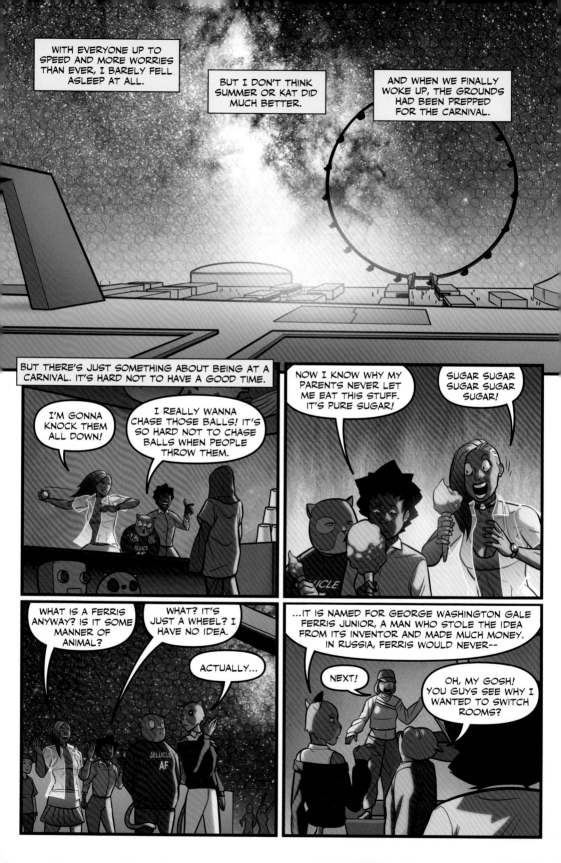

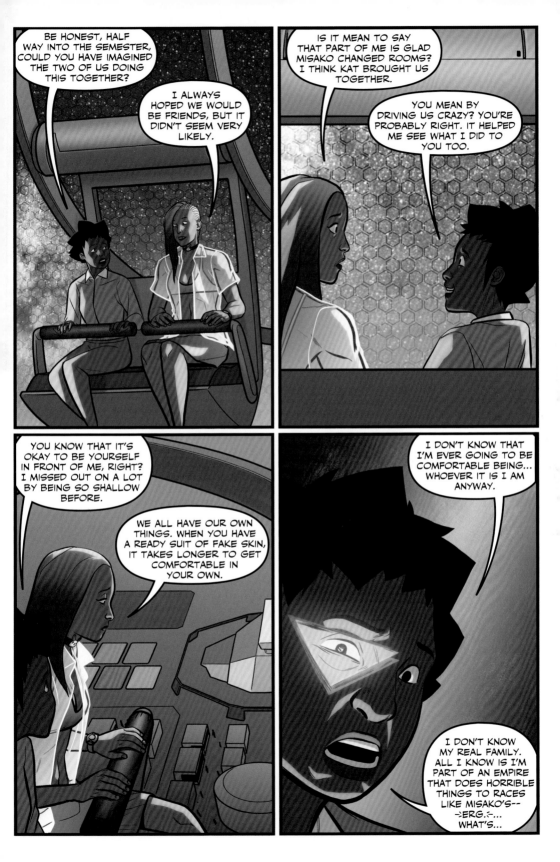

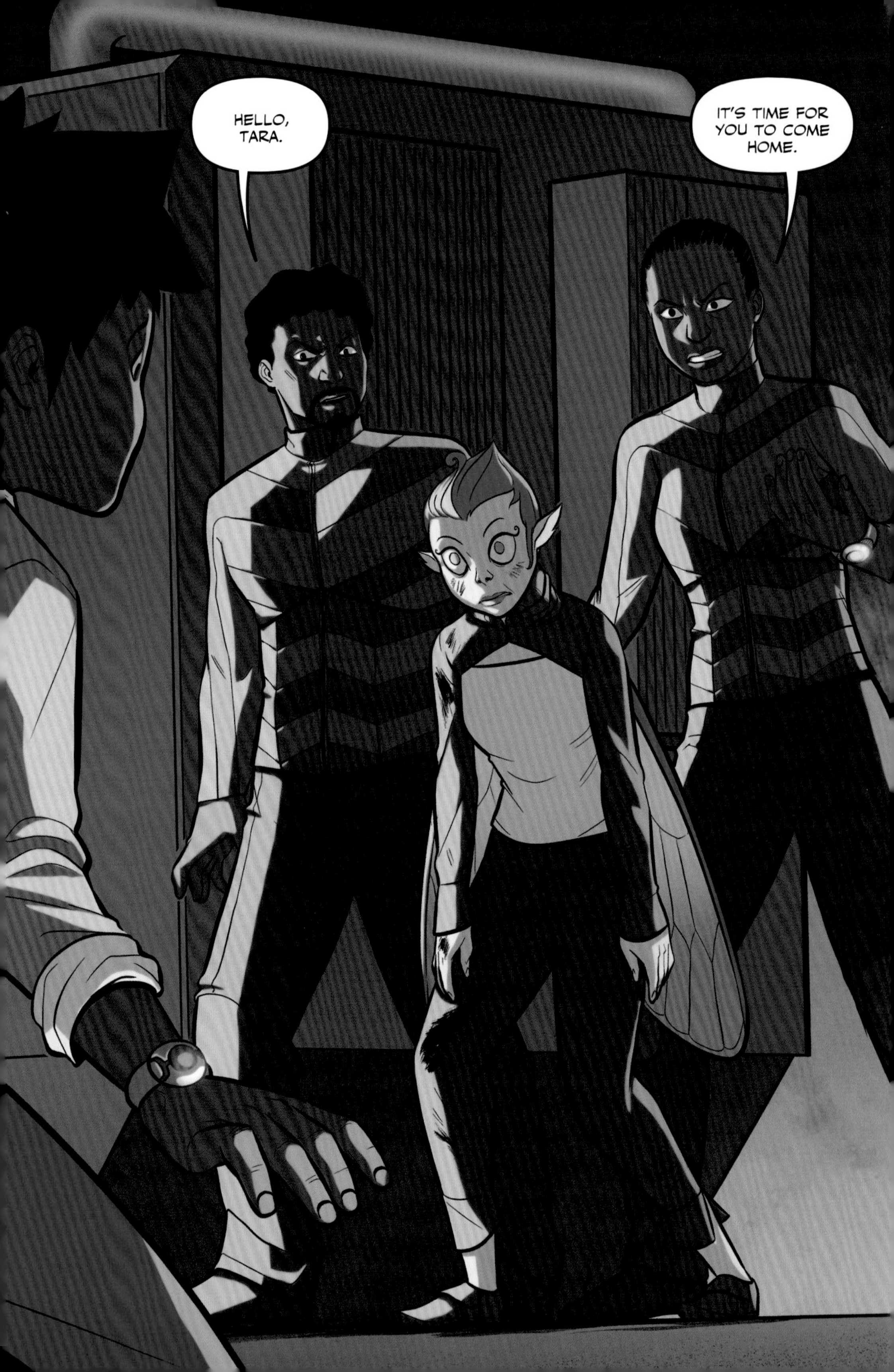
HELLO, TARA.
IT'S TIME FOR YOU TO COME HOME.

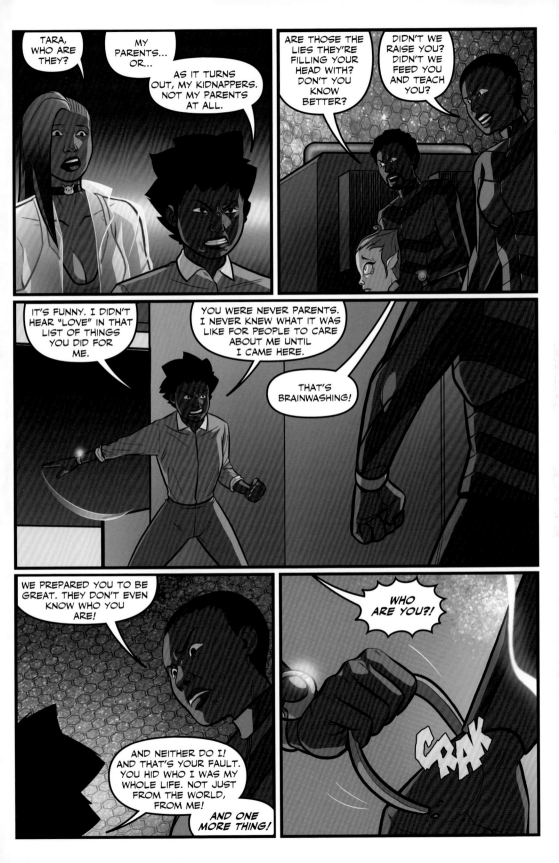

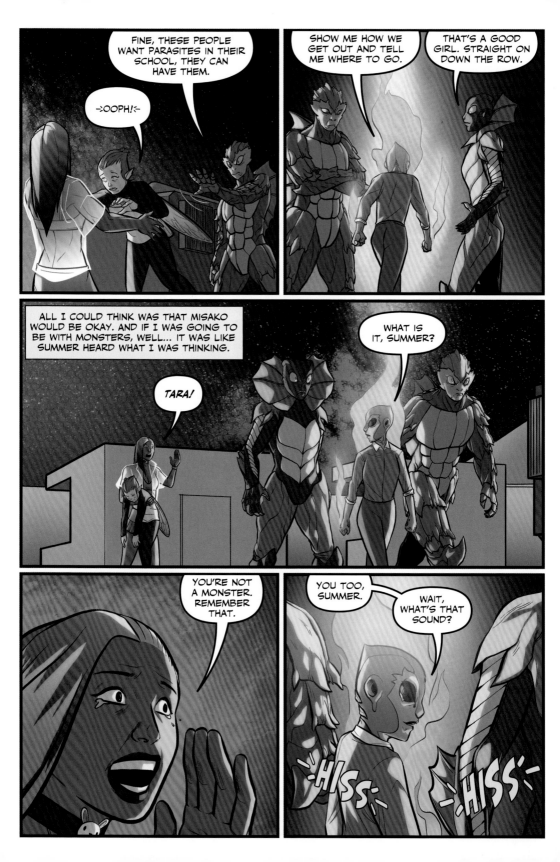

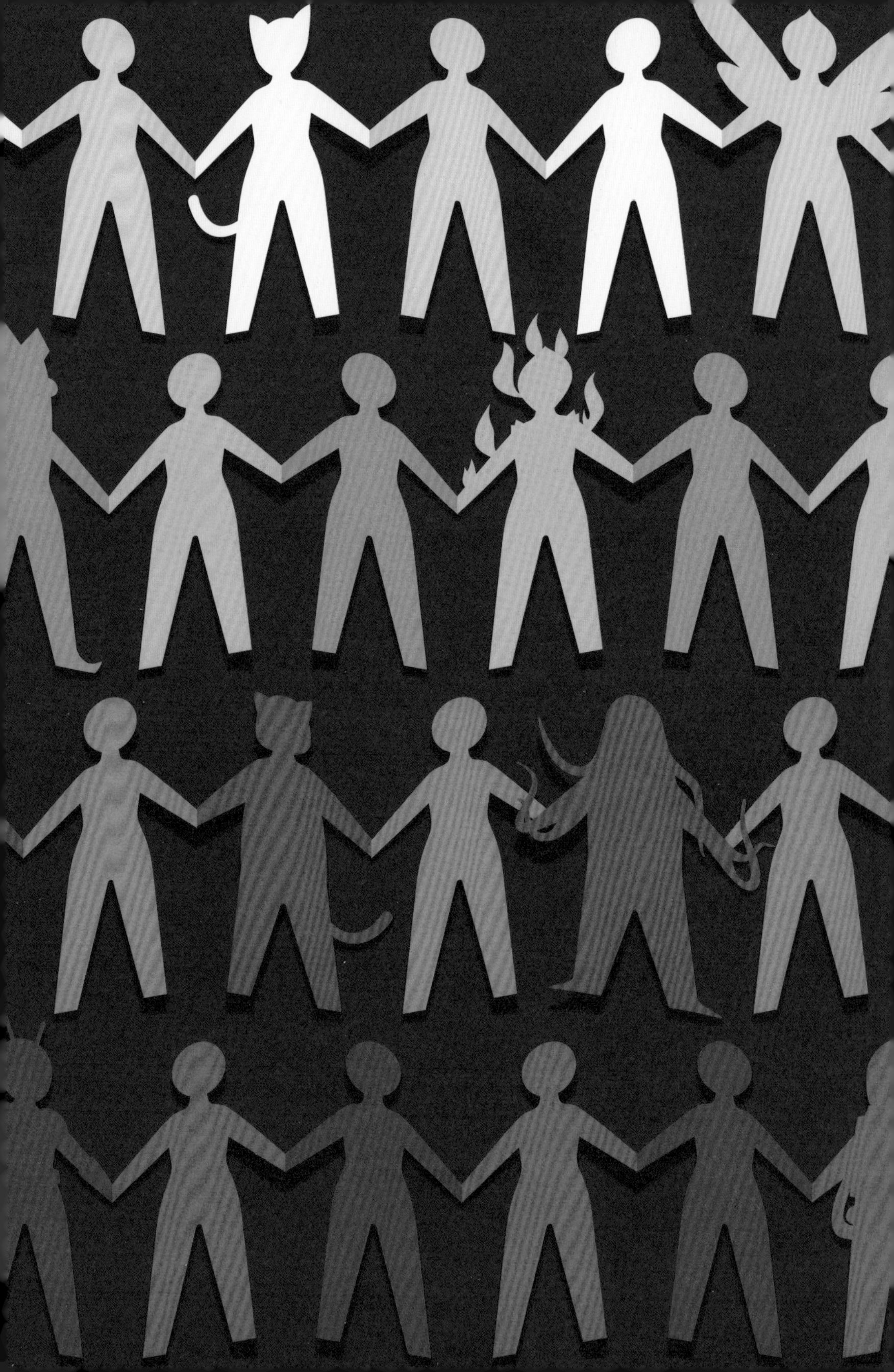